The Secret Hen House Theatre

Look out for the
second novel by

Helen Peters

Evie's
Ghost

The Secret Hen House Theatre

Helen Peters

nosy
crow

First published in the UK in 2012 by Nosy Crow Ltd
The Crow's Nest, 10a Lant Street
London, SE1 1QR, UK

Nosy Crow and associated logos are trademarks and/or registered
trademarks of Nosy Crow Ltd

A CIP catalogue record for this book will be available from the
British Library

1 3 5 7 9 10 8 6 4 2

Printed and bound in the UK by Clays Ltd, St. Ives Plc
Typeset by Tiger Media Ltd, Bishops Stortford, Hertfordshire

Papers used by Nosy Crow are made from wood grown in
sustainable forests.

ISBN: 978 0 85763 065 0

www.nosycrow.com

To my parents
and in memory of my grandparents

H. P.

Chapter One

The Stranger

BANG, BANG, BANG!

Somebody was trying to smash the scullery door down.

Hannah sat cross-legged on her bedroom floor, hunched over a piece of paper, her pen racing across the page. Even inside the farmhouse her breath came out in white trails, and the cold sneaked its way right through her woolly hat and three jumpers.

BANG, BANG, BANG!

Her right hand didn't leave the page as she glanced at her watch. Five to two. But it couldn't be Lottie. She never knocked. She just walked right in and yelled up the stairs.

One of the others could get it for once. She had to finish this by two o'clock.

BANG, BANG, BANG!

"Will someone answer that blasted door!" shouted her dad from the farm office.

There! Finished at last. Hannah wrote "THE END" in large capital letters. This play would win the competition, she just knew it.

BANG, BANG, BANG!

"Hannah!" called Dad.

"Oh, *OK*." Hannah slid her mother's copy of *Putting On a Play* under her bed and scrambled to her feet. She must remember to put that back in Mum's bookcase later.

"If it's for me, tell them I'm not in," Dad called as she passed his office door. "And get the others ready. There's a pig wants bringing up from the Anthill Field."

Hannah ran down the splintered back stairs, script in hand, ducking the cobwebs that hung from the crumbling ceiling. Her little brother, Sam, was already at the door, fumbling with the latch.

"It's stuck again," he said.

"I'll get it, Sammy," said Hannah. Sam moved aside. His laces were undone and his shoes were on the wrong feet.

BANG, BANG, BANG!

As Hannah wrestled with the battered latch, her sister Jo came through from the kitchen, a flat cap pulled down over her curls. A ginger guinea pig nestled into her left arm, nibbling a cabbage leaf.

"Who's come?" she asked.

The latch shot up. Sam glued himself to Hannah's side as she opened the door. Jo hovered by the stairs.

Looming in the doorway, stamping his feet against the cold, was a stocky man with a red face and a puffed-out chest. He looked like an irate turkey. His shiny dark hair was greased down on his head and he grasped a clipboard with his thick red fingers.

He stared at the children. "Flippin' heck," he

muttered. His breath h⸱ ng in the air.

What's wrong with him? thought Hannah. She looked round but there was nothing, only the three of them in their holey jumpers and torn jeans. Had he never seen farm clothes before?

Click, clack, click, clack.

They all turned. At the top of the steep staircase, in a white minidress and red stilettos several sizes too big for her, stood ten-year-old Martha, one hand on her hip and her chin in the air.

"Martha," said Hannah, "you'll die of pneumonia. Go and get changed. And take Mum's shoes off. Dad'll go ballistic."

"Oh, shut up," said Martha. "You're just jealous cos I look like a model."

The man raised his eyebrows. Martha tottered down the stairs and pushed past Jo to get a good look at him.

"I'm looking for –" The man glanced at the clipboard. "Clayhill Farm."

They said nothing.

"Is this Clayhill Farm?" he asked, louder now. "There's no sign."

"The sign blew down," said Sam.

Hannah noticed a very new, very big, very shiny black BMW parked in the farmyard. At least, the top half was shiny. The bottom half was plastered in mud, like every vehicle that came up the farm track.

"In the records, it says it's a working farm," he said.

"It is," said Hannah. Was he really thick or

something? And who was he anyway, coming up here on a Sunday afternoon asking nosy questions?

"Really? Then what's all this junk lying around for?" He flicked his hand around the yard. At the horse ploughs half buried in grass, the collapsed combine harvester rusting in the mud by the pigsties, the old doors, oil stoves and tangled barbed wire heaped up outside the house. "I mean, what's with that old rust bucket?" He pointed towards the tractor shed where Dad's vintage tractor stood. "What is it – an engine from the Age of Steam?"

"It's Daddy's Field Marshall," said Sam proudly. "It's really old."

"Huh. You don't say."

Sam turned puzzled eyes to Hannah, and Hannah felt her cheeks flushing. How dare he be rude to Sam? And how ignorant was he? Didn't he know Field Marshalls were collectors' items?

"Can we help you?" she asked.

"I hope so." He consulted his clipboard again. "I'm looking for Arthur Roberts."

"Who shall I say is calling?"

"Just get him for me, will you?"

They all spoke at the same time.

"He's out," said Hannah.

"He's milking," said Jo.

"He's in the office," said Sam.

"I see," said the stranger. "Busy man."

They nodded.

"Well, is your mum in then?"

They were silent. Hannah had already seen quite

enough of this stranger and she didn't want him to know any more about their lives than he did already. What else was written on that clipboard?

Along the lane a bell sounded. Hannah looked up. Lottie Perfect was bumping up the track on her brand-new bicycle, weaving around the puddles and potholes.

"Can I take a message?" Hannah asked. She had to get rid of him. She needed every second of her time with Lottie.

"Give your dad this," he said. "Make sure he gets it."

Hannah took the envelope. Printed across the top were the words "Strickland and Wormwood, Land Agents". And then, in red capital letters, "URGENT".

Thank goodness she hadn't called Dad. This man must be the agent for the new landlord. Hannah pulled on her coat and stuffed the letter and her script into one of the pockets.

The agent strutted off. Lottie, waving at Hannah from her bike, almost ran into him. She swerved wildly through a puddle. The children stared open-mouthed as a great brown wave of muddy water splattered all over the man's trousers. Sam giggled, and that made his sisters laugh too. The agent glared at them as he opened his car door, and they laughed even more.

Lottie braked at the garden gate. She jumped off her bike and yanked the gate open. "Look at the state of me," she said. "Have you got something to wipe this mud off, Han?"

"Right, you lazy lot!" shouted Dad down the stairs. "Look sharp!"

Oh, no, thought Hannah. If she got caught up in Dad's pig chase, she'd be gone all afternoon and they'd never get the play done.

She threw Lottie a threadbare towel from the draining board, then grabbed Jo's arm and pulled her outside, around the corner of the house. The guinea pig scrabbled across Jo's jumper.

"Hey, careful with Carrots!"

"Jo, you have to cover for me. *Please*. I've got to read through the play with Lottie. We need to make sure it's right so she can type it up. The competition closes on Tuesday – we have to send it off tomorrow."

"Oooh, I've got to read my play with Perfect Lottie," said Martha in a high-pitched singsong voice. "As if you'd win a prize with your stupid play."

Hannah swung round. "Martha, get lost. It's none of your business."

"Like I care anyway," said Martha. She stuck out her tongue at Hannah and teetered back inside.

Hannah turned to Jo. "Just tell him you don't know where I am. Please, Jo. I've *got* to do this play – if we win, it actually goes on the radio and it might be my chance to be an actress!"

Dad's heavy tread sounded from the stairs.

"I won't tell," said Jo. She placed Carrots in his hutch, sat on the scullery step and tugged on her muddy wellingtons. "Come on, Sam. Let's get your boots on."

Hannah skulked around the corner. Dad strode out into the yard with Sam trotting beside him. Jo followed them. And, finally, Martha emerged.

"Martha, please don't tell him! I'll give you anything!"

Martha shot her a contemptuous glance. "Like you've got anything I'd want."

She kicked off the red stilettos and rammed her feet into an old pair of Jo's boots. They were so much too small for her that she had to walk on tiptoe in them.

She staggered into the farmyard. "Dad, wait up!"

Dad was a good ten metres ahead of her and walking twice as fast. Hannah was spared. But not for long.

Chapter Two

The Pig

Once the others were a safe distance away, Hannah pulled Lottie into the yard. She could see her dad's back as he strode across North Meadow with the others behind him, Martha swaying precariously in her squashed-down wellies.

"OK," said Hannah. "Tractor-shed loft."

Halfway across the yard, she looked back. Lottie was still at the garden gate. She looked as panic-stricken as a person stranded on a sandbank with the tide coming in all around them.

"Come on, they've gone now," said Hannah.

"Can't we just go in the house?"

"Don't be stupid. That's the first place he'll look for me. Come *on*."

"I can't. I've got my new trainers on. I promised I'd keep them clean. If they get ruined my mum will kill me."

Hannah let out an exasperated sigh. They were wasting precious minutes. She could go and get her trainers for Lottie but they had holes in the bottom and they'd be miles too small. Lottie was tall for eleven, and Hannah was little.

Little but strong.

She squelched back through the mud. "All right, hop up."

"What?"

"I'll give you a piggyback."

Lottie giggled. "You're mad. You'll break your back."

"I've carried heavier things than you. Get up, quick. They'll be here with the pig in a minute."

Hannah staggered across the yard, her thick straw-coloured hair falling into her eyes. Lottie clung on to her neck, half laughing, half screaming.

"Lottie, you're strangling me!"

"Aargh, you're going to drop me!"

"Stop squealing; you sound like a stuck piglet. Right, get off."

She dumped Lottie on the floor of the tractor shed and sank down into the dirt, rubbing her shoulders and pushing the hair out of her face. Lottie's smooth dark bob was as sleek as ever. She always looked as though she'd just stepped out of the hairdresser's.

Lottie brushed the dust off her new coat. "Oh, guess what? You know the Linford Arts Festival's coming up? They've got a youth drama competition – I saw a poster round the shops. We could do our play there."

Hannah dragged the rickety ladder out from behind the Field Marshall. "We can't," she said as she propped it up against the trapdoor.

"Why not? You're a brilliant actress. And then we could win, and that would serve Miranda Hathaway right for going on and on about how her drama group has won it for the last fifty million years."

"But we can't enter," said Hannah as she stepped on the ladder. "It's for proper youth drama groups. You have to have an actual theatre. Don't you remember Miranda saying how the judges come out to your theatre and watch your play?"

"Oh. I forgot. Shame. It looked really good." Lottie climbed up into the loft. "So have you finished the radio play?"

"I'll show you."

The loft was dark except for the far corner, where a narrow slit let in a shaft of grey February light. They groped their way across, ducking the beams and the cobwebs. Nobody ever came up here.

They clambered over mounds of rusty tractor parts and empty calf-medicine bottles to a pile of old feed sacks next to the window slit. Hannah's muscles tensed at the thought of what might be lurking under those sacks. She bit her bottom lip, screwed her eyes shut and stamped her foot down on them. She held her breath, listening for the horrible sound of scuttling rodents.

Nothing.

Phew.

She plonked herself down on the sacks.

Lottie settled herself beside Hannah. "So?"

"OK." Hannah reached into her pocket, pulled out the folded sheets of paper and flattened them on her lap. "Ta da!"

On the first page was written, in large flourishing

letters: "*By Her Majesty's Appointment.* A play for radio by Hannah Roberts and Lottie Perfect."

"You didn't have to put my name on it," said Lottie. "I didn't do anything."

Hannah had struggled with this herself, but eventually her more generous side had won. "Well, you had some really good ideas. And you are going to do all the typing up. And then we can send it off tomorrow."

Lottie clapped her hands in excitement. "Come on, let's read it now."

"We're going to win, I know we are," said Hannah. "Mum loved Radio 4. It's a sign."

Lottie reached for the script but her arm froze in mid-stretch as a cacophony of squeals and grunts blasted their ears.

"What's *that*?"

The squealing got louder and more piercing as it was joined by the sound of running boots and thunderous swearing.

They looked down through the narrow slit.

Hannah's father, holding a muddy board in front of him, was herding an enormous pink pig into the farmyard. As they watched, it shifted its huge weight on its tiny trotters, flicked around so quickly that no one could stop it and bolted back up the track.

Martha shrieked and jumped out of the way.

"Martha, you useless tool!" shouted Dad. "Joanne, get round behind her. Move!"

Jo ducked under the electric fence and raced through the field, trying to outrun the speeding sow.

"Sam, stand on the path there. Don't let her past you, whatever you do. Martha, get down there and open the pigsty door. Move it!"

"Hadn't you better go?" asked Lottie. "He'll go mad at you later."

"He'd go mad anyway. I'd only knock something over or get trampled by the pig. He's moodier than ever at the moment."

"Here she comes!" yelled Dad. "Sam, hold that board out! Martha, get her in the sty. Where the blazes is Hannah?"

"She's in the tractor-shed loft with Lottie," called Martha. "They've been there all the time."

Hannah's heart stopped. She stuffed the script back into her pocket. "Hide!" she hissed to Lottie. "Quick!"

But there was no time. She heard him shout, "Hold that!" and in three bounds he was up the ladder and in the loft. He glared through the gloom at the girls trying to disappear into the pile of empty sacks.

"What the hell do you think you're playing at?" he shouted at Hannah. "Get down in that yard this instant!"

"Should I—" Lottie started to say.

"No, no, you stay here," Hannah muttered. Clumsy with embarrassment, she heaved herself off the sacks and followed her father down the splintered ladder. The sow was racing up the track again, and Jo was trying to turn her round, leaping from side to side like a goalkeeper defending a penalty.

"Get over there!" Dad barked at Hannah, pointing

at the entrance to the horse paddock. "Keep your wits about you and don't let her past."

Head down, Hannah trudged across the yard. A thin layer of mud, patterned all over with the spiky footprints of chickens, coated the concrete. Tractor tyres had churned the gateway into a mass of brown puddles. It was impossible to tell how deep they were until you stepped in them and the water slopped over the tops of your wellies.

Half a gate hung jaggedly off the one remaining hinge. If Dad ever got anything mended, Hannah thought, he wouldn't have to use his children as fences.

Standing up to her shins in a pool of water, Hannah let her imagination take over.

"It is a great pleasure," the radio interviewer would say, "to have with us the youngest ever winner of our playwriting competition, who also, of course, starred in the wonderful performance of her play which you have just heard. Hannah Roberts, you clearly have a great future ahead of you. What inspired you to write a play?"

"Well," Hannah would say, "my mum loved acting, so maybe I get it from her. And in Year Six I was in the school play. . ."

How could she describe the joy of it? The fun of rehearsals. The excitement as the play starts to come together. The magic of creating a world from wood and words and fabric and sound effects. The buzz backstage, the butterflies in your stomach, the dazzle of the lights—

"Hannah, look sharp!"

Hannah looked up.

The sow was charging straight towards her. Its muddy snout and huge yellow teeth loomed closer. And closer.

She knew exactly what to do, and if she had been Dad, or Jo, or even Sam, she would have done it: leapt right into its path and stood her ground, confident that it would sense her dominance and change direction at the last moment.

If she had been Martha, she would have jumped out of the way.

Hannah did neither. She turned and ran. Lurched across the sodden ground, the pig sploshing and squealing behind her. Thick wet clay, heavy as concrete, clung to her boots.

Dad crashed through the hedge just ahead and ran full tilt towards the enormous sow at her heels.

And Hannah tripped over his boot and fell flat on her face into a gigantic puddle.

She staggered to her feet, soaked to the skin. Freezing water cascaded down her back and legs. The world had gone dark. Her eyes were stuck together with mud. She tried to wipe them but her hands and sleeves were coated with mud too. She could feel her hair plastered to her face. Through the muddy water in her ears she heard Martha's laughter.

"Hannah, are you OK?" It was Jo's voice.

"Yeah, great, thanks, how are you?" Hannah tried to say, but the mud got into her mouth and she had to stop to spit it out.

Jo wiped at Hannah's cheeks with what felt like her coat sleeve.

"Eyes!" spluttered Hannah. "Wipe my eyes."

Jo wiped her eyes. Hannah blinked them open. And let out a cry of horror.

"No, no, no!"

Scattered all around her, floating in the puddles, trampled into the mud, lay the pages of her script.

"Oh, no, no, no!"

Hannah scrabbled wildly about, picking up all she could see. Some pages had already been ripped by the pig's hooves. Others tore as she tried to peel them off the ground.

Jo bent down to help but there was clearly no point. Barely a single word was legible.

"Have you got a copy?" she asked.

"It's all handwritten – of course I haven't got a copy."

"Ha ha, you've lost your play," said Martha. "Serves you right for trying to hide."

Her dad strode over. Somehow he had managed to get the pig into her sty.

"Good grief, you look a state. Get up out of that puddle, for goodness' sake. What's all this fuss for, girl?"

Hannah said nothing. She stared down at the soggy brown scraps of disintegrating paper.

"It's her play," said Jo. "It fell in the mud and Gertie trampled on it."

Dad looked at Hannah as though she'd just landed from another planet.

15

"Your *what*?"

"My play," said Hannah. "I wrote a play."

"Oh, for goodness' sake. This is a farm, not a theatre. Get out of that mud, girl."

He shook his head. Then his eye lit on an envelope floating in the puddle. The words "Strickland and Wormwood, Land Agents" and "URGENT" were just visible at the top.

"What's this?"

"Oh," said Hannah. "A man brought it. From the new landlord."

"Ha! Good. Best place for it." Her father tramped to the pigsty, and the letter sank deep into the mud under the weight of his boot.

He leaned over the wall and scratched Gertie behind her ears. "There you are, old girl. All safe and sound again. You just make yourself comfortable and I'll fetch you some meal. I expect you're thirsty too, eh, after all that running about? Let's get you some more water." He picked up a battered bucket and clumped across the yard towards the water tank.

Hannah stood completely still in the middle of the puddle, muddy water dripping from her hair, sodden clothes clinging to her skin. Lottie was standing open-mouthed at the bottom of the loft ladder. Hannah looked at Lottie, and at the loft, and she heard her dad's words again.

"This is a farm, not a theatre."

Her eyes were shining. She squelched across the yard as fast as she could under the weight of the mud and water. Her heart thumped with excitement.

Lottie's look of pity and concern changed to one of bewilderment as she saw Hannah's expression.

"Oh, my lord, Hannah, look at the state of you. What on earth are you smiling at?"

"Lottie," said Hannah, grabbing her arm, "I've just had the most amazing idea."

Chapter Three

The Poetry Competition

Miss Francis, Head of English, smiled around at the sea of navy blue and grey assembled in the school hall.

"Welcome, everyone, to our very first Key Stage Three Poetry Competition. We are most honoured to have with us as our judge a celebrity guest, local actress Monica Rowse, whom you will no doubt recognise from her numerous TV appearances. Thank you so much for coming, Monica."

Monica Rowse crossed her slim legs and smiled graciously. Hannah, sitting next to Lottie in the middle row, scrutinised the actress's face for clues as to her taste in poetry.

Hmm. Chicks and bunnies.

On the little table in front of the judge stood a small shiny silver cup. Hannah imagined the look of amazement on Dad's face if she pulled that cup out of her school bag at teatime and showed it to him. Maybe then he wouldn't think her writing was just a waste of time.

Her knuckles were white as she clutched her English exercise book. She had spent hours on her poem – poring over her thesaurus, writing and rewriting lines, trying out different rhythms and phrases, until it felt just right.

"This year's theme was The Natural World," said Miss Francis.

Danny Carr, sitting behind Lottie, yawned loudly. Hannah noticed that there was an empty seat next to him. Was he saving it for. . .?

Hannah's heart thumped. How could she possibly concentrate if *he* came and sat right behind her?

Miss Francis consulted her list. "The first person to recite will be Miranda Hathaway, from 7B. Come up to the front, Miranda."

Miranda didn't have far to go. She was already sitting in the front row.

She made a great performance of taking her English exercise book from an expensive-looking bag printed with the words *Hathaway Fine Art, Bond Street*. Miranda liked everyone to know that her father owned a London gallery.

She opened her book and announced, "'My Golden Retriever'."

Miranda's parents had probably hired a tutor and a poet to help her, Hannah thought. And they would have already entered her poem for the Nobel Prize for Literature.

Miranda flicked back her long shiny auburn hair and began to recite.

"*His eyes of topaz jewels*
His coat of shimmering hues. . ."

Hannah had seen that golden retriever. It was

massively fat, with a permanent stream of dribble trailing from its mouth.

Lottie made gagging motions. "Did you think any more about the you-know-what?" she whispered.

"Of course I did," said Hannah.

She had thought of little else since the idea had exploded like fireworks in her head as she stood in that puddle yesterday afternoon.

We could have a theatre in the tractor-shed loft!

She had been dying to talk about it since she got to school but it had been far too dangerous. Miranda and her best friend, Emily, sat right in front of them at registration and they must never, *ever* get wind of this.

Miranda continued to read her poem as if she was performing for the Queen.

"*His ears of silken threads*
His paws with velvet treads. . ."

Lottie nudged Hannah. "Look at this."

She took from her bag a shiny red notebook. On the first page she had written *The Tractor-shed Theatre Club*. She flicked the page over.

"This is how I thought we could set it up," she whispered.

Across the double page, Lottie had sketched a floor plan. Dressing room, wings, stage, auditorium.

Hannah stared at the sketch and her heart beat faster. The pictures leapt into her imagination: swishing curtains, lavish costumes, sumptuous scenery. She heard the wild applause from the audience as the actors took their curtain calls.

Lottie glanced up. The judge was gazing adoringly at Miranda as she wittered on about her big fat dog. "I've done costume designs too," she whispered. She started to turn the page.

Applause broke out at the front of the hall. Miss Francis stood up.

"Thank you, Miranda. That was a beautiful tribute to your pet. Your use of metaphor was lovely. It is a shame," she said, looking pointedly at Lottie, "that some people were not paying full attention. Perhaps you would do us the courtesy of listening properly from now on, Charlotte."

Lottie dropped the red notebook into her bag and folded her hands in her lap, the picture of studiousness.

"Now, our next entrant is Emily Sanders from 7B."

Emily rose from her seat next to Miranda and stood facing the audience. Miss Francis smiled and nodded for her to begin.

"'My Horse, Starlight'," announced Emily.

"Starlight is my best friend.
My love for him will never end.
I visit him every single day
To groom him, ride him and give him hay. . ."

Hannah gripped her exercise book and tried to concentrate on the poems. For the next twenty minutes her heart thumped against her ribcage as an endless succession of students praised dogs and cats, bluebell woods and willow trees, autumn leaves and summer sun.

21

Had she made a massive mistake? What on earth was the judge going to think of her poem?

But the natural world *wasn't* all sunny and fluffy, was it?

Some people lived right in the middle of the mud.

Vishali Patel, from 8M, finished her poem about snow and returned to her seat. Miss Francis looked at her list and said, "And finally we have Hannah Roberts from 7B."

Hannah felt sick. Lottie squeezed her hand and whispered, "Good luck."

Somehow Hannah got to the front of the hall. She found Lottie's friendly face in the crowd and fixed her eyes on it.

"'The Promise'," she announced. She took a deep breath.

And as soon as she began, the hall and the people melted away and she was back in the farmyard.

"All day, a driving, slashing rain
Swirls through the yard in clouds. Rain tips
From broken gutters, pours along the cracks
In ancient concrete, churns
With dung and straw and soil to form a paste
Of claggy, stinking, filthy clay-grey mud.

We stay inside. It's better there. But he,
In mud-encrusted, tattered waterproofs,
Wind-whipped, head bowed against the gusts
That stab like knives of ice, trudges through mud,
Buckets in oak-gnarled fingers, crimson-cold.

And in the barn, a slime-grey tangled mass
Lies in the straw. A steaming, rancid stench
Of rotten flesh. Twin lambs, too early born,
To be slung on the dung lump with the waste.

Outside, the silhouettes of hollow oaks
Darken and sharpen against the evening sky.
Impossible that brittle bare black twigs
Could metamorphose into fresh green life.

But spring is creeping upwards through the soil,
Along the roots and branches of the oaks.
Sharp silhouettes will soften into leaf
From tiny, tight brown buds. And April's warmth
Will heal his winter-battered face again."

Hannah's throat was tight when she finished. She had been far away as she read her poem. She had forgotten all about the audience.

Now she risked a glance out across the rows of chairs.

She wished she hadn't.

Because all she saw when she looked up was Danny Carr. He was leaning back on his chair and letting out the most enormous yawn.

She bent her head down and, cheeks burning, hurried back to her seat through the jagged applause.

Lottie squeezed her arm. "That was great, Hannah. You'll definitely win."

Danny leaned forward. "Nice one. You should have seen that judge's face when you were talking about dead lambs. I thought she was going to puke."

Hannah looked down at her muddy shoes. She wanted to curl up and disappear.

She sneaked a look at the judge and Miss Francis. They were talking in low, intense tones.

She should have written a prettier poem.

She should never have mentioned dead lambs.

Eventually, Miss Francis stood up and smiled. She thanked everyone for entering, and then she said, "It was very difficult to single out one poem among so many excellent entries, but our judge has chosen a winner."

Monica Rowse stood up, smiling her benevolent smile, and started on another speech. Hannah's stomach twisted into knots.

"And so," she finished, "I am delighted to announce that the Walters Cup for Poetry is awarded to . . . Miranda Hathaway!"

Of course.

Miranda's gang in the front row cheered.

Lottie put her arm around Hannah's shoulders. "Yours was miles better. That judge doesn't know what she's talking about."

Sweet of Lottie to say that.

But it didn't make any difference.

Maybe Dad was right after all. Maybe her writing was just a pointless waste of time.

Chapter Four

Homework

Miss Francis walked over as they were stacking chairs.

"That was a wonderful poem, Hannah."

Hannah stared at her.

"I think the judge's taste was perhaps a little more ... conventional, shall we say, but I have to say that, for me, yours was the one that stood out."

Hannah stood there, trying to take this in. The Head of English liked her poem best?

"Do you read a lot of poetry?" asked Miss Francis.

Hannah's eyes lit up. "Yes, loads. I love Ted Hughes and Seamus Heaney. I love that they write about the countryside in a real way, you know? Not all fluffy bunnies and chicks and daffodils, but mud and blood and death. Not that the countryside's always like that, obviously. But it's a mixture – sometimes it's beautiful and sometimes it's ugly. And that's the point, isn't it? Spring wouldn't be so beautiful if it didn't come after winter."

She stopped. She was talking too much.

But Miss Francis smiled at her. "Yes, absolutely. And I'd love to see more of your writing, if you'd

25

like to show it to me."

"See?" said Lottie as they left the hall. "I said it was really good, didn't I?"

Hannah was glowing. The Head of English liked her writing!

She turned left towards their form room, but Lottie said, "We have to hand in our maths homework, remember?"

Hannah's hand shot to her mouth.

"Didn't you do it?"

"I was going to do it last night, but the sheep got out again. Oh, no, Mr Nagra's going to kill me. I promised I'd hand it in on time this week. He said he'd phone my dad if it was late again. Oh, I'm so dead."

"Just copy mine when we get to the classroom. It won't take long."

Hannah breathed a sigh of relief. "Oh, Lottie, thank you so much. You're the best friend ever. You can copy mine next time."

"So," said Lottie, "do you really think your dad will let us have the loft?"

The wonderful vision of the theatre flooded into Hannah's head again. "Why wouldn't he? He doesn't use it for anything."

"We need to ask him today, though. I've got to email the entry form to the festival people by tomorrow. And we have to put the name and address of our theatre on it."

Hannah skipped with delight. "Can you believe it? We're going to enter the Linford Arts Festival!

We're going to have our own theatre!"

"So can I come up after school? Will he be around?"

Hannah stopped in her tracks and her eyes lit up. "Actually, that's perfect. He's taking the Field Marshall to a steam fair today."

"To sell it?"

"No, don't be silly. He'd never sell it. To show it. The point is, he loves the steam fair. He stands there all day showing off his Field Marshall and all these old blokes in tweeds come up and admire it and ask him questions about it. He goes every year and he's always in a good mood when he gets back."

"Fantastic. So I'll come up after school."

Lottie pushed open the door of their maths room. It was also 8M's tutor room and, since the sky was hurling sheets of rain against the windows, most of 8M were in there. They huddled in groups around the tables, chatting and texting.

Hannah did a quick scan of the room.

No. He wasn't there. He must be off sick today.

Was she relieved?

Or disappointed?

It was so hard to tell.

There was a pile of 7B's maths books already on the homework shelf in the corner. Lottie sat down at the empty table in front of the shelf and pulled her maths book out of her bag. She opened it to reveal a page of work so neat that it deserved to be blown up to poster size and displayed to the world right there and then.

Hannah knew as certainly as she knew her own name that every single answer was right. Lottie had never in her whole life got a maths question wrong.

Hannah opened her own book and wrote yesterday's date at the top of a clean page. She started to copy the first question.

The classroom door swung open and cracked against the wall. Every head turned.

Hannah looked up and her stomach did a back flip.

Into the room sauntered Jack Adamson. And, if it were possible, he looked even more gorgeous than usual. His wavy hair was all messed up and he had a cheeky grin on his face.

"Better late than never," grunted Danny, looking up from his phone.

"Yeah, well," said Jack, rearranging his expression into one of deep sorrow. "It's just, I was a bit upset. Family tragedy."

Vishali Patel was sitting at the table next to Hannah and Lottie. Her eyes widened in concern. "Oh, no. What's wrong?"

Jack gave a heavy sigh and plonked himself down in the chair beside Vishali's. He looked deeply into her eyes. Something stabbed at Hannah's chest.

"It's my goldfish," said Jack sadly. "He got run over."

The room erupted into giggles. Except for Lottie, who raised her eyes to heaven. Hannah looked down at her feet so Lottie couldn't see her smiling.

Vishali smacked Jack on the shoulder. "You pig.

You really had me going."

"Aw, sorry, Vish. Hey, you couldn't give us a lend of the geography homework, could you? I was going to do it but my mum's on a life support machine and I had to go and put another 50p in the slot."

Vishali giggled. "Oh, go on then." She fished in her bag.

"Thanks, Vish, you're a lifesaver." He winked at her. Hannah felt that stab in her chest again.

"Loser," muttered Lottie.

Jack looked up and caught Hannah's eye. Hannah felt herself going red. Jack grinned at her.

"Saw you all pedalling to school this morning, Roberts."

Danny snorted. "What, in that skip they call a car?"

Jack turned to his friend. "Don't be mean, Dan. Her dad built that car himself. It's all made from bits that fell off his tractors. One day he's going to put an engine in it, then they won't have to pedal any more."

Hannah put her head down to hide her smile.

"You're not funny, Jack," said Lottie.

"Shame you missed the poetry competition," said Danny.

"Yeah, I was really upset about that."

"No, really. It was hilarious. She did this poem all about mud and rotting lamb corpses. The judge nearly threw up."

Jack nodded respectfully at Hannah. "I like your style, Roberts. There's not enough poems about dead animals in the world, that's what I say."

Hannah was a mass of confusion. She bent right down over her maths book so that her hair curtained her face.

"It was really good actually," said Lottie. "I bet you couldn't write a poem to save your life. You probably can't even write."

"As it happens," said Jack, "I wrote a poem this very morning. It was inspired by the tragic death of my only goldfish."

The class giggled again.

"Huh," said Lottie. "Sure you did."

"Want to hear it?"

"No," said Lottie.

"Yes," said 8M.

Jack took out his English book, stood up and looked around the class expectantly. They all looked back at him. When Jack performed, everybody watched.

Hannah gazed at him adoringly. He was so good-looking. And so funny. How could Lottie not see that?

"'Ode to my Goldfish'," declaimed Jack.

Danny snorted.

Jack allowed a generous dramatic pause before continuing.

"Bubble, bubble, swim, swim."

Another dramatic pause.

"Verse Two," he announced. "Bubble, bubble, swim, swim.

"Verse Three," he continued through the laughter.

"Bubble, bubble, swim, swim."

"How many verses are there?" somebody asked.

"Thirty-seven."

"And they all go, 'Bubble, bubble, swim, swim'?"

"Yep. Hey, it's not my fault," he protested, dodging a book hurled at his head. "Goldfish only have four-second memories. He really wants to say more but he keeps having to go back to the beginning."

"Idiot," muttered Lottie as Jack sat back down, ducking a blizzard of flying objects. "Honestly, I don't know how you can like him."

"I don't like him!" said Hannah, suddenly aware that she'd been grinning like a halfwit.

"Oh, come on, Han, you so obviously do. You go red every time he looks at you. And you've been in such a love trance that you haven't even finished question one and the bell's going to go any minute."

Oh, my goodness. Lottie was right. Hannah pulled Lottie's maths book closer to her and started scribbling furiously.

"What are you doing in our classroom anyway?" Jack asked Hannah.

He leaned his chair sideways and glanced at the two maths books open in front of her. "Ooh, what's this? Copying homework? In Year Seven? Tut tut."

Lottie leapt in like a lioness protecting her young.

"At least she had a proper reason, Jack. Unlike someone I could mention. So don't you dare say anything."

"Shut up, pudding head," said Jack. "You're not

31

her babysitter."

The door opened and Hannah looked up.

Oh, help.

Mr Nagra was heading straight towards them.

Hannah slammed shut the two exercise books spread out on the table. She slipped Lottie's on to the top of the pile on the shelf. But what could she do with her own? All she had written was the date and half of question one.

"Just in time, you two," said Mr Nagra. "Right, let's have those books."

He picked up the pile of books and tucked them under his right arm. Hannah hid her book behind her back.

Honestly, what was she – five years old?

Mr Nagra stretched out his left hand. "Come on, Hannah. It can't be that bad."

Hannah stood as if turned to stone. If she confessed now and got told off in front of Jack and his friends, how humiliating would that be? But not to confess and then to be found out later. . .

Mr Nagra would phone Dad. And that would be worse.

And then, as she stood there dithering, the book was snatched out of her hand.

Hannah swung round.

And there was Jack, holding her maths book, strolling away from her towards the window, rifling through the pages.

She couldn't believe it.

He was looking for the page with her unfinished

homework.

He was going to show it to his form tutor.

So that she'd get into trouble and he'd get brownie points for grassing her up.

How could he?

Hannah ran over to get her book back but he held it out of her reach and carried on flicking through the pages.

"Stop horsing around, Jack, and bring that over here," said Mr Nagra. "I haven't got all day to waste."

And then the most amazing thing happened.

Holding the book with the covers facing the teacher, Jack found the page of unfinished work.

With a dramatic flourish he ripped it out, tore it into tiny pieces and threw them out of the window.

Hannah stared, frozen, as the wind blew the shreds of paper out of sight.

Jack turned to Mr Nagra and shrugged. "Just saving your time, sir. It was all wrong anyway. She's rubbish at maths, isn't she, sir?"

Mr Nagra was speechless for a moment. Then he said, "Jack Adamson, go to the Head's office. This minute. I've just about had it up to here with you."

Jack ambled out of the classroom.

Just before he closed the door, he turned and winked at Hannah.

Hannah couldn't stop smiling for the rest of the morning.

Chapter Five

Dad

Clayhill Farm was shaped like a shallow bowl, with the farmstead at its centre and the fields rising gently all around it to the woods on the north side and the Downs in the south. As Hannah and Lottie walked down the track after school, the silvery winter sun was setting in streaks of pink and orange cloud.

Hannah nudged Lottie. "Look! Aren't they beautiful?"

A charm of jewel-bright goldfinches, flashing scarlet and gold, pecked the seeds from the winter-blackened teazels by the woodpile.

But Lottie was absorbed in what looked like a complicated game of hopscotch.

"I don't know why you bother," said Hannah. "You're going to get covered in mud anyway."

"It's not so much the mud. I just don't want to get covered in cowpats and sheep droppings and chicken dung."

"Well, it's all mixed up together so you haven't got much chance of avoiding them. You should keep a pair of wellies here."

"Where will he be?" asked Lottie.

Hannah glanced at the tractor shed. "The Field Marshall's there, so he's back from the steam fair. We might catch him in his office before he does the milking."

They ran up the back stairs and squeezed past the clutter of filing cabinets in the corridor. Then they froze as they heard Hannah's dad's raised voice.

"So that's it then? You're saying he has every right to double the rent and there's nothing we can do about it?" There was silence for a moment. Then a grunt and, "Goodbye."

The phone slammed down on its receiver. Hannah looked at Lottie in alarm. She had heard that tone in his voice more often lately. Angry phone calls, letters from the land agent. . .

"Go on," whispered Lottie.

Hannah pushed the anxiety from her mind. She braced herself, placed both palms flat on the office door and shoved. The hinges squeaked and the bottom of the door scraped along the floorboards. It opened halfway and ground to a halt against some obstruction on the other side. Hannah squeezed into the room, stepping over a heap of cardboard files, and pulled Lottie in after her.

The farm office looked like the long-lost treasure hoard of a tribe that worshipped paper. There were files of papers, folders of papers, boxes of papers, and thousands and thousands of loose sheets of paper, all covered in dust and all heaped around the room in gigantic tottering piles. The table under the ivy-covered window was completely obliterated by stacks of paper. The wallpaper hung off in strips, bowing down to the paper on the floor. A cupboard door had burst open several years ago from the pressure of the boxes of papers stacked up inside it. No one had tried to close it since, so it still gaped open, with the papers tumbled crazily across the floor. One heap was suspended in mid-fall: a Leaning Tower of Paper.

The only thing in the room that wasn't filled with paper was the waste-paper basket.

It was empty.

In the middle of the room, like an island in a foaming paper sea, was an old oak desk. And at this desk, banging out a letter on an ancient black typewriter, sat Hannah's father. He wore torn blue dungarees with a frayed leather belt. He looked older than usual, his face stern, his forehead deeply furrowed. He looked thinner too, Hannah noticed.

"Dad?"

She couldn't tell if he had heard her. He stopped typing and frowned at a letter lying beside the typewriter. Hannah read the letterhead at the top. Goldman and Co., Solicitors.

"Dad?" she said again, a little louder this time.

"What's that, Joanne, er, Martha, er, Hannah?" He didn't look up.

Hannah looked at Lottie. "Go on," Lottie mouthed.

Her stomach clenched, Hannah navigated her way between a tower of box files and a pile of brown envelopes to reach his desk.

"Dad, me and Lottie were wondering if we could maybe use the tractor-shed loft?"

"Use it? For what?" His voice was tetchy. Hannah took a little step backwards.

"Well, errmm, as a theatre." Even the word theatre sounded strange in that room.

"Theatre?" Her father mouthed the word as if it had an unpleasant taste. "Ha!"

He went back to his typing. Bash, bash, bash, with his huge rough fingers.

Hannah turned to Lottie, hovering in the doorway. Lottie stepped back out of the room and beckoned. Hannah tiptoed around the heaps of paper and followed her into the corridor.

"We've got to tell him why we want it," Lottie whispered. "Describe how good it's going to be."

"Why would that work?"

"Well, your mum used to act before she was married, didn't she?"

"Yes, exactly. Before she got married."

"Well, maybe if he knew how much you love theatre? He knows you won the Year Six Drama Cup, doesn't he? So he knows how good you are. Go on, talk to him."

"Hmm," said Hannah, but she weaved her way back through the obstacles, her heart beating faster. Over the past two days, the wonderful vision of her theatre had taken over her head. Lottie was right. It was worth a try.

"Dad, you know I wrote a play?"

"Eh?"

"It fell in the mud but I'm writing it out again. And we've got loads of ideas for more. You see, there's this drama competition we really want to enter, and we thought if we made a real theatre in the tractor-shed loft we could act the plays out properly, and Lottie can sew and she could make amazing costumes, and we'd make scenery and—"

Now he raised his head, a deep frown on his face. "You want to take over the tractor-shed loft to use as a *theatre*?"

"Yes."

"And what about everything that's in there?"

Hannah glanced at Lottie, who had stayed in the doorway. "Well, we thought maybe we could help you sort through it."

"Oh, did you?" He glared at Hannah. "Do you think I haven't got enough on my plate at the moment? I've just had Martha pestering for a television in the house. A television! So she can sit about night after night goggling at drivel. And now you come up here asking for the tractor-shed loft! Have you all gone mad?"

"We could clear it out ourselves."

He banged his fist on the desk, raising clouds of dust from the disintegrating blotting paper. "Don't you even think of messing about with all that stuff yourselves! You've got no idea what any of it is; you'll get yourselves injured. And that floor up there isn't sound. You'd end up falling through it and breaking your legs, and the last thing I need is to be taking one of you to hospital. For goodness' sake, this is a farm, not a playground. Haven't you got better things to do than mess about with plays?"

Something in Hannah made her persist.

"*Please*, Dad. I know you don't like theatre, but I love it. I love it just like Mum did." She saw his face tighten, but she had to go on. "I can't be just the same as you. You love your animals. This is what I love. Please, could I just have this?"

Her father jumped up from his chair and suddenly he was towering above her, silhouetted by the dim light from the window.

Hannah took a step back.

Was he angry?

Or was he upset?

"Get out!" he yelled. "Just get out! I've got work to do, for goodness' sake. Just leave me in peace!"

Hannah was already stumbling out of the room. Her vision blurry with tears, she caught her foot on a pile of folders.

"Aarghh!" she cried as her knee crashed on to the splintered floorboards. "Ow!"

She shot out her hand and pushed over a heap of plastic wallets. They slithered across the floor, spilling their contents like an oil slick.

Hannah scrambled to her feet, trying to pile the papers back together.

"Leave them alone!" shouted her dad. "Don't touch anything! Just get out!"

Chapter Six

The Photograph

Hannah limped into the corridor, pushed past Lottie, stumbled to the stairs and slumped on the top step, her hands shielding her face.

Lottie came and sat beside her. "Are you all right?"

Hannah bit her cheeks to stop herself from crying. Why had Dad just lost it with her like that?

Click, clack, click, clack.

"Martha!" hissed Hannah. She jumped to her feet and wiped her cheeks with her sleeves. "Quick!"

But it was too late.

"Ha ha ha-ha haa!"

Martha tottered down the corridor. She was wearing the red stilettos again, this time with black tights, denim hotpants and a tiny red vest top.

"Dad wouldn't let you have a theatre, ha ha ha-ha haa! Dad's angry with Hannah, ha ha ha-ha haa!"

"Have you been spying again?"

"Spying? It wasn't exactly hard to hear. Ooh, Daddy, can we have a theatre? Ooh, *please*, Daddy?"

"Oh, shut up, Martha. Come on," said Hannah to Lottie. "Let's go to my room."

They walked past Martha and back through the

jungle of filing cabinets. Martha clacked off down the stairs.

As Hannah passed the office door, she couldn't help glancing in.

Her father sat with his head in his hands, staring at a picture on the desk in front of him.

Hannah knew that picture. It usually hung on the wall behind the desk.

It was a photograph of her grandfather, taken in the 1940s. He was perched on the seat of a brand-new, bright-green tractor. He was grinning broadly. It was his first ever tractor, Dad had said. His beloved Field Marshall.

Why had Dad taken the photograph off the wall? And why was he sitting staring at it, looking so miserable?

Had something happened at the steam fair?

But what could have happened to upset him like that?

Hannah pushed the questions aside. She opened her bedroom door and then, without going in, slammed it very loudly.

"Follow me!" she hissed to Lottie. "Tiptoes!"

"Where are we going?" mouthed Lottie as they crept down the carpeted front stairs.

"Sitting room."

"But you're not allowed in there."

"Have to get away from Martha. She'll think we're in my room. She'll go and try to listen at the door."

"Oh. Clever."

The sitting room hadn't been used since Christmas.

A scattering of soot rattled down the chimney as Hannah opened the door. The ancestors on the wall did not look amused.

Hannah's great-grandparents had been wealthy Londoners. They'd wanted their only child, Hannah's grandfather, to be a lawyer. But on family holidays in Sussex he fell in love with the land and made up his mind to become a farmer. While in the army during the Second World War he took an agricultural correspondence course. And when he came back from the war he rented Clayhill Farm. It was badly neglected. There was no electricity or mains water, the fields were full of weeds and there wasn't even a farmyard, just a sea of mud right up to the back door.

Over the years, all the family money was spent on the farm. All the silver and the good furniture was sold to pay the bills, but Hannah's mother had tried to keep the sitting room nice and now Dad wouldn't allow anything in there to be touched. The rich ancestors sat haughtily in their chipped gilt frames, and their stern painted eyes seemed to say: "We're not supposed to be in a farmhouse, you know. We deserve better than this."

The children had been banned from the sitting room after Hannah smashed into the china cabinet during a game of Tag in the Dark. Their mother's collection of china pigs lived in the cabinet. Three of them had been broken. That was probably the last time Hannah had seen her father as angry as he was today.

Lottie stared nervously at the portraits. She shivered and pulled her coat more tightly around her.

"That's a lovely picture." She pointed at the only painting that wasn't a portrait. It was of a beautiful bay horse, all saddled up but riderless, with a spaniel standing beside it.

Hannah glanced at it. "That was my mum's favourite." She slumped on the sagging Victorian sofa and picked at the torn gold brocade. "I can't believe he won't let us have the loft. It would have been so amazing to enter the festival. He never even uses it! I bet he hasn't been up there for years."

Lottie wandered over to the mantelpiece and picked up one of the ornate silver candlesticks. "Wow, it's really heavy. Are they real silver?"

"Oh, be careful with those," said Hannah. "They were my great-granny's."

Lottie put the candlestick back. "Why did your dad get so mad just now? I didn't think he'd go that crazy just because you asked to use the loft."

Hannah shrugged. "I don't know. It's weird. He's so moody at the moment. He hates the new landlord. That always sets him off on one. But I never mentioned the landlord, did I?"

Lottie drew in her breath sharply.

"What?" said Hannah.

Lottie grabbed Hannah's arm. "I forgot. I meant to tell you. My mum's friend – you know, Jeanette, she's a real gossip – came round last night. And – and I know this can't be true – but . . . it's just . . . I heard her telling my mum that your new landlord wants to demolish the farm. And build houses on it."

Hannah burst out laughing. "Don't be stupid! He can't do that – we live here!"

Lottie's shoulders relaxed. "I know. I told you it was just a silly rumour." She dusted off a baby photograph of Hannah. "Look at those fat cheeks!"

Hannah ignored this. She picked up a picture of her father and grandfather standing outside the granary. They were dressed identically in patched blue dungarees with leather belts. They both had their heads thrown back, laughing. Her dad must have been about fourteen. Shortly after that picture was taken, Grandfather died and Dad left school to take over the farm. Usually the picture made Hannah feel sorry for him, but today she just felt cross.

"I can't believe he won't let us have a theatre. How can I get to be an actress if I can't do any acting? It's so rubbish that we don't do drama at school."

"We can't just give up. Isn't there anywhere else we could use?"

"Everywhere's full of stuff. Animals or machinery or feed. Well, there's the old stables, I suppose."

"They wouldn't work," said Lottie. "There's partitions everywhere."

"Anyway," said Hannah, "they're right in the middle of the yard. If we tried to turn them into a theatre he'd notice straightaway."

Lottie took a breath as if she was going to speak. Then she shut her mouth again. She wandered over to the window sill and drew patterns in the dust with her fingers.

"What?" said Hannah.

Lottie hesitated. "It's just – well, Mum said I could join the Linford Youth Theatre if I wanted. You know, the one Miranda and Emily go to. It's supposed to be really good."

Hannah stared at Lottie.

"I'd only join if you came too," Lottie said.

Hannah shook her head. "I can't. You know I can't. You have to pay to join."

"My mum would pay for you."

Hannah's voice came out louder than usual, as it always did when she was irritated. "I wouldn't let her do that. And neither would Dad. And he wouldn't let me go anyway. Drama is a waste of time, remember? And I have to be home to get the tea ready, you know that."

"All right, don't bite my head off. It was only an offer. It's your dad you're mad at, not me, remember?"

Lottie wiped the dust off a faded photo with her sleeve. Then she frowned and peered closely at it. She took it into the middle of the room and stared at it under the light.

"What are you doing?" said Hannah.

"Hannah, what's that?"

Hannah looked at the photo. Then she looked at Lottie. How could she be so insensitive?

"It's my mum."

"I know it's your mum. I meant, what's that behind her?"

Hannah took the faded photograph. Her mother stood in a field, a bucket in one hand and baby

45

Hannah balanced on the other hip. Hens pecked around in the bushes.

That was all Hannah had ever seen in the picture. But now she saw that in the background was a long, low shed, surrounded by bushes.

"Which shed is that?" asked Lottie.

"I don't know. How weird. I've never noticed it before."

"Maybe it's on another farm."

Hannah held the picture closer to the light. "No, look, that's the wood behind. And those look like the orchard railings. So she must be standing in North Meadow."

"But there's no shed around there now, is there?"

Hannah shook her head. Then she opened her eyes wide and stared at Lottie. "Unless. . ."

"What?"

But Hannah was already halfway out the door, the picture in her hand. "Come on! We've got to see!"

She ran across the hall and into the gloomy back passage, her heart racing. If they went out this way, they were less likely to bump into anyone and be waylaid with chores.

But as they passed the kitchen, she heard a plaintive, "Hannah, is that you?"

She stopped. "I'll just check he's OK."

Sam was sitting at the big table in the middle of the kitchen. He had cleared a space amid the piles of unironed laundry, unopened post and oily tractor parts and was drawing a large picture of a tractor pulling a plough.

"Oh, Sam, that's lovely," said Hannah.

Sam looked up proudly. "It's a Kverneland 4 Furrow Reversible."

"Wow. Well done."

"What's for tea?"

Hannah shot a hand to her mouth. "Blast, I forgot to get the casserole out of the freezer."

"I'm starving."

"Sorry, Sammy. We'll have to have scrambled eggs again. Have you collected the eggs?"

Sam nodded. Hannah looked at the clock. Was it really five already?

"I'll be back in a second, Sam."

Lottie followed her out to the scullery.

"Sorry, Lottie, I've got to get tea."

Lottie's eyes widened. "No way!"

"But if we go out now," Hannah whispered, "someone's going to come looking for me and then they'll all find out and then it's all over. You saw what Dad was like. If we do find anything, we're going to have to keep it secret."

Lottie groaned in frustration. "But if we're going to enter the festival, we have to send the entry form tomorrow, remember? With the name and address of our theatre on it."

Sam's voice came from the kitchen. "Hannah! I'm really, *really* hungry."

"Coming!" She lowered her voice. "Can you come up later?"

"Sure." Lottie's mum worked in London. She didn't get home until late, and even when she was at home she was too tired to notice where Lottie was most of the time.

"Meet me by the orchard fence. I'll say I'm taking Tess for a walk."

They jumped back as the scullery door opened. "Hello," said Jo, kicking off her boots. "What's for tea? I'm starving."

"Scrambled eggs."

"*Again?*"

"Sorry. Casserole tomorrow."

Jo went into the kitchen. Hannah shut the door.

"Seven thirty," she whispered. "And bring a torch."

Chapter Seven

The Search

The farmyard was pitch-black except for a dim light in the pig shed. Through the darkness came muffled grunts and snuffles from the sties. Hannah heard the distant clanking of buckets and her father's voice saying, "There you go, old girl. That'll sort you out."

She couldn't risk switching her torch on yet. She let her eyes adjust to the dark and then she crept through the yard and on to the track.

A sudden shriek pierced the night and made her gasp.

Only a Little Owl, she told herself. Get a grip.

She ducked under the fence into North Meadow and climbed on to the orchard railings to wait for Lottie.

It was a really dark night. No moon and no stars. She was still too near the pigsties to use her torch. The icy wind cut right through to her skin. She pulled her scarf up over her mouth.

What was that?

Something rustled in the long grass at the edge of the field. All Hannah's muscles tensed. Please not a rat. What if she stepped on it in the dark? What if it ran up her leg? She drew her legs up higher on the railings.

Come on, Lottie. Please don't be late tonight.

A light appeared at the top of the track. Was it a bike light or a torch? The track was a public footpath and people used it to walk their dogs. It could be anyone.

But then the light started to swerve madly from one side of the road to the other. Hannah relaxed. Definitely Lottie on her bicycle. No one but Lottie would swerve around in that crazy way just to avoid a bit of mud on their clothes.

Hannah listened to make sure her dad was still in the pigsties and then flashed her torch on and off three times. Lottie braked at the railings.

"Bring your bike into the field," whispered Hannah. "Dad might see it if you leave it there."

"It's so dark up here," whispered Lottie as they lifted her bicycle over the fence. "It's spooky."

"It's fine," said Hannah. She felt much braver now she wasn't alone. "Have you got a torch?"

Lottie took one out of her pocket and switched it on. "So where's the shed?" She shone the torch around in every direction.

Hannah grabbed her arm. "Don't do that!" she hissed. "Dad'll see it!"

"Oops, sorry."

Hannah shone her own torch down the field. The beam illuminated a dense black tangle of bushes in the bottom corner of the meadow.

"See there?"

"You think the shed's in there?"

Hannah reached into her other coat pocket and took out the framed photograph of her mother. She moved the light on to it.

"See? There's the orchard railings and there's the wood behind. And there's that big oak tree by the bottom fence."

Lottie shone her torch beam on to the thicket and shuddered. "No way am I going into those bushes."

"Lottie! Don't be crazy. Imagine how amazing it would be if we found a building in there. Our own secret theatre that no one else even knows exists!"

"But it's so dark. Anything might be lurking in the bushes."

An image of glinting rodent eyes flashed into Hannah's head. She forced it out again. "There won't be anything bad. Come on."

Hannah didn't voice her worst fear, because she didn't even want to think it.

What if the shed had been demolished?

Or blown down in a storm?

What if there was nothing there at all?

Lottie stayed close to Hannah as they stumbled down the muddy field. The wind whipped against their faces and made strange noises in the treetops. They kept their torch beams trained on the treacherous ground, where rabbit holes and molehills lay ready to send them sprawling into cowpats at every step.

Hannah caught a rabbit's eyes in the beam of her torch. It froze for a second, then bolted away. Something fluttered across their path. Lottie screamed and jumped backwards.

"Sssh," said Hannah. "Do you want Dad to find us? It was only a bat."

She hoped Lottie hadn't noticed how the bat had made her jump. Bats were a little too close to mice for Hannah's liking.

"What was your mum doing down here anyway?" asked Lottie.

Hannah shrugged. "I think she kept chickens once."

"Why did she stop?"

"A monster crawled out of the woods one night – a dark February night, very like this one – and devoured all the chickens."

"Stop it!"

A piercing shriek split the darkness.

"What was that?" cried Lottie. She grabbed Hannah's arm so tightly it hurt.

Hannah was glad of the distraction. She didn't want to talk about her mother. "It's a Little Owl. Your dad would love it."

Lottie laughed. "Yes, he'd be recording it in his notebook right now."

Lottie's dad was a mad-keen birdwatcher. His monthly Clayhill Bird Survey was the highlight of Hannah's dad's life. The two of them would discuss the results for hours – how many species there were that month and whether some exciting new bird had been spotted on the farm.

They had reached the edge of the thicket now. They stopped, and Lottie tightened her grip on Hannah's arm even more. Funny how Lottie, so confident at school, could turn into a gibbering wreck when put into a field at night.

Hannah shone her torch over the thicket. It was a mass of bare black thorny twigs, crowded together like living barbed wire.

"There must be a way in somewhere. Let's investigate."

They walked the whole way around the thicket, scanning it from top to bottom with their torches. But there was no way in.

"I don't understand," said Lottie. "Your mum must've got in to feed the chickens."

"That was ten years ago. It's just got really overgrown, I guess. We'll have to push our way through."

"But there's no gaps."

"Follow me."

Hannah ducked under a branch. Holding the torch in her mouth, she inched forward, snapping twigs and moving brambles aside with her gloved hands. The gloves were thin and the thorns pierced through them. Brambles clawed into her coat and hat and she had to keep stopping to pull herself free. Lottie followed her, letting out shrieks and moans as twigs sprang back and scratched her face.

"What will they say at school tomorrow? We're going to look like we've been in the First World War trenches."

Hannah wriggled under a hawthorn bush and out the other side. She shone her torch in front of her, expecting more brambles. But the beam illuminated what looked like a hedge of ivy.

Hannah's heart raced. "Quick. Shine it over here."

Lottie squeezed through the bush and got to her feet, rubbing her bleeding face. She moved the beam of her torch up and along the ivy-covered surface.

"Oooh!"

"Do you think it is?"

Lottie pulled at the ivy tendrils.

"Look! A wooden wall! It's a shed, I know it is!"

She turned to Hannah. They could just see each other's faces in the glow from the torchlight.

"I can't believe it," said Lottie. "It's been here all this time and we never knew it existed."

Hannah said nothing. Goose pimples sprang up all over her body.

"We have to find the door," said Lottie.

They felt their way along the low ivy-covered wall, shining their torches slowly all over its surface. Suddenly Hannah's beam lit up a metal runner, near to the ground. Her heart thumping, she moved the light to the top of the wall. Another runner. She zigzagged the beam downwards and across, searching, searching.

And then she saw it. A rusty iron door handle.

"Here! It's here!"

Hannah held the torch steady and they stood there for a few seconds, just staring at the handle.

"Wow," said Lottie.

Hannah looked at the door, her stomach churning. What was inside?

"Do you dare to open it?" whispered Lottie.

"You do it."

"No way. It's your farm. You do it."

It was clear from Lottie's tone that she wasn't going to change her mind. Hannah would have to go in first.

It was only rats that frightened her. If there weren't rats, it would be all right.

She banged hard on the door with her fist and held her breath.

No sound at all. She banged again. Still silent.

"OK. I'm going in." She grasped the handle and braced herself to pull the door along its runners. But it didn't move.

"It won't budge. There's too much ivy."

They started to rip off the clinging tendrils. And then, reaching out to grasp a stem, Hannah's gloved hand hit metal. She shone her torch on to it.

It was a horseshoe. A large iron horseshoe, carefully nailed to the door.

A lucky horseshoe.

It was a sign.

A sign from Mum.

This had been Mum's shed.

And now it was meant to be theirs.

Suddenly Hannah was desperate to get inside. She had to see what was there. She grasped the handle again and yanked it.

"It still won't budge. It must be rusted up."

She dug her heels into the ground as if for a tug of war and pulled with all her strength. Slowly she felt the door start to give. It creaked back on its rusty runners, centimetre by reluctant centimetre.

Hannah's heart was thumping so fast now she was sure she could hear it.

"Go on," whispered Lottie. "Shine your torch in."

But now Hannah didn't dare. Because as long as she didn't look inside, she could still imagine it was going to be perfect.

What if the roof had fallen in?

What if there was only this one wall and the rest of the shed had collapsed?

It had been ten years, after all.

A lot could happen in ten years.

"I can't," she said. "What if it's all fallen down?"

"OK, let's do it together. One, two, three. . ."

Hannah took a deep breath and shone her light into the blackness.

For a moment there was complete silence. Then Hannah spoke, so quietly it was barely even a whisper.

"It's here," she breathed. "It's still here."

In hushed reverence, as if they were entering a great cathedral, they stepped inside and shone their torches around.

"Oh my goodness," said Lottie. She was fidgeting with excitement. "It's perfect!"

She paced the shed, shining her torch along the walls and on to the ceiling.

"It's really big – we can divide it into three to make a dressing room and a stage and an auditorium. And look, there's a door at the other end for the audience.

There's a few gaps in the walls, but we can easily mend them. And the floor's dry, so the roof doesn't leak. It's perfect!"

The strangest sensation flooded over Hannah.

It felt like coming home.

This was Mum's shed, she thought. She left it here for us to find.

"What shall we call it?" said Lottie. "We need a name. Then I can e-mail the form off when I get home. I can't believe it! We can enter the festival! What about the Theatre in the Shed? Or, I know, the Rusty Horseshoe Theatre?"

"No," said Hannah. "I already know what it's called."

"What? Tell me! Tell me!" Lottie shone her torch directly into Hannah's eyes. "Tell me, Hannah Roberts, or there will be consequences."

Hannah smiled and grabbed Lottie's hands. "This was my mum's hen house. So it's called the Secret Hen House Theatre. What do you think?"

Lottie tried it out. "The Secret Hen House Theatre. Yes. It sounds just right."

Chapter Eight

A Letter

Friday morning, eight thirty-five. Hannah sat in the far corner of 7B's tutor room, racing through her history homework and trying not to be distracted by the presence of Jack Adamson, who for some reason was perched on the edge of Miranda's desk.

"Hey, Miranda," said Emily. "Did you know the prize money's gone up? For the festival? Five hundred pounds for the winning theatre!"

Five hundred pounds!

Imagine having five hundred pounds to spend on the theatre.

Red velvet chairs in the auditorium. . .

A huge dressing-room mirror with lights all around it. . .

Gold curtains. . .

"Five hundred pounds?" said Miranda. "How strange, that's the same amount I had for my birthday." She gave a little tinkling laugh.

Imagine Miranda's dumbstruck face when the Secret Hen House Theatre won the five hundred-pound prize. . .

"You know what else is strange?" said Jack.

Hannah glanced up. Jack sounded deeply thoughtful.

"Ronaldo's transfer fee is eighty million pounds," he said, "and that's the same amount *I* had for *my* birthday."

Hannah giggled. So did everyone else. Miranda looked unsure whether to be offended or join in the laughter. She settled for a tight little smile and a toss of her head.

Lottie walked in and Hannah wiped the smile off her face. Lottie flung her bag on to the classroom table, sat down and dropped an envelope in Hannah's lap. "Look at this," she murmured. "The post came just as I was leaving."

Hannah glanced at the clock. Still ten minutes to go and she was on the last question. There was plenty of time.

She picked up the plain white envelope. "What is it?"

"Look and see," whispered Lottie. She drummed her fingers on the table in excitement.

Hannah prised the letter out of its envelope.

Dear Miss Roberts and Miss Perfect

Many thanks for entering the Linford Arts Festival's Youth Theatre Celebration. We are delighted that your drama group has chosen to participate in this exciting event and enclose the complete festival programme and competition rules for your information.

We very much look forward to seeing your play, *By Her Majesty's Appointment*. Mrs Fran Butler, one of our team of adjudicators, will visit your theatre to watch your performance at 3p.m. on Saturday 20 March. . .

"What!" Hannah jerked her head up, wide-eyed. "That's only—"

"Three weeks. I know. Keep your voice down – Miranda will hear."

"Three weeks!" whispered Hannah. "There's no way we'll be ready by then. We haven't even had one rehearsal. Oh, my goodness, I can't believe we've entered this."

"Think of how much we've already done, though. The theatre's nearly ready, isn't it?"

They had spent every evening since Monday hacking a path from the back of the thicket to what they now called the stage door, and then smuggling all the junk out of the shed and concealing it around the farm.

"It's not exactly ready," said Hannah. "We haven't even built the proscenium arch yet."

"The what?"

"Proscenium arch. You know, the walls at the front of the stage, either side of the curtains. Can you come for the whole day tomorrow? We can make the arch with fence posts and sacking."

"Won't the others be around, though?"

"Martha's going to Jade's house in the morning."

"Jade? Danny's sister Jade?"

"Yeah, can you believe it? Typical Martha to be

60

best friends with Danny's sister. But at least she'll be out of the way."

"Cool," said Lottie. "Then on Sunday we can start rehearsing. And the performance date's a week into the Easter holidays, so we can rehearse every day then. Oh, and the new script's brilliant."

"Really? You like it?"

"It's great. Although I didn't understand half the words the queen uses."

"I did use my thesaurus a lot. Good words though, aren't they? My favourite was 'mellifluous'. And 'serendipity'. And 'solipsistic'."

Lottie shook her head. "Your granny should never have given you that thesaurus. It's like a deadly weapon in your hands."

Hannah looked at the letter again.

The winners in each category will be announced and the prizes awarded at the festival's closing ceremony on Thursday 25 March, to which all participating groups are warmly invited.

The Linford Arts Festival Committee wishes you the best of luck and much enjoyment with the preparations for your play.

Yours sincerely

Martin Dean
Chairman, Linford Arts Festival Committee

"What do you think the judge will think?" said Lottie. "When she comes and finds a theatre in a hen house?"

"She'll love it. It's original. And we're doing everything ourselves."

"Yeah. All two of us."

"Exactly! I bet Miranda's group has adults doing everything for them."

Miranda had drifted across the room and was flicking through a magazine with Emily. At the mention of her name she turned round.

Lottie slapped her hand over the letter and slid it off the table, but not before Miranda had seen the logo at the top.

"The Linford Arts Festival. How come you've got a letter from them?"

"Mind your own business, Little Miss Nosy," said Lottie.

Miranda narrowed her eyes. "Are you entering? Are you in a drama group?"

"Oh, which one?" asked Emily.

"Yes, which one?" said Miranda, her eyes fixed on Hannah. "I didn't know you went to a drama group, Hannah. Is it a special group for farm animals?" Her eyes lit up. "What play are you doing? *Animal Farm*?" She nudged Emily, who giggled on cue.

Hannah felt a blush rise from deep inside her and start to spread all over her cheeks. Oh, why couldn't she control it?

Lottie tilted her chin and challenged Miranda's stare. "It's none of your business which group we're in, Miranda. And we're certainly not going to tell you."

Miranda tossed her head like a mare in a temper. Hannah could almost see her stamp her hoof. "Well, I wouldn't bother entering the festival if I were you. Our group's won it for the last three years and my mum's written the best play ever this year, hasn't she, Ems? And she's got her friend who's a professional West End director to help direct it. No one else stands a chance."

"Really?" said Lottie. "Well, you'd better prepare for a disappointment, because you might just have some competition this time."

Miranda smirked. "I very much doubt that, Charlotte. I can't imagine that our group is going to be seriously challenged by you two losers and a bunch of farm animals." She flicked her hair over her shoulder and turned back to the magazine.

"Oh, I wouldn't be too sure about that," retorted Lottie. "You'll just have to wait and see, won't you?"

Chapter Nine

Curtains

When Hannah got to the theatre on Saturday morning Lottie was already there, perched on an upturned barrel of Cooper's Dairy Ointment (The Number One Udder Cream), drawing in her red notebook. Shafts of sunlight poured through the gaps in the walls and illuminated her work.

"You're early!"

"I know," said Lottie. "My mum was still asleep and it's so boring at home. What's udder cream? It sounds really gross."

"There's nothing wrong with udder cream. It's what you rub on cows' udders if they get sore when they're being milked or when their calves are sucking from them."

"Cow moisturiser?"

"Exactly. Also a cure for every human skin problem, according to my dad. What are you drawing?"

Lottie held out her notebook. "An idea I had for the queen's costume."

"Wow," said Hannah. "That's amazing."

She took the notebook reverently. The page was filled with a detailed design of a full-length gown:

a riot of clashing colours and patterns, frills, bows and lace.

"I thought it would suit the queen's over-the-top personality," said Lottie. "She has no taste so she just goes for the gaudiest design possible and she thinks she looks great."

Hannah stroked the paper. She imagined how it would feel to act Queen Matilda in that dress: the way she would draw herself to her fullest height; the arrogant tilt of her head as she looked down her nose at the poor maid; the rustle of silk as she paraded across the stage.

"It's fabulous," she said. "Are you really going to make it?"

"Sure. We'll need to go to jumble sales and get material, then I'll use Mum's sewing machine."

"It'll be amazing." Hannah hesitated. "Have you thought about costume changes, though? We're going to have to change really quickly, with just the two of us doing all the parts."

"Don't worry," said Lottie. "I'll use Velcro. So what's in that file?"

Hannah had read in one of her mother's theatre books that the director of a play keeps a file of notes about every aspect of the play she is working on. So she had gone to the newsagent's after school yesterday and spent half of Granny's Christmas money on a shiny purple ring binder, a pad of paper and some brightly coloured dividers. She had labelled each section: Costumes, Props, Scenery, Hair and Make-Up. In the last section, labelled The Play, she had filed a photocopy of the script, single-sided to keep the facing pages blank for her director's notes on the actors' movements and gestures.

Lottie nodded in approval. "Cool. Let's get started."

They spent the morning making two tall frames out of fence posts. They nailed hessian sacking over them so they looked like huge artists' canvases. Then they wedged the frames vertically on either side of the shed, from floor to ceiling, to make two side walls for the front of the stage.

"There!" said Hannah, standing out in the auditorium to admire the effect. "Our proscenium arch. We'll have wings behind the side walls for our exits and entrances – we'll make them the same way as we did the proscenium – then hang a backcloth at the back, and then, between the front walls – swish!" With a grand sweep of her hands, she mimed a pair of curtains opening.

Lottie frowned. "Where are we going to get curtains?"

Hannah paused, her hands still in mid-air. "Hmm. Has your mum got some old ones somewhere?"

"Definitely not. She doesn't keep anything old. It's a miracle I haven't ever been bagged up for the wheelie bin in one of her clear-outs. Don't you have any old ones?"

"All ours are old," said Hannah. "But they're all torn. And they're all still on the windows."

Then she stared at Lottie. "Oh, but—"

"What?"

Hannah clapped her hands. "What about the sitting-room ones? They're not torn. And they're red and silky. They'd look amazing."

Lottie stared at her. "You have got to be joking."

"No one will notice. Nobody ever goes in there."

"Hannah, you can't take your dad's curtains. That's stealing."

"It's not stealing, it's just borrowing. We'll put them back for Christmas; that's the only time the room's used. He'll never know."

"They *would* look amazing," said Lottie, looking at the bare proscenium arch.

"Exactly."

"What if he finds out, though? He'd kill us."

"He'd only kill me. And he'll never find out."

The sitting room had two wide windows, each hung with crimson curtains.

"Which pair shall we take?" whispered Lottie.

"These ones," said Hannah. "They're not so faded."

She dragged a carved mahogany chair dotted with woodworm holes over to the furthest window and climbed on to the torn velvet seat.

A shrivelled holly branch sat on top of the curtain rail. When Hannah's mother was alive, the whole room sparkled at Christmas. There was always a huge tree covered in lights and an enormous log fire that crackled and shot sparks up the chimney. Candles burned on the mantelpiece and silver tinsel glittered on the picture rail. Her father cut down great swathes of ivy and holly branches to drape over the gilt picture frames.

He still decorated the house with greenery and they still made a show of having a happy Christmas. But everybody knew it wasn't the same.

Lottie folded each curtain carefully as Hannah handed it to her. Then they carried them through the silent house and into the yard.

"Oh, no!" said Hannah. Tess, her father's springer spaniel, was bounding towards her, tail waving like a windmill. "Dad must be around."

As she was speaking, her father strode around the corner from the milking parlour.

"Quick! Hide them!" hissed Lottie.

Hannah looked around frantically. A dented wheelbarrow, coated with dried-up pig dung, stood outside the garden gate.

"In there!"

They threw the curtains into the wheelbarrow. Hannah pulled her coat off and flung it on top of them.

"Look casual," she muttered. "We've been cleaning out the guinea pigs, OK?"

They strolled through the yard, trundling the barrow in front of them. Dad passed them and turned up the path towards the pigsties without a glance.

"Phew," mouthed Hannah.

"Oh, no – look."

Hannah looked up towards the farm track. The farm's one working gate was bolted shut across the track. Sitting on the gate, grinning triumphantly, were Jo and Sam. In front of the gate sprawled Jasper, a sheep so fat that he looked like a giant snowball. Jo had looked after him since he was orphaned at two days old, and now he followed her everywhere. He even had his own pet, a half-grown duck called Lucy, who spent her days riding around on Jasper's back. She was there now, tucked into her vast woolly nest.

"Uh-oh," said Hannah. "What are they up to?"

Jo and Sam didn't take their eyes off Lottie and Hannah as they approached with the wheelbarrow. When they were nearly at the gate, Jo thrust out her arm, palm up towards Hannah.

"Stop, in the name of Bean!"

"What?"

"The correct password is required to pass through this gate."

Hannah rolled her eyes and looked around her.

"Pig dung?"

"Incorrect password."

"Big fat sheep?" suggested Lottie.

Jo narrowed her eyes at Lottie. "Incorrect password. Also rude and hurtful."

Hannah sighed. "Crazy mad people who call each other bean names?"

"Incorrect password and an insult to the great and mighty Society of Bean."

Hannah turned to her brother. "Sam, please let us through. It's important."

Sam looked at Jo. Jo gave him a stern stare.

"Do not relent, French Bean. The question is, *why*

is it important? And *what* is important? That is what the Society of Bean must find out."

Hannah blew out her cheeks impatiently. "Sam, why do you do this mad Bean thing?"

Sam shrugged. "She makes me."

"All password attempts unsuccessful," said Jo. "Entry denied."

From the pigsties came a sound of clattering metal, followed by, "Get down, girl! Behave!"

Lottie glanced fearfully towards the pigsties. "Just stop being so stupid and let us through."

She grabbed the bolt and tugged it. It didn't move.

"There's no point," said Hannah. "It won't budge with those two sitting on it and Jasper in front like a great fat door stop."

"Don't listen to them, Jasper!" cried Jo.

"Let us through," said Lottie in as menacing a voice as she could manage. "Or the sheep gets it."

Jo laughed. "I wouldn't threaten Jasper if I were you. He's a trained killer. He butts people I don't like."

"Oh, please," said Lottie.

There was the sound of wood being dragged across concrete. Dad was shutting the pigsty door.

"Let us *through*!" hissed Lottie, glancing at the wheelbarrow.

Jo caught the glance. "If you want to get through, show us what you've got in that barrow."

Hannah said, in a higher voice than she'd intended, "We've been cleaning out the guinea pigs."

Jo snorted. "You?!"

70

"Why have you put your coat on top of guinea-pig droppings?" said Sam.

"Good point, French Bean," said Jo. "Let's see what's under it."

She jumped down from the gate and reached for the coat.

Hannah spreadeagled herself across the barrow. "No! Get off!"

"Guess I'll have to call Dad then." Jo opened her mouth wide and took a deep breath.

"No!" shouted Hannah and Lottie together.

Jo folded her arms and looked at them through narrowed eyes. "So. Here's the deal. We won't call Dad and we'll let you through this gate if you show us what's in that wheelbarrow."

"And," said Sam, "you have to tell us what you've been doing all morning."

Hannah looked at Lottie in despair. Was the theatre over before it had even begun?

Clomp, clomp, clomp. Dad's boots coming down the path towards them.

"Hannah!" he shouted. "Have you taken my barrow?"

Jo cocked her head and smiled sweetly. "Shall I talk to him?"

"Fine," spat Hannah. "You win. Now open up."

As Jo unbolted the gate, Hannah and Lottie grabbed the curtains from the barrow and sprinted off up the track.

"Hey!" called Jo. "Come back! I'm telling Dad!"

"Just follow us!" shouted Hannah. "Quick!"

Chapter Ten

Spying

The curtains, strung on a length of washing line that Hannah had taken from the garden, glimmered and danced as they caught the winter sunlight. Hannah gave a long murmur of contentment. "Now it's really starting to look like a theatre."

"We can attach strings to them so we can open and close them from the wings," said Lottie, her hands clasped in admiration.

"I guess that's one good thing about having the Beans in the theatre. We couldn't do the curtains *and* be on stage."

"And if Jo's in the play, at least we won't have to do so many costume changes."

"She'll be good as Prince Rallentando too."

"The hardest thing," said Lottie, "is how I'm going to manage the costume changes from the maid to the princess."

"I can always write some extra lines for the queen to say while you're changing."

"Or the footman can come on. Although we'd better not give Sam too many lines."

"Sshh," said Hannah, putting a hand on Lottie's

shoulder.

They froze and listened. Twigs snapped and cracked in the thicket. Something or someone was outside the theatre.

"Push harder, Baked Bean; it's stuck."

It was Jo's voice. Hannah breathed again. She pushed the stage door open. She had oiled it this morning and now it moved a lot more easily.

Jo was staggering up the path, dragging a large piece of furniture. Behind it Hannah could see Sam's little face, his cheeks red with effort.

"Look what we've got," said Jo.

She stepped aside so Hannah and Lottie could see. It was a pine chest of drawers without any drawers in it.

"The drawers are down there," said Jo, pointing to the bottom of the thicket. "We had to bring them over separately."

"Have you two just dragged a chest of drawers across the yard?" said Hannah. "Don't you remember what we said? About keeping the theatre secret and not letting Dad suspect anything?"

"Don't worry," said Jo. "He didn't mind."

"What?!" Hannah's voice rose about an octave. "You *asked* him?"

"No, of course not. But he saw us taking it across the yard and he didn't say anything."

Hannah and Lottie looked at each other. This made no sense.

"Did he see you coming down here?" asked Lottie.

"No," said Jo. "He was going to the milking

parlour."

"But Mar—" began Sam.

"Shut up," hissed Jo.

"What?" asked Hannah. "What were you going to say, Sam?"

Sam looked at Jo, who was glaring at him.

"Nothing," they both said.

Hannah looked at them suspiciously. "If you two get us caught. . ." She tailed off, unable to think of a single punishment severe enough for that offence.

An enormous woolly ball with a duck on its back squeezed along the path and nuzzled up to Jo.

"No way, Jo!" said Hannah. "I told you yesterday, this is a theatre, not a farm. Do you think they let sheep into the Old Vic?"

"I don't know, I've never been there," said Jo. "Don't be mean, Hannah. It's bad enough that he's alone all day when I'm at school. He has to be with me at weekends, otherwise he pines. Animals can pine to death, you know."

"Not ones with as much fat on as that."

Jo put her arms round Jasper and her cheek on his huge woolly back. She stroked Lucy's glossy feathers sadly.

"Oh, OK, fine," said Hannah. "But you clear up after them. That's the rule at the Old Vic too."

Lottie had moved past Jo to get a proper look at the chest of drawers.

"This thing is disgusting. What's all that stuck to the top of it?"

Hannah looked. Three large mounds of dried-up

bird droppings sat on the pine surface.

"We found it in the bottom stable," said Jo. "There were swallows' nests above it."

"Great," said Lottie. "You've brought us a swallows' toilet."

Jo fixed her hardest stare on Lottie. "You're very rude and ungrateful sometimes, Lottie Perfect. We're going to clean it and paint it and then we can keep things in it."

Hannah clapped her hands together, her eyes shining. "Yes! It's perfect for backstage! For make-up and hair stuff. We can put a mirror on top and it can be our dressing table. It will be like a proper theatre dressing room!"

Lottie raised her eyebrows and shook her head. "You're all mad. It's gross."

Hannah rubbed a filthy drawer handle with her sleeve. "These are china. They're gorgeous. It'll be lovely when it's cleaned up."

"Exactly," said Jo. "Come on, Baked Bean."

"I thought he was French Bean," said Lottie.

"That was *this morning*," said Jo, as if she were talking to a particularly dim toddler. She lifted one end of the chest.

"Oh, no," protested Lottie. "You're not bringing that inside the theatre until it's completely clean. We just swept the floor."

Jo sighed. "Fine, we'll do it outside."

"I'll go and get you a bucket of water and some rags," said Hannah.

"We'll go," said Jo.

"No. Martha's back. I saw Jade's mum driving down the track. You might give something away."

"I wouldn't!"

"Well, I'm going on my own." She walked towards the front-of-house door. Then she stopped and turned round. "Actually, Sam, will you be lookout? With Dad and Martha around, we need someone to stand guard at the top of the field."

"Cool!" said Sam, beaming with excitement and importance. "I'll get my stick. And my binoculars." He hurried down the path. His trousers flapped around his ankles. I must go to the Scouts' jumble sale next Saturday and get him some new clothes, Hannah thought.

"Can you bring me some nails too, Han?" asked Lottie, who was patching up gaps in the theatre's walls. "I've nearly run out."

"Sure," said Hannah. She pushed the front-of-house door hard. She had oiled this one yesterday too.

"Owwww!" came a piercing screech from outside. "Owwww!"

No! Oh, no!

Martha!

It was over.

All over.

Everything was ruined.

Hannah couldn't bear it. She turned to Lottie, who was frozen to the spot, her hammer in mid-bang, staring at the door in disbelief.

Martha appeared in the doorway, a vision of

fury, hopping on one foot and clutching the other. There were red scratches all over her bare legs. She obviously hadn't found the path.

"You evil pig, you did that on purpose!"

Lottie unfroze. "What are you doing here?" she asked, striding to the door.

"Ha! I've been spying on those two idiots ever since I got home, and I followed them here."

Hannah remembered Sam's "But Mar—", and Jo hastily shutting him up.

So they knew Martha was spying on them and they'd still lugged a chest of drawers across the farmyard to the theatre in broad daylight.

"I knew it!" she burst out. "I knew we couldn't trust them!"

How could they have been so stupid? After she and Lottie had been so careful, creeping about in the dark for a week. She should have known it would never work, having the Beans in the theatre.

"So now I know everything," Martha said. "And now I can just go and tell Dad and—" She stopped in her tracks, her eyes fixed on the curtains that hung so splendidly across the proscenium arch. For a fraction of a second Hannah thought she saw in her sister's face something like excitement, admiration even. Then her eyes and mouth opened wide with a dawning realisation.

"Whoa," she said. "The sitting-room curtains. You've taken the sitting-room curtains that Mum made. Dad's going to go so mental."

"Martha, don't tell him. Please." Even as Hannah

said this, she knew it was useless. Of course Martha would tell him.

"You've set up a whole theatre without me, you horrible pig. You've all been doing your pathetic secret things and you've left me out of everything. You've even got stupid little Sam in it, and he's only six. You're mean and evil and I hate you and I'm going to tell Dad all about it, so there."

She turned and started to push her way out through the brambles. Hannah stood there, unable to move or speak. Their wonderful secret theatre, the chance to perform their own play in a real drama competition – all destroyed. Back to muddy grey reality with nothing to look forward to.

But suddenly Lottie ran to the door. She called out, "Martha!"

"What?" snapped Martha, still pushing through the brambles.

"Martha," asked Lottie, "would you like to be in the theatre?"

Martha turned her head. "What?"

"WHAT?!" shrieked Hannah.

"Would you like to be in the theatre? We need someone to play the princess."

"Why would I want to be in your stupid poxy theatre? You don't even like me."

"Esmeralda wears really beautiful dresses," said Lottie. "Actually, she wears the nicest clothes of any of the characters."

"Shut up," said Martha. "You're lying. You don't want me in your stupid theatre."

"Actually," said Lottie, "we were just saying how we really need someone to do hair and make-up."

No we weren't, thought Hannah. Has she gone mad? Does she want to ruin the theatre?

"No, you weren't," said Martha. "I never heard you say that."

"Well, it must have been before you started spying on us. The Beans found this chest of drawers, you see, for our make-up and hair things, but none of us is any good at it, and we thought you'd be the best."

"You haven't even got any make-up."

"No, but we're going to get some. Please, Martha, we really do need you. And then it will be *our* secret."

And then Hannah realised what Lottie was doing. Of course. Clever Lottie. If Martha was in the theatre, she would have to keep it secret from Dad. She would be on their side.

Martha opened her mouth to speak. But it wasn't her voice they heard.

"Help! Hannah, come here! Help!"

It was Sam. It sounded like he was running. He sounded breathless – and he sounded as if he was crying. And Sam never cried.

Chapter Eleven

The Man With the Angel Tattoo

Hannah raced past Martha and down the path, her heart thumping against her ribs. She sprinted up the field, the others at her heels. Sam was hurtling down the field towards them, his eyes wide with fear.

Hannah grabbed his shoulders and crouched beside him. "What is it? What's wrong?"

"They're stealing Daddy's Field Marshall!"

"What?"

"There's two men in the yard and they're putting it on a lorry."

"They can't be."

"They are! Come and stop them, quick!" He tugged at Hannah's hand with both of his.

All five children ran up the field like a tribe of warriors. They turned, panting, on to the track and raced into the yard, Jasper trotting behind them.

An enormous flatbed lorry, spurting black fumes and juddering with menace, straddled the yard. It dwarfed the ancient buildings and the farm machinery. Their father's Field Marshall sat hunched on the back of it, strapped up like a captive. It looked tiny up there.

A bulky man with a shaved head was throwing a long canvas strap over the Marshall to a second man standing on the other side of the lorry.

"Ratchet it in tight," shouted the first man. On the back of his thick neck was a tattoo of a pair of angels' wings. "It looks like a heap of scrap but it's worth a few grand."

Hannah's whole body tingled with rage. She strode up to the man with the tattoo.

"Hey! Take my dad's tractor off that lorry!"

He didn't even turn round. He couldn't have heard her over the noise of the engine.

Hannah felt as if she was about to explode with anger. She grabbed the man's arm. "What are you doing? You're stealing my dad's tractor!"

He turned and looked down at her. He glanced at the others, and at Jasper, gasping for breath. A dribble of saliva plopped from Jasper's mouth on to the man's oily wellington boot. He looked at it in disgust and shrugged his arm out of Hannah's grip. "Out of the way. We've got a job to do."

Lottie stepped up to him, her hands on her hips. "We know exactly what sort of job you're doing. How dare you come up here and attempt to commit robbery in broad daylight? I hereby do make a citizen's arrest. You do not have to speak but anything you do say may be taken down and—"

He had already turned his back on her. He picked up another strap. "Ready, Barry?" he shouted. The strap thudded on to the smooth curved bonnet of the old tractor.

"Jasper, attack!" hissed Jo.

Jasper sat down.

"Stop playing games!" cried Hannah. "This is serious. We have to stop them." She looked around the yard wildly. "Where's Dad?"

"All done," shouted the man on the other side of the lorry.

Suddenly Martha jumped up and down in her sparkly heels. "I know! Stand in front of the lorry. All of us, in a line. Then they can't move."

Hannah stared at Martha in amazement. "Genius!" she said. "Come on!"

As one person, they sprinted to the front of the lorry. Then Jo turned around. "Where's Sam?"

Hannah stopped in her tracks. Where *was* Sam?

The lorry's engine cut out.

Everybody looked up at the cab. And there was Sam, bouncing up and down on the driver's seat, throwing his head back and laughing, waving the ignition key in his hand.

Hannah laughed in delight. Jo and Martha cheered.

"Sam!" shouted Lottie. "That's fantastic!"

"You cheeky blighter!" yelled the tattooed driver. "Get out of my cab!"

Sam pushed the key deep into his jeans pocket and climbed down the steps. The others ran round to meet him.

"Come here, Sammy," said Hannah. She lifted him off the steps and gave him a huge squeeze. "Well done! You're brilliant."

Jasper nuzzled Sam in approval and Sam ruffled his wool.

The driver barged through the children and held an oily hand out to Sam. "Right, sonny boy, stop horsing around and give us that key."

Sam looked up at him with his big blue eyes. "No," he said. "Not until you take Daddy's tractor off the lorry."

The man's face darkened. Hannah saw his hands curl into fists.

"Get the key off him."

"No," they all said.

Sam's face was pale now, but he didn't move. The driver lunged towards him. Hannah leapt between them and spread her arms out wide.

The others were all shouting at once.

"No!"

"Leave him alone!"

"Get off, you big fat bully!" Martha ducked under Hannah's arm and kicked the man hard on the leg.

"OW!" he yelled, grabbing his shin. "Jeez, what was that?!" He glared at Martha's mud-caked red stiletto and raised his arm. "You little—"

With superhuman strength, Jo shoved Jasper forward. Crushed in the throng, Jasper planted one big front hoof squarely down on the man's wellington boot.

"OWWWW!! What the—" Judging by the swearing, Jasper was pretty much resting his entire weight on that hoof.

Suddenly a voice behind Hannah said, "What on

earth's going on?"

She swung round. There was Dad, hands on hips, staring open-mouthed at the scene in front of him.

Jasper took his hoof off the man's boot and sat down, unblinking, as the man clutched his foot and hopped up and down. "Your blasted kids! Bunch of hooligans!"

Sam ran to his father. "Daddy, we saved your Marshall!"

Dad looked blankly at him.

"Look!" said Hannah, pointing to the tractor. "They were stealing it. We've stopped them."

Dad shifted his gaze so that he seemed to be looking far away across the fields. When he spoke, his words sounded flat and final.

"Nobody's stealing it."

"Yes, they are. Look!"

"They're not stealing it. I've sold it."

"What?" said Hannah. What was he talking about?

"Right," said the driver. "So give me that key."

Sam looked at Dad, who was still staring out across the meadows. He turned to Hannah.

Hannah put her hand on Dad's arm. "What's going on? I don't understand. You can't sell your Marshall. It was Grandfather's. And you love it."

She looked into his face, trying to meet his gaze, willing him to say something that would put it all right.

But he didn't move.

The driver blew out his cheeks. "Are we taking

this thing or not?"

Dad kept his eyes fixed on the silver horizon as he spoke. "Give him the key."

Sam, white-faced and bewildered, looked at Hannah. Feeling sick, she nodded.

The driver snatched the key from Sam's palm and swung himself up into the cab. The other man climbed into the passenger seat. The engine roared into life.

The children watched the Field Marshall get smaller and smaller as it bumped away up the track. Then Hannah turned to her father.

"You sold your Marshall, Dad? Why?"

For a brief moment, he met her gaze. "Got to pay the rent," he said.

Then he turned away. He ruffled up Sam's golden hair with his huge rough hand.

"Come on, boy. Let's go and milk those cows."

Chapter Twelve

The Changing Room

The freezing wind cut Hannah's cheeks like a whip as she walked off the hockey pitch. The other girls were talking and laughing, congratulating each other on goals scored and gossiping about the other team. Hannah kept at the back of the group. Her head was a tangled mess of worry and she was desperately trying to unravel the knots.

Why on earth would Dad need to sell his Field Marshall?

What was going on?

And then she remembered.

That afternoon when they had asked Dad for the tractor-shed loft. His harsh voice on the phone as they crept along the corridor.

"You're saying he has every right to double the rent and there's nothing we can do about it?"

The new landlord had doubled the rent!

Hannah's mind whirled. That couldn't be true, could it? People couldn't just double things like that. If you went into a shop and everything was twice the price of the day before and they said, we've doubled the prices . . . I mean, people just couldn't do that, could they?

Could they?

It seemed like they could.

But how can someone suddenly pay twice the rent they were paying before?

And if they can't . . . then what happens?

From deep down where she had tried to bury them, Hannah heard Lottie's words in the sitting room that day.

"*Your new landlord wants to demolish the farm. And build houses on it.*"

No.

It's not true.

It can't be true.

He can't do that.

He won't be allowed to.

I mustn't think about it.

Dad will sort it out.

She buried the words again.

In the changing room, Hannah took off her boots and picked her way through the muddy hockey sticks, smelly socks and random bits of clothing.

There was nothing worse than communal showers.

Still in her kit, Hannah stood as far back as she could from the shower head and briefly stuck her head under the jet of hot water. She shook out her hair like a spaniel after a paddle in a pond and walked back to the changing room. That would be enough to convince Frostbite if she came in for one of her interrogations.

"What's up, Emily?" asked Priya, who had had a

proper shower and was now getting dressed. "You've been really quiet all day."

Emily was sitting on the slatted wooden bench, carefully folding her hockey kit. "Oh, it's nothing. I'm just a bit worried about Starlight."

"Your horse?"

"Yes. It's just, the stables where I keep him – they told me yesterday they're closing down. And there's nowhere else round here – all the other places are too far to walk or cycle to, or they're too expensive. I don't know what—"

"Oh, Ems," said Miranda in a voice that could have shattered crystal. "I forgot to tell you *the* most exciting thing. I'm going skiing at Easter!"

"Oh, wow, lucky you," said Emily.

"I know, isn't that just so cool? Mummy booked it last night. Daddy sold this painting at Sotheby's yesterday and he made a fortune. We're staying in this amazing chalet in the Italian Alps with a cook and everything. Come round to mine before drama tonight and I'll show you the website."

"OK, cool. Can you believe we've got a dress rehearsal on Saturday, though? We're nowhere near ready."

Dress rehearsal? This Saturday? Hannah shot Lottie a horrified look. They hadn't even got fabric for costumes yet, and they hadn't had a single proper rehearsal.

Miranda arranged herself in front of the mirror and started to brush her glossy hair. "I think it's exactly what we need. Last week's rehearsal was a mess. I mean, half the cast haven't even learned their lines yet. It's pathetic. They need a dress rehearsal in front of an audience to make them take it seriously."

"Yes, you're right," said Emily. "That is so true. I was thinking—"

"Oh, and did I tell you Jack's going to come?" Miranda flicked a glance at Hannah, who felt a blush rise to her cheeks. She leaned over the bench to fold her hockey kit so that her hair covered her face.

"To the dress rehearsal?" said Emily. "Oh, no, how embarrassing."

"That's the whole point though, isn't it? It'll make people learn their lines at last. Anyway, I asked him and he said he'd come. Right, let's go." Miranda tossed her hair back and wafted across the changing room. Emily picked up her bags and scurried out after her.

"Oh, by the way, Hannah," said Miranda, turning at the door so that Emily nearly skidded into her, "I *love* your trousers."

"Cow," said Lottie as the door banged shut.

"What's wrong with my trousers?"

"Nothing. She's just evil. What are you doing?"

Hannah's voice came out muffled from beneath the bench. "I can't find my sock."

"Oh, Hannah, can you never get changed without losing something? Hurry up, we're last again."

The door burst open as if a cannon had fired at it and their PE teacher, Mrs Frost, launched herself into the changing room. She looked like she was made from pipe cleaners, but despite that she somehow seemed to fill the room.

"Come on, you two!" she barked. "Always the same ones, isn't it? I've never seen such slowcoaches. Hannah Roberts, you've got mud on your face. I hope you've had a shower, young lady."

"Yes, miss," Hannah said. She raised her head from under the bench and pointed to her damp fringe.

"Huh. Well, get a move on. The caretaker's locking up in ten minutes. And put those hockey sticks in the basket on your way out. Well played on the wing today, Charlotte," she called as the door swung shut behind her.

"How come she never loses her voice?" asked Lottie. "How can a person shout non-stop for eight hours a day and not get a sore throat?"

Hannah scrambled to her feet, red-faced, her hair standing out all around her head.

"It's nowhere. How can a sock just completely disappear? That was the only pair I had without holes in."

"Is this it?" said Lottie, holding out a grubby grey sock between her thumb and forefinger.

Hannah took it gratefully and pulled it on.

From the corridor came the sound of jangling keys.

"Let's go," said Lottie.

Hannah took her coat off her peg and headed for the door.

"Aren't you going to take your bag?"

Hannah turned round. Her school bag was still hanging on the peg. She heaved it on to her shoulder.

It was heavier than usual – she had several textbooks and a science project in there as well as all her exercise books. She noticed that the stitching was unravelling on the strap. She must sew it up tonight.

Except she knew she wouldn't. Last night she had started reading the most fantastic book and there was no way she was doing any mending until she'd finished it.

Dusk was falling as they left the PE building and walked towards the school gates. The wind stung Hannah's face. She pulled her gloves out of her coat pocket. "Do you want a lift home? My dad's at a meeting – he said he'll pick me up from the bus stop at six."

"No, I'm going into Linford to meet my mum, remember. She's getting an early train for once."

They walked past the bike sheds towards the main entrance. Attached to the railings was a laminated poster for the Scout jumble sale on Saturday. Lottie stopped to read it. "Hey, why don't we go? I bet there'll be loads of stuff for costumes."

Hannah hesitated. She was planning to go anyway, if Dad would give her some money to get clothes for Sam, but she couldn't spend that money on costumes, and she didn't want Lottie to have to spend her pocket money when she herself could contribute nothing. She couldn't wait to be fourteen so she could get a Saturday job.

Oh, but wait a minute. She still had five pounds left from her Christmas money.

"That would be great. I'll probably have to bring

the others, though."

"That's OK," said Lottie. "They can help us find stuff."

"I think we should have a dress rehearsal," said Hannah, not quite knowing what she was saying or why she was saying it. "With an audience."

"With an audience! Hannah, we're not the Linford Youth Theatre. I can't believe you're trying to copy Miranda."

"I'm not. I just think it's a good idea. It will give us something to aim for – make us more organised."

"But the competition's in three weeks."

"So let's have the dress rehearsal in two weeks."

"But we haven't made a single costume!"

"I'll come to yours every night after I've put Sam to bed and help you make them."

Lizzie snorted with laughter. "You! What use would you be?"

"I can sew! I'm always sewing."

"Sewing buttons back on doesn't count. And you haven't even sewn on a name tape since my mum gave you that fabric marker. Anyway, there's no point arguing. There's no way we can be ready in two weeks. I mean, the queen alone has three costumes, and Esmeralda—"

"You can show me what to do," said Hannah. "I'll help you with anything I can. I'll really concentrate, I promise. And it doesn't matter if they're not all finished – we'll have another week before the actual performance."

"Well, we're not doing it to an audience if the

costumes aren't finished. It would look ridiculous."

"We *need* a rehearsal in front of an audience, Lottie. We need to get used to people watching it. We can't perform for the first time to an audience on the day the judge comes. And at least it will force Martha to learn her lines."

"But who will we invite? And what if your dad sees them arriving? No, it's a crazy idea, Hannah. No. No way. The end."

"There's your bus," said Hannah. "Go on. We'll work it all out tomorrow. Have a good evening!"

Chapter Thirteen

A Lift Home

Alone, Hannah felt the fears swirl into her head again. She pushed them away, crossed the road and trudged up the pavement to the bus shelter. A shadowy figure leaned against the far side of it.

Wait a minute. . .

Could it be. . .?

It was!

Her heart missed a beat. Jack Adamson! And she, Hannah Roberts, was about to be alone in a bus shelter with him!

Hannah was suddenly painfully aware of every single cell in her body. Her mouth felt dry. Her stomach fluttered like there was a family of sparrows trapped inside it. She didn't know how to walk. What should she do with her hands? Should she look at him or not? Oh, no, had she brushed her hair after the match? She put a hand to her head, then instantly removed it. Act casual, she told herself.

Would he speak to her?

What would he say?

What if he ignored her?

Anything, any amount of teasing, was better than

being ignored.

Jack glanced up as she approached.

"All right?" he said.

Hannah's heart leapt. He had spoken to her! Maybe they were about to have a conversation!

Be casual, she told herself sternly. Be nonchalant.

"All right?" she replied. He was more good-looking than ever in the dim light with his hands in his pockets. Not that she dared really look at him.

"Just had a guitar lesson. You?"

"Hockey match. Away, against Tidemills."

"Oh, right. You win?"

"Yes, three–two." She didn't mention that Miranda Hathaway had scored the winning goal.

"Cool."

Cool. He's being nice to me! And he smiled! I'm sure he smiled!

Silence.

That's because it's my turn. Say something! Make a witty remark! Keep the conversation going!

"So, are you getting the bus home?" she asked.

What a moronic thing to say. Of course he was getting the bus home. He got the bus home every single day. What sarcastic comment would he make now?

But he just said, "Yeah. You too?"

"No, my dad's picking me up."

Why had Jack asked her that? Had he hoped she was getting the bus? If she had been, would he have sat next to her? He must really like her if he wanted to sit next to her on the bus. She hoped that both the

95

bus and her dad would be a very long time coming.

But that seemed to be the end of the conversation. Jack said nothing. Why had she said her dad was picking her up? That made her sound like such a baby.

Jack reached into his jeans pocket and pulled out a box of matches. He struck a match and looked at the flame as it flared up with a little hiss. The wind blew it out and he dropped it on the pavement.

Hannah looked at the matchbox in his hand. There was something scrawled in biro on the cardboard. A mobile number. And a name. Hannah strained her eyes to make it out.

Miranda.

Jack had Miranda's name and number written on his matchbox. In Miranda's handwriting.

Of course. He was going to Miranda's dress rehearsal on Saturday, wasn't he?

The silence thickened. Hannah fished desperately inside her paralysed brain for something to say. How many times had she dreamed of being alone with Jack? And now that she was, all she could do was stand there like an idiot.

She plucked nervously at the frayed strap of her canvas bag. It was slipping off her shoulder. She hoisted it back up. There was a loud ripping sound and the bag thudded on to the pavement.

"Oh, no!"

In nightmarish slow motion, the entire contents of her bag slithered on to the ground. Books, pens, calculator, scrunched-up tissues and crumpled sheets of paper rolled all around her. She dropped to her knees, scrabbling to pick up her fountain pen before it fell off the kerb. Oh, wasn't Jack going to love telling this story in the canteen: Roberts and her inability to do the simplest thing without looking like a halfwit.

And then the strangest thing happened. Jack moved across the bus shelter. His shoes were on the tarmac beside her. And then he knelt. Jack Adamson knelt on the ground, gathering books and stationery into his arms and ramming them back into the broken canvas bag.

"There you go." He held out the bag so she could tip her meagre catch of pencils into it.

Hannah finally dared to lift her eyes from the pavement. And there he was, his face just centimetres from hers, her green eyes level with his brown ones. "Are you OK?" he asked awkwardly.

"Yes. Fine. Thank you." She held his gaze for a second frozen in time, looking at his lovely face, framed by his curly hair and silhouetted by the yellow streetlight, and his strong hand, outstretched to help her up. And then, suddenly, she blurted out, "Do you want to come to our dress rehearsal next Sunday?"

What?

What had she just said?

"What?" said Jack.

The words tumbled out of her before she knew what was happening. It was like watching somebody else rush headlong into a pit in the dark. "Our theatre group. We're having a dress rehearsal for the Linford Arts Festival. You know, like Miranda's. On the first weekend of the holidays. Sunday the fourteenth. Three o'clock. On my farm. In a hen house. I mean, it's a theatre but it used to be a hen house. It's in a little wood in North Meadow – the field on the right as you come up the track. I mean, you don't have to or anything. . ."

Finally, her mouth seemed to have stopped spilling out words. She didn't dare look at him.

Miraculously, though, he smiled. "Sure. Why not?"

Her heart soared. He really did like her!

Suddenly, a honk-honk like an angry goose pierced the air. No, not now! Not now! Go away!

Jack looked up.

"Isn't that your dad?"

Hannah made herself look. There it was. Her father's ancient, mud-encrusted Vauxhall Chevette, signalling to pull in at the bus shelter. But what was that on the . . . no, surely not.

Oh, my sweet lord, it really is. Please let this be a nightmare. Earth, please swallow me up. Right now. Oh, please don't let Jack see it. *Please.*

"Flipping heck," said Jack. "*What* is that thing on the roof of his car?"

"No way," said Lottie. "You have *got* to be kidding."

It was eight thirty on Tuesday morning and they were huddled against the hot-water pipes in the girls' cloakroom.

98

"Oh, if only I were " said Hannah. "Can you imagine it?"

"That is unbelievable. A dead duck. No way."

"A massive dead Muscovy duck. Huge. Just sprawled across the roof of the car with its giant wings outstretched. I nearly died."

"But why did he have it up there?"

"He said he'd found it in the yard – a fox had got it – and he'd slung it there to stop the dogs eating it, until he got a chance to bury it. And then he'd just forgotten all about it. I mean, what sort of person just *forgets* they have a dead duck on the roof of their car? It was the most embarrassing moment of my entire life. And that's saying something. And it's going to be all round the school by lunchtime."

Hannah curled up and buried her head in her hands. Lottie hugged her.

Don't be nice to me, thought Hannah. I haven't told you everything. If you knew that I'd invited Jack Adamson to watch our non-existent dress rehearsal, you wouldn't be comforting me right now. You'd be strangling me to death with your bare hands.

Chapter Fourteen

Secrets and Threats

Hannah sat on a wobbly milking stool in the auditorium and opened her notebook. "I hereby declare this meeting of the Secret Hen House Theatre open. Date: Sunday 7th March. Present: all members of the theatre.

"Item one: Programme. To be produced by Miss Lottie Perfect, as agreed at the meeting of Saturday 6th March."

Lottie, perched on the udder-barrel on the other side of the circle, reached into her bag and took out a folded piece of straw-coloured paper.

"Wow," said Hannah. "That looks so professional."

"Cool," agreed the Beans. They were sharing an upturned chicken crate and using Jasper, sprawled in front of them, as a giant woolly footstool.

Martha glanced up briefly from her magazine, curled her top lip and said nothing.

Lottie had drawn a border of brambles around the edge of the cover. Inside the border was typed:

The Secret Hen House Theatre Presents
By Her Majesty's Appointment
Saturday 20th March
3.00 p.m.

In the bottom right-hand corner she had drawn a hen wearing dark glasses and carrying binoculars under one wing.

"Why does the hen have sunglasses and binoculars?" asked Sam.

"Because we're the Secret Hen House Theatre. She's a secret hen."

The Beans giggled. Martha flipped over the page of her magazine with a vicious crack.

"And then inside," said Lottie, opening the programme, "there's the list of scenes and the cast list." She started to read it out. "Cast, in order of appearance: Queen Matilda – Hannah Roberts; Lady's maid – Lottie Perfect; Footman—"

"Oh, surprise, surprise, yours and Hannah's names are first," said Martha.

"They're in order of appearance," said Lottie through gritted teeth. "Like it says. I'll do extra programmes for the dress rehearsal. Since apparently we're now having a dress rehearsal. With an audience."

She raised her eyebrows at Hannah. Hannah smiled innocently. It had taken a bit of persuasion, but she'd known Lottie would come round in the end. Hannah had just needed to convince her that a dress rehearsal would make the play more professional.

101

Professionalism mattered. To both of them.

There was one thing she hadn't told Lottie, though. One really quite major thing.

And that wasn't very professional, was it?

"Who's going to be in the audience?" asked Sam.

Hannah's stomach churned. She couldn't believe she'd invited Jack. It was *such* a crazy thing to have done that she could sometimes almost convince herself it hadn't happened at all. Especially since Jack had never mentioned it since.

It was horrible, though, having a secret from Lottie. It gnawed away at Hannah's conscience.

She couldn't tell her, though, could she? Lottie would go crazy.

And anyway, there was no way Jack would actually come. Not after the dead duck fiasco.

"My mum's coming," said Lottie. "Don't worry, my dad isn't," she added in response to Hannah's look of alarm. Lottie's parents were divorced and they didn't always manage to be civil to each other in public. "And my mum's going to bring your granny. And my auntie and uncle and cousins are coming."

"But how," asked Jo, "are all those people going to come here and park their cars and walk to the theatre without Dad finding out?"

"I've told them we're keeping it a secret from your dad because we want to surprise him at the actual performance. They're going to leave their cars at the end of the track and act like they're just having a walk on the footpath. So as long as he's not actually in this field, he won't see anything suspicious."

"And what if he *is* actually in this field, freak?" said Martha.

"Why isn't Daddy coming?" asked Sam.

"Well," Hannah said slowly, "Daddy didn't want us to have a theatre, remember? So this is all a secret."

"But Daddy would want to come and see our play. I want Daddy to come. It's mean not to invite him."

Hannah looked at Sam's face. If only it were that simple.

"We can't, Sammy. If he didn't like it, he might make us stop it and then we wouldn't be able to enter the competition and all our work would be ruined."

Sam opened his mouth to reply.

"Right," said Hannah quickly, turning back to her notebook. "Item two: Costumes. The members of the theatre spent a very successful afternoon buying fabric and make-up at the Scouts' jumble sale on Saturday 6th March. Miss Lottie Perfect to report on progress with costume production."

Lottie pulled some items from a plastic bag. "OK, this is what I did last night. I've made my own costumes first. Just because I know my own measurements," she said pointedly to Martha. "So, this is for the maid."

She held it up. The maid's blouse had originally been a white school shirt. Lottie had chopped off the collar and cuffs and sewn on lacy ones instead, made from a net curtain. She had made a white apron from an old sheet and altered a long black skirt from the jumble sale.

"That's great," said Hannah.

The Beans looked impressed.

"Gross," said Martha.

"I'm going to wear black trousers underneath, then all I have to do is whip off the skirt and apron, put on a black jacket and I'm Prince John. His costume's very plain because he's modest and hates show-offs – so it will contrast with Prince Rallentando's, which will be really gaudy. I'm going to use that satin jacket we got yesterday and sew on loads of lace – actually, you can do that, Hannah; it'll be quite simple."

"It will have to be, if Hannah can manage it," said Martha.

"Now, I'll need you to try this one on, Martha." Lottie reached into her bag and took out a costume. Hannah recognised some of the things they had found at the jumble sale. The bodice was the top half of a swirly brown and pink print dress. The sleeves were shiny orange curtain fabric and the long skirt was made from a flowery bedspread on to which Lottie had sewn several large green bows.

"Ugh!" said Martha. "That is disgusting!"

"It's brilliant," said Hannah. "Perfect for Esmeralda."

"What do you mean, perfect for me?" snapped Martha. "Are you calling me ugly? Have you looked in a mirror lately? Do you know what your face looks like? Like a mouldy apple with a maggot sticking out of it for a nose."

"She wasn't calling you ugly," said Lottie. "This dress is meant to be over the top. The whole point is that the queen has terrible taste and she forces Esmeralda to wear it. The one she chooses herself will be really nice."

"Where is it? Show me."

"I haven't finished it yet."

"Well, it'd better not be skanky like this one. Or there's no way I'm going to be in your poxy play. People might think I chose it."

"On the notice board in the dressing room," continued Lottie, "there's a list of times for all members of the cast to report to me so that I can take their measurements."

"Thank you, Lottie," said Hannah. "Now, item three: Rehearsals. As you all know, the dress rehearsal is a week from today, so everybody should be off the book from now on."

"Off the what?"

"Martha, I explained yesterday. It means no scripts. Everyone should have learned their lines. Right, let's go from Esmeralda's first entrance."

"OK then, Jo, I need to do your measurements," said Lottie, moving backstage.

"Ready, Martha?" said Hannah.

Martha ignored her.

"Martha!"

Martha kept her eyes on her magazine. "What?"

"We're going from your entrance. You need to be in the wings, stage left."

Martha sighed, picked up her script and dragged herself into the wings.

"I said stage *left*."

"I am on the left."

"No, *stage* left means left from the actors' point of view, remember? So you need to be on the other side."

Hannah positioned herself in a queenly manner on top of a pile of crates that was going to be her four-poster bed. "*Come in, Esmeralda, my dear,*" she said in her most regal voice.

Martha held the script up in front of her face and spoke her lines in a flat, halting monotone, like a five-year-old struggling with an Early Reader.

"*You . . . wanted . . . to . . . see . . . me . . . Mama?*"

"Why are you doing that?" asked Hannah.

Martha made her eyes wide and innocent. "Doing what?"

"Pretending you can't read. Or act. When I know you can do both really well. And why are you still reading from your script when you're meant to have learned your lines?"

"This isn't school, you know! You're not my teacher. I don't have to do anything you say, so shut up."

Hannah took another deep breath. "Let's start again." She changed her voice back to the queen's.

"*Come in, Esmeralda, my dear.*"

"*YouwantedtoseemeMama?*"

"Martha!"

"What? You said it was too slow before. I was doing it faster."

Hannah decided to carry on.

"*In a year, on your sixteenth birthday, you will*

106

be married to a prince, who, at this moment, my faithful servants are setting out to find."

"*But,Mama,Iwanttochoosemyhusbandbymyself.*"

"Martha!! We've got one week! Will you just do it properly!"

Martha raised her eyebrows and drew herself up to her full height. "Are you being horrible to me? Because if you are, I'm just going to tell Dad all about your little secret. Is that what you want?"

Hannah looked at her. For the first time in her life, Martha held all the cards, and she was loving every minute of it.

"Let's carry on, shall we?" said Hannah, making her voice as calm as she could. "*Silence, child! Before your beloved father died...*" Hannah paused and bowed her head. "*We both decided what would be best for you. You will obey me or you are disregarding his wishes. Do you understand, Esmeralda?*"

Martha looked at Hannah demurely, the picture of obedience. She moved her lips but no sound came out.

"That was your cue, Martha."

"I said my line."

"You didn't say it, you mouthed it."

"You don't like my voice, so you don't have to listen to it. Now you can't complain it's too fast or too slow."

Hannah put her head in her hands. "Martha, what is your problem?"

"*My* problem! What is *your* problem?"

"What do you mean?" said Hannah.

107

"Isn't it enough for you that you boss me around every minute of the day at home, without bossing me around in the stupid play too?"

"Oh, is *that* it?" Hannah stared at Martha. And suddenly a light flicked on in her head. "Martha, who's the main character in Cinderella?"

"Cinderella, stupid."

"Exactly. Not the bossy stepmother, even though she has more lines. And it's the same in this play. Esmeralda is the main character. The play is her story, and in the end she gets the prince she wants, doesn't she? She stands up to her mother – only she doesn't do it by screaming and shouting. She's cleverer than that. You've got the main part in this play. But, you know what, if you want to swap and play the queen instead, that's fine. You'll just have a lot more lines to learn and a really gaudy dress to wear."

Martha stuck her chin out and looked away.

"Well? What's it going to be, Martha? Beautiful princess or ugly old queen? It's completely up to you."

Chapter Fifteen

Finishing Touches

By four o'clock they had been through the whole play twice and Hannah called an end to rehearsals.

"Right," she said to Lottie as the others left, "shall we finish this panelling?"

Using bits of old doors, planks and crates that they had found around the yard, Hannah and Lottie had built a wooden wall for the back of the stage. On the reverse side there were nails and strips of wood all over the place, but from the stage it looked quite solid and smooth. Now they had to nail a grid of thin strips of wood on to it to create a panelling effect. And finally, they were going to paint it with a can of brown paint Lottie had found in her dad's garage.

"Then the only thing that isn't right will be the floor," said Hannah. "We really need a rug."

"And we need some ornaments for the dressing table," said Lottie. "And we should hang a picture on the panelling. There's always old oil paintings on the panelling." Lottie visited a lot of stately homes with her mum.

Hannah looked at her and raised her eyebrows.

"I know where we could get one of those."

Lottie read her face. "Oh, no. No way. Don't even think about it."

Hannah was already pulling back the front-of-house door. "Come on! It'll take two of us to carry it."

"Hannah! Don't be ridiculous! Come back!"

But Hannah was halfway down the secret path. "Come on. It'll be perfect!"

Hannah stretched up to the grimy picture rail in the sitting room. "Imagine how great this will look in the queen's bedroom." She gripped the sides of the frame.

"Hannah!" said Lottie, out of breath from the chase. "We can't take this to the theatre. Your dad'll go crazy!"

"He'll never notice it's gone," said Hannah. "We'll put it back straight after the competition."

She lifted the horse and dog painting off its hook. The string had been hanging there so long that it stayed as stiff as wire in its upside-down v-shape.

"Come on, take the other end."

Lottie groaned, but she picked up the other end of the frame.

"Tell you what," said Hannah as they carried the painting through to the hall. "I'll bring those silver candlesticks out later too. They'll look amazing on the queen's dressing table. I'll put new candles in them."

"Hannah, you nutter, you cannot—"

The back door rattled open. Both girls froze.

"Tess! Stay outside, you bad dog."

Lottie's eyes gleamed in terror. "Your dad!" she whispered. "Oh, my goodness, you're going to get us killed."

"Hannah!" called Dad.

Hannah propped the picture against a chair. She grabbed a moth-eaten picnic rug from the hall cupboard and thrust it at Lottie, who looked like she had been turned to stone. "Cover it up," she hissed.

Hannah walked innocently into the kitchen. "Yes?"

Dad was standing in the doorway in his wellies.

"Get some antibiotics from the fridge, would you, Hannah?"

"What's up?"

"Calf with pneumonia in the barn."

Hannah went back through the hall.

"What's going on?" mouthed Lottie.

"Ssshh," said Hannah. She found the box of antibiotics and took it to her father. As casually as she could, she walked back into the hall. "Through the garden," she whispered to Lottie. "He's going out the other way."

"I was nearly sick waiting for you," said Lottie, sidestepping a cowpat as they scurried across the yard. "Don't you *ever* do that to me again."

"It was worth it, though," said Hannah. "Won't it look great?"

Hannah made Dad's cocoa at nine o'clock as usual,

but he still hadn't come in. She pulled her coat and boots on and stepped out into the farmyard.

The farm was cloaked in velvet darkness and the sky was dotted all over with tiny stars. The only sound was the occasional muffled grunt of a well-fed pig. As Hannah breathed in the silence, a barn owl swooped, feather-light, across the yard.

A dim glow came from the back barn. As Hannah approached, she heard the low murmur of her father's voice. She tiptoed round behind the machinery to the far end of the barn, where a pen of calves was housed. One calf, bolder than the others, wandered over to the bars and sniffed at Hannah's hand. She stroked its velvet back and let it lick her fingers with its sandpaper tongue.

The light came from an old-fashioned lantern strung over a beam with baler twine. It hung above a small enclosure made of straw bales. "There you are then," Dad was saying to the sick calf. He heaved a bale from the stack at the side of the barn and added it to the straw wall. "Soon have you warm as toast. Don't want any draughts, do we? We'll put a few more bales around you here, get you nice and comfortable. Good girl, well done. I'm just going to see to the cows."

He picked up a bucket in each hand, straightened up and saw Hannah. A look of fear crossed his face.

"What's up? Something wrong?"

"No, no," said Hannah quickly. "Everyone's fine. Your cocoa's ready."

"Righty-ho. I'm just finishing here." He moved

towards the cows' winter barn.

All of a sudden Hannah felt she had to talk to him.

She forced the words out through the tightness in her throat. "Lottie says the landlord wants to demolish the farm to build houses on. He can't do that, can he?"

Her father gave a short laugh, like a bark.

"Don't you worry about that. Cashmore's a greedy money-grabbing snake, but as long as we pay the rent every quarter, he can't lay a finger on this place."

"But how will you—"

"See that old thresher over there?" He pointed to an ancient, ramshackle machine at the side of the barn. It was so old that it was built entirely from wood, even the wheels. It had once been salmon-pink but its peeling paint had faded to a pale pastel.

"What about it?"

"Bloke who bought the Field Marshall wants the thresher as well. They're fetching it in a couple of weeks. Saves insuring it too. Costs a fortune to insure these old machines. So next quarter's rent's all covered. Don't you worry for a second, all right?"

"All right," said Hannah. "Night, Dad."

"Goodnight."

Hannah walked back across the yard with a spring in her step. So Dad *did* have it all sorted.

She could hear him talking to the cows. "Hello, Clover. There you go, old girl. Plenty there to keep you going. All right, Bluebell? Good girl, here you are."

He gave each of his cows a name on the day they were born. All the names were chalked up on a board in the milking parlour, and he knew every one of them.

She should just have trusted him. There was no way Dad would ever let anything happen to the farm.

Chapter Sixteen

The Dress Rehearsal

Hannah and Lottie spent every spare minute of the next week working on scenery and costumes. On Monday after school they made the queen's four-poster bed. They tied fence posts to the corners of the chicken crates and cut up a big purple bedspread. Draped in purple damask, with matching curtains at each corner tied with gold ribbon, the bed really did look fit for a queen.

On Tuesday they painted a woodwormy old blanket box. Hannah had found it on the log pile and thought it would make a perfect window seat. Above it they fixed an old sash window they had found in a shed.

"That looks fantastic," said Lottie. "And I've got a piece of blue fabric at home – we'll hang that behind the window for the sky."

On Wednesday Hannah led Lottie backstage and unveiled a surprise. "See," she said, gesturing with a sweep of her arm to a sawn-off broom handle, suspended horizontally from the ceiling with baler twine. "Our costume rail. And the genius of it is, it doesn't take up any floor space. When we don't need to use it, we won't even know it's there."

As she had promised, Hannah cycled to Lottie's house every evening after she had put Sam to bed, and as the week went on the rail started filling up with costumes, each labelled, as Mum's theatre books advised, with the character's name and the scenes in which they were to be worn.

Hannah loved every second of the preparation. Each day at school dragged more than the one before, as she watched the clock until the time when she would be released to work on the theatre. And on Sunday afternoon, the day of the dress rehearsal, when she stood backstage and looked around at all they had achieved, she thought: Mum would be proud of us. This really is a theatre now.

It was fifteen minutes until curtain up. Hannah was dressed in her Scene One costume: a long frilled pink nightdress with pastel-blue bows. It was made of a satiny material, which made her feel very regal and changed her walk into a kind of glide. The hair helped too. Martha had put it up in a bun. The hairgrips had been shoved in slightly harder than necessary and her hair scraped back a little forcibly, and the hairspray need not perhaps have gone into her eyes quite so much, but the result was effective. And the make-up – orange lipstick, puce blusher and purple eyeshadow – was certainly striking.

"Jo, have you checked off all the props?" she asked. "Are they on the table in scene order?"

"Yes, I've just done a last check," said Jo, shrugging Prince Rallentando's flowery silk jacket on to her

116

shoulders. "And I've ticked them all off on my list."

"Where's the letter from Prince Rallentando?"

Lottie, who was sitting by the window having her make-up done, patted the pocket of her maid's apron. "In here, ready to bring on. Hannah, take your watch off! Martha, you're going to have to hurry – you haven't done Jo yet."

Martha grabbed Lottie by the chin. "Stop talking, stupid, or I'll smudge your make-up."

Hannah put her watch on the dressing table and slipped through the wings to give the stage a final check. The wooden panelling looked totally authentic now it was painted, and the horse picture, in its gilt frame, gave the room real grandeur. The silver candlesticks looked amazing on the dressing table in front of the painting. Hannah gave a deep sigh of satisfaction.

She peeped through the curtains into the auditorium. The only members of the audience so far were Jasper and Lucy, sitting in prime position in the very centre. Jasper was chewing the cud thoughtfully. Lucy was nestled into his back.

Oh, well. At least Jo hadn't sat them on chairs.

Where was the rest of the audience, though? What if they hadn't managed to find the hidden path?

Suddenly she heard a murmur of voices from somewhere in the thicket. Her heart leapt into her throat.

What if it was Jack?

But it wouldn't be, would it?

Of course it wouldn't. He hadn't made the slightest

mention of the dress rehearsal. He had probably forgotten she'd ever invited him. It was only one stupid remark, after all – the whole hideous dead duck incident would have swept it clean from his mind.

And he hadn't gone to Miranda's rehearsal either. Miranda had been really annoyed with him about that.

Somebody laughed.

A woman. Phew. Hannah ran backstage. "People are coming!"

Everyone stopped what they were doing and listened. "That's Auntie Cath," said Lottie.

Leaves rustled and twigs snapped. A child wailed, "Ow, it stung me!"

"Ugh," said Lottie. "My cousin Jeremy. He'll probably cry for an hour now."

The front-of-house door slid open. Hannah crept onstage and peeped through the gaps at the sides of the curtains. Lottie's auntie Cath stepped cautiously over the threshold. A little girl held her hand.

"Isn't this fun!" said Auntie Cath. "Look at those lovely curtains, Evie!"

A very grumpy-looking man stepped into the auditorium. He had two folding chairs under each arm and a whimpering boy behind him.

"Great fun," he said, "when you have to carry your own flipping chairs through a blasted forest to get here. What is this, boot camp?"

"Sshh, Andrew," said his wife. "They'll hear you. Stop moaning and enjoy it."

A pale girl of about ten, holding a paperback book in front of her face, appeared at the door. She glanced up from the book for long enough to pinpoint the spare seat, sat down in it and started reading again.

"Where's everybody else?" asked Uncle Andrew. "We're not the only ones who've got to suffer this, are we?"

Charming.

But where *was* everybody else? Surely it must be three o'clock by now? What if Granny and Lottie's mum were wandering lost around the thicket?

The others were fussing with costumes and make-up. Hannah slipped out of the stage door and down the path, where bright-green leaves were uncurling all over the blackthorn bushes and wood anemones were opening up on the ground like little earthbound stars.

And then she heard a sound that stopped her blood in her veins.

"A theatre? In these bushes? You having a laugh, Adamson?"

Jack and Danny! Hannah felt her leg bones dissolve like tablets in a glass of water. She clutched at a hazel branch. No, no, no!

Deep inside her, so deep that she couldn't really admit it even to herself, Hannah had had a secret fantasy that Jack *would* come to the play, and that, once there, he would be so wowed by her acting that he would see her in a whole new light and fall madly in love with her.

What a ridiculous idea. He *had* come, but he'd

brought Danny with him. Of course he had. They'd come to point and laugh, to gloat and make fun, and then to spread it all round the school on Monday morning that Hannah Roberts spends her weekends playing at theatres in an old chicken shed.

And what would Lottie say?

Lottie would never speak to her again after this.

As Hannah stood there clutching the hazel branch, she heard Danny's voice again.

"There's nothing in there, mate. She must've been having you on."

And then Jack. "Who cares, anyway? Let's get out of here."

Hannah clung to the branch, not moving, not even breathing, as their voices faded away. Even when the only sound left was the rustle of the grass in the breeze, her legs still trembled and she couldn't move. She hardly dared believe they had gone.

But they didn't come back. There wasn't another sound.

She was saved. And she would never, ever be so stupid again.

"Here we are, Dora. This must be the path."

Lottie's mum. And Hannah's granny with her. Weak with relief, Hannah scurried back to the theatre before they saw her.

Jo and Lottie took up their positions in the wings, each holding the string of a curtain. Lottie caught Hannah's eye. "Ready?" she whispered.

Hannah laid her head on the queen's pillow and closed her eyes. Lottie and Jo pulled the curtains open.

Hannah, snoring loudly, heard surprised and appreciative noises from the audience. She heard her granny say, "Goodness, haven't they got it looking nice!"

Hannah stretched elegantly and gave a huge yawn. Slowly she sat upright, opened her eyes, raised her chin and called: *"Maid! MAID! Come here at once! I command you!"*

Halfway through the play everything was going pretty well. Lottie's Prince John moustache had dropped off a couple of times and Jo had fluffed one of her speeches (though, to be fair, it hadn't helped that her breeches had fallen down halfway through). But there had been no real disasters. Martha was charm itself as Princess Esmeralda and, best of all, the audience really seemed to like it. They were laughing in all the right places.

Lottie entered now in her maid's costume, with a letter on a tray. Hannah was lounging on the bed, admiring herself in a hand mirror.

"A letter for you, Your Majesty," said Lottie with a curtsy.

Hannah extended a hand and took the paper between her thumb and forefinger. *"Oh, marvellous. It is from my nephew, Prince Laurence."* She scanned the letter. *"Oh, how utterly vexing. His malingering wife is indisposed and he will be unable to grace my birthday celebrations."* She looked at the letter again. *"I wonder who his hosts are in Shropshire. He speaks of them most highly. You are from*

121

Shropshire, maid. Which are the families of consequence in the county?"

Lottie, who was dusting the window frame, looked up thoughtfully. "*Well, Your Majesty, there are Lord and Lady Dingly-Wilson, or—*"

"*Imbecile!*" screeched Hannah. "*Do you not know that Lord and Lady Dingly-Wilson only own nine castles? How can you insult my dear nephew so by implying that he would stay with people who only own nine castles? You should be executed for treason.*"

"*Of course, Your Majesty,*" said Lottie, bowing her head. "*I beg your pardon, Your Majesty.*"

And then Sam burst through the wings on to the stage.

What was he doing? His entrance wasn't for ages.

He tugged at Hannah's skirts. "There's a fire!" he gasped.

Hannah stared at him. His face was white and his eyes were huge with panic.

"What?" she said.

Lottie turned away from the audience and put her hands on his shoulders. "Sam, you're not on yet," she whispered.

Sam shook her hands off. "No!" he shouted. "In real life, the farm's on fire!"

Chapter Seventeen

Fire

Hannah hurtled down the secret path, dodging the thorns and ducking the branches. She emerged into the meadow.

And gasped.

Behind the tractor shed rose a huge column of black smoke. And as she stood there, gaping, from across the yard came a rapid series of loud cracks, like machine-gun fire.

Hannah tried to scream, but nothing came out. She couldn't think. She just ran. Ran with all her strength, her legs drumming across the open field, her heartbeat loud and fierce in her ears.

The smell in her nostrils was growing stronger – a bitter, choking, poisonous smell. Dimly aware of the others behind her, Hannah raced through the yard, around the corner and skidded to a halt at the sight of the back barn.

She drew in her breath in a shuddering gulp. The barn was a vast black cavern of smoke. Through the smoke shot gigantic tongues of blue and orange flame, almost licking the roof.

CRACK! CRACK! CRACK!

Hannah felt Sam's hand clutch hers. She saw Martha open her mouth in a scream, but she could hear nothing above the explosions and the roaring.

Lottie's face drained of colour and her mouth formed the words, "What's that noise?"

Hannah pointed upwards. The barn's corrugated roof was exploding in the heat, expanding and popping with violent cracking sounds. As the flames spread, the sides of the barn started to bulge and writhe.

"Get back!" came a shout in her ear. Hannah turned around. It was Lottie's mum, followed by the rest of her family. "Get back, all of you! That barn could collapse any second!"

They grabbed the children and pulled them away from the barn. Hannah looked behind them, but there was nobody else.

"Where's Dad?" she cried.

"Has anybody called the fire brigade?" yelled Lottie's Uncle Andrew. He waved his mobile phone around wildly. "I can't get reception. Can anybody get a signal?"

Jo's eyes and mouth widened in horror. She clutched Hannah's arm. "The calves!" she shouted.

Hannah's stomach plummeted as if the earth had slid away from under her feet. She looked into the smoke-filled barn again. The calves – the wobbly-legged calves with their big blue eyes – were shut in a pen at the far end of that barn.

And she knew there was only one place her father would be.

"Dad!" she screamed, but no sound came out. She raced towards the barn. But it was as if she were in a nightmare. She was straining every muscle to move forward but something was pulling her back. She flailed her arms and kicked but she was getting nowhere.

"Get back over there!" yelled a voice in her ear. "Don't be an idiot."

Lottie's Uncle Andrew had his arms around her waist, dragging her away from the barn. She lashed out but his grip was too strong and she was pulled away. But she kept her stinging eyes fixed on the smoke-filled cavern, searching, searching.

And then the shape of her father appeared through the darkness and the flames. His face was completely black. Under each arm he carried a writhing, kicking calf.

Uncle Andrew had loosened his grip when Hannah stopped fighting, and now, with one massive thrust, she broke free of his hold and catapulted towards Dad.

At that moment, a fire engine swept around the corner and stopped by the milking parlour. Another one pulled up behind it. Firemen poured out of them. Some started unrolling hoses. Some pulled on breathing apparatus. Others went up to the adults and seemed to be asking them questions.

A fireman ran up to Dad. Coughing and wheezing, Dad thrust one calf at him and the other at Jo. "Get these two down into the bottom yard. Show him the way, Joanne."

He turned back towards the roaring cavern.

The fireman grabbed his shoulder with the hand that wasn't holding the calf. "You can't go back in there. That smoke's poisonous. And the fire's spreading."

Dad took the fireman's hand away. "Put it out then. Do your job and I'll do mine."

"You can't go in. Nothing in there's worth risking your life for."

CRACK! An explosion like a gunshot blew a huge hole in the barn wall. Flames surged out. Dad pulled a rag out of his pocket, dipped it into the water tank, tied it round his nose and mouth and disappeared into the smoke.

"No!" screamed Hannah. She raced in after him, but a fireman lifted her off the ground and carried her, screaming and choking, out of the barn.

"Don't you dare go in there," he said.

"But Dad—"

"We'll deal with him. You stay with your brother and sister."

Hannah turned round. Martha and Sam were standing behind her, their faces huge-eyed and rigid with terror. She held out her arms. Martha shrank away. Sam flung his arms around her waist and burst into sobs.

"Dad, Dad!" screamed Martha.

Hannah whipped her head around. The back half of the barn was engulfed in flames. And, seemingly through the flames themselves, his back bent and his head down, stumbled Dad. Next to him came a fireman, wearing breathing apparatus. Each of them carried two terrified calves under their arms.

And then everything went into slow motion. A vast concrete beam crashed down from the roof directly above her father. Hannah watched in paralysed horror as it smashed on to the ground.

Her stomach tightened in pain and she doubled over. She felt Lottie's arm round her shoulder. "It's OK, Hannah. Look, he's OK."

Hannah looked up. By some miracle Dad and the fireman had emerged into the open air. Dad was wheezing and coughing. Two firemen rushed forward and took the calves from him. Two others led him away from the burning barn.

The children ran over to their father. He was bent double and his chest heaved as he gulped in air.

"Stand back," said a fireman, shooing them away. "We need to check him over."

Jo came racing up the yard. "What's happened? Is Dad OK?"

A fireman raised his head. "Stand back, kids. Give him some air."

They moved back half a step. Hannah watched in terror as firemen rushed around with oxygen masks and breathing apparatus, giving instructions to each other in words she didn't understand.

Finally Hannah said in a tight little voice that didn't sound like her own, "Will he be all right?"

"We're doing all we can," said a fireman. "The ambulance is on its way."

Hannah's throat closed up and only Lottie's arm

round her shoulder kept her upright. "Ambulance? What do you mean?"

But her voice came out as a tiny croak. The fire crackled and roared as it devoured the barn, and nobody heard her.

Chapter Eighteen

A Discovery

"Yuck!" Sam spat a mouthful of porridge back into his bowl. "That's disgusting."

"It's burned," said Jo, pushing her bowl away and pulling towards her a yellow exercise book. On the cover she had written in large multicoloured capitals, "BEAN STEW". This was the magazine of the Great and Mighty Society of Bean. "And lumpy."

Hannah had hoped they wouldn't notice. She sighed. "Do you want toast instead?"

"Is Daddy going to be put in jail?" asked Sam.

Hannah's stomach churned. "No, of course not."

"You've given me milk and Sam water," said Jo, swapping the cups around.

"Why are the police here then?" asked Sam.

"They're just trying to find out how the fire started, that's all."

Yesterday afternoon, standing in terror outside the burning barn as her father disappeared into the flames, Hannah had been certain that if he came out of that barn alive, she would never worry about anything else ever again.

And he had come out alive. He hadn't even gone

to hospital. When the ambulance came, he had refused to get into it. "I've got a farm to look after," he said, and even when every other adult offered to look after the farm and the children, he wouldn't budge. So the ambulance crew had stayed until they were satisfied he was going to be OK, and then they left. He must have a fantastic pair of lungs on him, they said.

So she ought to be completely happy, shouldn't she?

"Jo, get your drawing stuff out of the way." Hannah pushed two plates of toast across the table.

"Hey, Broad Bean, look at this," said Jo, moving the open book towards her brother.

"Cool," said Sam. "Where's the butter?"

"In the fridge," said Hannah.

Sam slid off his stool as Dad's raised voice came from the dining room.

"You think I'd torch my own barn? With my livestock in it?"

"Is there any jam?" asked Jo.

"Sshh," said Hannah. But she couldn't make out any words in the policewoman's reply.

What did that mean? Did the police suspect Dad of causing the fire himself? But why on earth would anyone do that?

"Hannah, is there any jam?"

"For goodness' sake, Jo, get it yourself!"

The hall door banged open and Martha crashed into the kitchen, Princess Esmeralda's eyeliner smudged over her cheeks.

"Ugh, it stinks in here."

"Hannah burned the porridge," said Jo. "You look like a badger with that make-up all round your eyes."

"Shut up, you little weirdo. I've got beautiful eyes. Yours look like the bottom of a murky pond."

The door to the dining room opened and Dad and the policewoman walked out. Neither of them looked at the children. Dad's face was grim as he showed the policewoman to the scullery door.

"Well, thank you very much for your time," she said as he pulled the door open. "We'll be in touch. And if you find anything or hear anything that might help us discover the cause of the fire, let me know straightaway. Anything at all. If this was arson, we need to find out who was responsible."

Arson!

Did the police think someone had burned Dad's barn down on purpose?

But who on earth would do that?

Dad walked back into the kitchen. The children avoided his gaze. Since the fire, his mood was worse than ever.

He stopped and stood by the table.

"Were any of you playing around with matches in that barn?"

Now they all looked at him. "No."

"Are you sure? What were you all up to yesterday afternoon?"

The Beans looked at Hannah. "We were nowhere near the barn," she said. "And we wouldn't do

131

anything like that. You know we wouldn't."

He grunted. "Hmm."

"Why are you asking?" said Hannah. "The police don't think we did it, do they?"

Dad frowned. "They think it must be arson. There's no other explanation for a livestock barn going up in flames like that. They even started asking me questions, for goodness' sake."

"You!" said Jo. "Why would you burn your own barn down?"

"Oh, don't worry, I soon put them right on that score. Not much point burning down your own barn if you're not insured. Well, must get on," he said, heading out round the back where he kept his boots and coats. "But if you lot see or hear anything, you let me know."

For the first time ever, Hannah wished it wasn't the holidays. All the noise and bustle of school might have crowded out the image that kept flashing back into her head.

Dad, groping his way out of the burning barn, And a concrete beam, falling, falling, falling. . .

As soon as she had cleaned up the breakfast stuff, she found herself heading back to the barn.

The foul stench of chemical smoke hung in the air all over the farm. But the sun was shining and sparrows chattered in the hedgerows. It felt wrong, like laughter at a funeral.

All that was left of the barn's structure were the steel uprights. The sun poured down on to the scorched ground, illuminating millions of ash flecks hanging in the air. Every little breeze blew up clouds of ash and soot, which got into Hannah's nostrils and made her cough.

She walked through what had been the barn and out the other side. The yard out there was black too. She walked on, down the back track that cut through the fields leading to the other side of the village.

There was a matchbox lying on the track. Hannah hated litter. She bent down and picked it up. She would put it in the bin when she got back.

She transferred it to her other hand to put in her coat pocket.

As she did so, something caught her eye.

There was writing on the back.

Hannah's stomach scrunched itself into a tiny ball.

Miranda, said the writing, in blue biro. And, below the name, a mobile phone number.

Hannah dropped the matchbox as if it was burning her fingers. Her heart thumping against her chest, she stared at it lying in the dust.

When she'd last seen that matchbox, in the bus shelter, it was full.

Now it was empty.

And the barn had burned down.

She heard Dad's words again. "Were any of you playing around with matches in that barn?"

And she heard Jack's voice outside the theatre. "Come on. Let's get out of here."

She looked back at the huge burned-out skeleton of the barn.

No.

No. Don't be crazy. They couldn't have done that. They *wouldn't* have done that.

They wouldn't have gone into the barn. The packet was here, on the track. They were probably just walking along the footpath. Nowhere near the barn.

Something else must have caused the fire. It couldn't have been them, could it?

Because if it was . . . then she was responsible. Because it was her fault that they were on the farm.

No. It couldn't have been them.

She looked at the matchbox on the ground.

It wasn't evidence, was it? She couldn't report that to the police. Just a stupid matchbox?

Was it a crime? Withholding evidence?

But she couldn't tell the police. She couldn't tell anyone. Because then they would know. They would know that she had invited Jack to the farm. And they would know that the whole fire was her fault.

Hannah looked at the matchbox again. She stretched her fingers out. Withdrew them. Stretched them out again.

Slowly she bent down, picked up the box with the tips of her fingers, put it in her coat pocket and trudged back towards the house.

A big black BMW was parked in the farmyard. That looked familiar too, but Hannah couldn't quite pinpoint why.

Chapter Nineteen

Dilapidations

The house was quiet. The others must all be playing in their bedrooms.

"Hi, I'm back," Hannah called up the stairs.

The sitting-room door opened and Jo crept out. She pulled a face and pointed back into the room.

"What's wrong?" Hannah started to say, but Jo put a finger to her lips and beckoned Hannah to follow her down the hall.

"That man's here again," she whispered.

"What man?"

"The one from the landlord. The agent."

"What's he doing in the house? Who let him in?"

"He said I had to."

"You *had* to?"

"He's got his clipboard."

Hannah marched into the sitting room. She would tell that man where to take his clipboard.

He was standing in the middle of the room, looking from one window to the other.

"Only fancied curtains on the one window then?" he said, not looking at Hannah.

Hannah asked herself the question she always

asked when confronted with rude adults. What would Mum say?

"Can I help you?" she asked coldly.

"Cup of tea would be nice," he said without looking up from his clipboard.

The cheek of him! She drew herself up as tall as she possibly could. "On what purpose are you here?"

He waved a hand around the room. "Dilapidations. Got a right job on my hands too. Should have scheduled a whole day for this place."

Hannah didn't know exactly what he was talking about but he was being rude about their house, that much was obvious. Every fibre in her body tingled with rage. "What does that mean – 'Dilapidations'? And why are you in the house when Dad's not here?"

"It means I'm inspecting Mr Cashmore's property to ensure it's being properly maintained by the tenant. Routine procedure for which the tenant is obliged to provide full and free access. And long overdue, by the looks of it. Goodness knows what the last landlord was playing at. The whole place is a tip. That fire was probably a blessing in disguise. I bet that barn was piled to the rafters with junk. And as for *your father* –" he pronounced those words with a contempt that made Hannah really hate him – "he was sent a notification letter a week ago."

He walked over to the curtainless window, picked at the peeling paint and made a note on the form on his clipboard. Then he noticed the loose electrical socket underneath where the horse and dog painting usually hung. For as long as Hannah could remember, that socket had been hanging off the wall by one wobbly screw. It was fine as long as you remembered to push it hard into the wall whenever you unplugged the heater.

The agent wiggled the socket. It came off in his hand. "Strewth," he said, and made another note. Then, leaving it dangling off the wall, he walked out of the door and started up the stairs.

"You can't go upstairs!" said Hannah, thinking in horror of her bedroom floor, covered with dirty clothes and whatever she'd tipped out of her school bag over the past several weeks.

"I have a duty to inspect the whole property." He poked the torn stair carpet with his shiny black shoe and made another note.

"It's not a property!" Hannah shouted. "It's our house!" He ignored her. She followed him up the stairs, hoping he wouldn't look upwards.

He did, though. "What a state," he muttered, staring at the cobwebs. Hatred surged through Hannah.

At the top of the stairs he turned left. Oh, no. Not Dad's bedroom. That was worse. Much, much worse. Her room was embarrassing but this would be painful.

But he walked into Sam's room instead.

Sam was farming. He was pushing a model tractor with a seed drill fixed to the back of it across the worn square of carpet in the middle of the room. When the man walked in, followed by Hannah and Jo, Sam frowned and hunched lower over his tractor.

"Got your tractor out, eh?" said the man. "I'd have thought you'd be playing with that big combine harvester over there."

Sam looked at him with an expression that plainly said: are you really, really stupid? "I'm just planting the spring barley. It won't be ready to combine until August."

The man cleared his throat and flipped the page on his clipboard. He pulled up the corner of the carpet to inspect the splintered boards, and revealed a sheet of paper. Sam snatched it away and clutched it to his chest. Hannah knew what was on the piece of paper. Every room in the house was a field on Sam's farm, and under every carpet was a field plan, listing the crops he had sown in that field.

He finished snooping round Sam's room and without a word went back out into the hall. Hannah and Jo followed him, and Sam followed them, probably to check that the agent didn't unearth any more of his field plans.

As the agent opened the door of Jo's room, Hannah's shoulders relaxed slightly. Jo was the tidy member of the family.

But this man clearly didn't care about the ordered desk, the animal books carefully arranged on the shelves, the perfectly straightened bedspread. He just zoomed in on the peeling paint and the bits where the plaster had crumbled.

Hannah glanced at Jo to see her reaction but her face was blank and unreadable. Hannah felt as though she was about to combust with hatred. Every tut, every frown, every prod and poke and snide remark cut into her flesh like a knife.

He crossed the landing to Martha's bedroom and turned the doorknob. The door didn't budge. He pushed at it.

"Get lost, you fat loser!" yelled Martha.

The man stepped back from the door. His face had turned even redder. He hesitated for a second, as if he might make another attempt, but then he withdrew his hand.

Oh, no. It was her turn. Hannah tensed up with mortification. What on earth would he say when he saw the state of her room?

But he turned left again, heading for the door with a clay plaque on it that Hannah had made at infant school. It was decorated with seashells, and it said "Mummy and Daddy's room".

He opened the door.

"Strewth," he muttered again as he stepped inside.

Jo and Sam stayed at the door. Hannah pushed past the agent into the room. If you say anything, she thought, if you dare make one snotty comment. . .

Hannah saw the room through the agent's eyes as he stared around it. Cobwebs covered the windows. Cobwebs hung from the ceiling. Cobwebs clung to a dress still on a hanger on the outside of the wardrobe. Mum's shoes, all grey now with dust, were neatly paired up along the wall. Only Dad's slippers, sitting next to Mum's, and the bed, with its covers still crumpled where he had got out of it this morning, were free from dust.

For six years the dust had silently fallen on to Mum's possessions. Dad had not moved one single thing of hers since the day she died. And nobody was allowed into the room.

The agent shook himself out of his trance. He moved over to the wall and prodded at the crumbling plaster. He tutted over the peeling wallpaper and picked at the paintwork. Hannah noticed a gap in the bookcase and remembered that Mum's copy of *A Handbook for Drama Clubs*, which she had been reading last night, was still under her bed. She must fetch it as soon as this man left. Thank goodness Dad hadn't spotted it was missing.

The agent moved over to Mum's dressing table. Half-empty perfume bottles, entwined with cobwebs and thick with dust, sat clustered by the mirror. There were still some of Mum's hairs in the hairbrush that lay on the grimy glass top.

He stretched out his fat red hand and picked up the bottle of Mum's favourite perfume. A perfect circle of shiny glass was left on the dressing table.

Hannah took the poker from the fireplace. No one was allowed to touch Mum's stuff. No one. And certainly not a mean-minded, sweaty-faced land agent.

"Jeez," he said, staring at the dust-coated mirror. "Looks like someone died in here."

Hannah held the poker straight out in front of her and moved towards him.

"They did. Now, put my mum's stuff down and

get out of our house."

He turned around and laughed. "Are you threatening me with a poker?"

"Get out of our house!" yelled Hannah.

Downstairs, the back door slammed.

"Dad's here," shouted Jo.

Still holding the poker in front of her, Hannah moved towards the agent. He started to back out of the room.

"Get out. Now. Because if my dad sees you in this room, it won't be a poker aimed at your chest. It will be a shotgun."

Chapter Twenty

Confrontations

Hannah stood in the scullery doorway and looked from the agent's shiny red face to Dad's dry, weathered one. Like plastic and leather, she thought.

The agent cleared his throat. "Mr Roberts, I work for Strickland and Wormwood. I'm the land agent for Mr Cashmore. You'll have had our letters."

"Have you been poking about inside my house?" asked Dad.

"I gave you notice that—"

"When I wasn't there? Thought you'd help yourself, did you? Muscle your way in past my children? You arrogant—"

"He came in our bedrooms," said Sam.

Dad's face turned purple. "He did *what*?"

Click, clack. Click, clack. Everyone turned around to see Martha, in a sequinned vest top, spray-on hotpants and her mother's red stilettos, wobbling down the stairs.

Dad caught the look of repulsed fascination on the agent's face. "Martha," he said in the quiet, stern voice that was far more scary than his yell. "Go and put some proper clothes on."

Martha jutted her chin out and didn't move.

"Do as I say. Now."

Martha sighed theatrically. "Fine!"

The agent puffed his chest out. "Mr Roberts, I have a duty to Mr Cashmore to report on the condition of—"

"He said the house was a state," called Martha from the landing.

"Oh, he did, did he?"

The agent gave a short laugh. "Oh, come on, I'm only telling the truth. It is a state. I could have it condemned before you could say Polyfilla."

Dad's voice was hard as flint. "Only telling the truth. Is that so? Well, there are many truths, Mr Whatever-your-name-is, and if you had a grain of understanding in your head you'd know that. There's the truth that there's a bit of dust lying around in my house, and then there's the truth that my wife isn't here any more but we do the best we can and this is our home. So clear off and write your snivelling report, and when you've finished, send it to me and I'll feed it to the pigs. Or I would, if I wasn't afraid they'd choke on it."

Dad turned his back and strode into the yard.

The man was scarlet now. He followed Dad out. The children followed him, a few metres behind.

"You can say what you like, Mr Roberts, but the bottom line is that if this quarter's rent isn't in my hands by Midsummer's Day, you won't have a home or a farm."

Hannah drew in her breath as though somebody

had slapped her. Dad whipped round, his face hardened with anger. "Are you threatening me?"

Sam gripped Hannah's hand. "What does he mean? Why is he saying we won't have a home or a farm?"

"Nothing, Sammy," murmured Hannah. She put her arm round his shoulder and drew him close. "He's just being silly. It's not true."

It can't be true, she thought. It just can't. You can't throw people out of their home just because they're late with the rent, can you?

Can you?

What if you can?

A tide of panic rose up inside Hannah. She looked at Jo to try to gauge her reaction, but Jasper had trotted across the yard to greet her and Jo was crouched down with her arms around him and her curly head nestled into his wool.

"I'm just reminding you," said the agent, "that whatever's happened in the past around here, there won't be any tolerance of late rent payments under Mr Cashmore. Rumour has it you're having a bit of trouble finding the money."

"Well, when rents double overnight, people do have trouble paying," said Dad.

"The estate isn't a charity. Rents have been too low for too long. This is prime development land, you know."

"Prime development land!" Dad practically spat the words out. "Prime development land! It's a working farm, that's what it is."

144

And our home, thought Hannah.

"People need houses, Mr Roberts."

"Of course they do, but not at the cost of destroying a farm. Once you lose a farm, it's gone forever. People need food too, and farms feed people."

"And what about the animals?" cried Jo suddenly. "And the wildlife?"

Everyone turned to look at her. She blushed and shut her mouth.

Go on, Jo, thought Hannah. Don't let him shut you up.

But Jo had buried her face in Jasper's wool again.

Dad looked at Jo for a moment. "That's right," he said. He turned to the agent. "Farmers have looked after this landscape –" Hannah followed his eyes across the meadows, the streams, the trees and the ponds – "for hundreds of years. And if we're late with our rent, you'll just get the bulldozers in and flatten the lot, is that what you're saying?"

The agent shifted his shoulders in his jacket. "I didn't come here to argue with you, Mr Roberts. I was just giving you fair warning that rent cheques need to be sent on time in future. And that fire won't help, I shouldn't think. I hope you had the contents properly insured."

Hannah drew in her breath in a gasp.

The thresher!

The thresher that was going to pay the rent. The thresher that Dad hadn't insured because he was going to sell it next week. The thresher that was now a pile of ash in the burned-out barn.

Wide-eyed with horror, Hannah stared at Dad. But his face was impenetrable. "Just get off my farm," he said.

"With pleasure," said the agent. "I've seen all I need to see. Goodbye, Mr Roberts."

He tucked the clipboard under his arm and sauntered towards his car. Hannah looked after his retreating back, boiling with impotent rage. But Jo whispered in Jasper's ear, "Jasper, attack!"

Jasper didn't move.

Jo whispered the command again, fierce determination in her voice.

And Jasper put his head down and charged.

He butted the agent squarely on the bottom. The man's feet slid out from under him and he landed with a thud on the concrete, arms and legs flailing, a stream of high-pitched swear words pouring from his mouth. The children watched, open-mouthed and spellbound.

The agent heaved himself to his feet. It hadn't rained for a while, and the mud had turned to dust. His black suit was covered all over with a mixture of powdery clay, wisps of straw and squashed chicken dung. His face looked like a ripe plum about to burst. "That ruddy sheep! Running around like that! Ought to be locked up!"

He pulled his car door open and bashed at his suit to beat the dust out.

Jo's golden curls with the sun behind them glowed like an angel's halo. "I'm really sorry," she said as the man plonked himself down into the driver's seat.

"I don't know what got into him."

The agent slammed the door shut and revved the engine. Hannah let out a huge snort. And that was that. They bent double over the concrete and laughed and laughed and laughed. They had to hold on to each other to stay standing. Sam cheered with joy and danced up and down on the concrete.

And then Hannah glanced at her father and did a double take.

She nudged Jo. Dad's eyes sparkled as he watched the agent's retreating car. His lips were twitching. He saw the girls staring at him and he bent down and ruffled Jasper's thick fleece. "Good boy," he murmured. "Good boy."

He headed into the house. And as he clumped up the back stairs a sound that Hannah hadn't heard for years floated out into the yard.

Her father was laughing.

Chapter Twenty-One

An Idea

It was a brief moment of triumph. But it was only a moment. And when it was over, Hannah was filled with an overwhelming need.

As soon as she had put Sam to bed she would go to Lottie's house. She had to see Lottie.

Lottie lived in a Victorian cottage on the edge of the village, just as the fields stopped and the houses took over. Right from the front gate, the place was immaculate. The gate was freshly painted and swung silently on its hinges. The lawn was a perfect grass carpet.

You had to take off your shoes the second you stepped inside the house. The gleaming floorboards were dotted with beautiful rugs and every wall was painted white. No speck of dust was allowed to settle on the polished antique furniture and there wasn't a stray piece of paper in sight. Lottie's mum hated clutter.

Lottie led Hannah straight up to her perfectly organised bedroom. The sewing machine was out on her desk. "I was just finishing off Esmeralda's Scene Three costume," she said, folding the fabric on the floor into a tidy pile. "So what's up? Is it about the fire? What's happened? How's your dad?"

Hannah shook her head. "Awful. Everything's awful. It's been a hideous, hideous day."

Pacing the room, she told Lottie what the policewoman had said that morning. She told her about the agent's visit and the threats he had made. She told her about the uninsured thresher, and how it meant that Dad's next rent payment had turned into a pile of ashes in the burned-out barn.

The only thing she didn't mention was finding the matchbox.

Lottie sat very still and listened. Then she said, "Has he got anything else to sell?"

Hannah had asked herself this question on the walk to Lottie's house. "I don't think so. The Field Marshall and the thresher were the only vintage things he had that actually worked. He's got other old stuff but it's all rusty or broken. You know. You've seen it all lying around."

Lottie was looking at the floor. After a minute she said, "How about—" And stopped.

Hannah looked at her curiously. It wasn't like Lottie to be hesitant. "What?"

Lottie met her eyes. "OK. I've been thinking for a while. The festival prize money's five hundred pounds, isn't it? And we're going to make sure we win."

"Yes?"

Lottie took a deep breath. "I think we should give your dad the money."

149

Hannah stared. "Give all our prize money to my dad?"

"He needs it more than we do."

But what about the theatre? thought Hannah. What about the red velvet chairs for the auditorium? And the gold curtains? And a fund to buy props instead of making them from cardboard? And . . . and. . .

"That is such a kind idea," she said. "But he'd never accept it."

"We'll call it rent. Rent for the theatre."

And another image flashed into Hannah's head. The Secret Hen House Theatre Company presenting her father with a cheque for five hundred pounds.

If they won that prize and paid the rent with it, Dad would have to see how important the theatre was, wouldn't he?

Lottie cut into her fantasy. "I mean, I know it wouldn't pay the whole rent, but it would be a help, wouldn't it? How much is the rent?"

Hannah stared at her. How much *was* the rent?

"I don't know."

"You don't *know*?"

"Well, do you know how much your dad's rent is?"

Lottie gave her a withering look. "They got divorced, remember? They spent about a year arguing over money. I practically know how much every brick in this house is worth."

Hannah winced. "Sorry."

"Anyway, those men who took the Field Marshall

said it was worth a few grand, didn't they? And your dad sold it to pay the rent. So that means the rent is a few thousand pounds."

"Thousands of pounds? Four times a year? How can anyone pay that much money?"

"Well, he can't, can he? Not any more. Because they doubled it."

Anger rose up in Hannah, and then a wave of despair pulled her down. "So five hundred pounds is nothing, is it?"

"It's not nothing. It's a lot better than nothing."

Hannah rubbed her face with her hands, trying to push her brain into action. "If we could think of something else that might be worth another five hundred, then we'd have a thousand pounds to give him."

"Sell something, you mean? Behind his back?"

A key turned in the lock downstairs. "Hello, darling! I'm home!"

"Hi, Mum," called Lottie. "Hannah's here. We're working."

"Hello, Hannah," called Vanessa. "You've got fifteen minutes, girls, then your dinner will be ready, Charlotte."

"If it was something he wouldn't notice was missing, maybe we could," said Hannah.

"But you said there's nothing else that's worth anything."

"I don't know though, do I? How can we tell what's valuable? I mean, maybe some of those old machines half buried in mud are actually worth something."

Lottie laughed. "The Antiques Roadshow."

"What?"

"You know. People take their stuff to be valued. I'd love to see their faces if we dragged in one of your dad's old ploughs."

"What sort of stuff do people take?"

"Oh, you know, furniture, silver, stuff that's been in their family—"

Hannah drew in her breath. "Like candlesticks? Silver candlesticks?"

"Yes, that kind of—" Lottie stopped and stared at Hannah. "But not – you're not – you can't sell your dad's silver candlesticks. I mean, you wouldn't do that, without telling him, would you? *Would* you?"

Hannah paced the room. "They're in the theatre already and he hasn't missed them, has he? And anyway, they're not my dad's. They're my mum's."

"That's even worse! And they are his now anyway. You can't take them and sell them behind his back. That's stealing. And—"

"Funny sort of stealing, selling somebody's candlesticks and giving the money straight back to them. Lottie, if it helps the farm, we have to do it."

And I have to help the farm, she thought. Because it's my fault that the barn burned down. It's my fault that Dad has nothing to pay the rent with.

"But then your dad should sell them," said Lottie. She was biting her nails now. "Not us. It's his choice."

"He'd never sell them. My mum inherited them. They were her great-grandmother's or something."

Lottie went white. "Then we definitely can't sell them. Hannah, you're mad. He'd go completely nuts. Especially how he is at the moment."

"Maybe they're not worth anything anyway."

"No," said Lottie hopefully.

"How can we find out?"

"Hannah, you *can't* sell them."

"Fine. But we could find out if they might be worth something. Just for fun. Your mum's into antiques, isn't she? How do you find out if something's valuable?"

"You have to take it to a valuer," said Lottie. "An antiques dealer or an auctioneer or something."

"Like Sotheby's?" said Hannah.

"What?"

"You know. Where Miranda's dad works."

"He doesn't work there. He sells stuff there."

"Whatever. It's an auctioneers', isn't it?"

"But it's in London. Are you planning to go to London with your dad's candlesticks now?"

Hannah growled with frustration. "Honestly, Lottie, you're so difficult. Do you *want* the farm to be bulldozed? I'm just trying to think of things."

"All right. But I'm not an expert. I don't know if Sotheby's sells candlesticks."

Hannah sat down on the edge of Lottie's desk chair. "Right. Budge up."

"What are you doing?"

"They must have a website. I'm going to look it up."

Lottie sighed. "OK, fine. We'll look it up. But get

153

off my chair. I'm going to do it."

"That's not fair! They're my candlesticks."

"My computer. And you're so slow we'd be here all night. We've only got five minutes."

"Oh, go on then, bossy boots. But at least let me sit next to you." Lottie started tapping at the keyboard. "Go to 'Departments and Services'," said Hannah when the home page came up.

There was a long list of departments. "'English and European Silver and Vertu'," said Lottie. "Your candlesticks are English, aren't they?"

"What's vertu?" asked Hannah. She made a mental note to look it up when she got home.

Lottie clicked on the department.

Both girls drew in their breath.

Because right under the title "English and European Silver and Vertu" was a single picture. It was of a set of silver candlesticks.

"So they do sell candlesticks," said Lottie.

"Oh, my goodness, look at that!" Hannah pointed to a box on the other side of the screen. In it was a smaller version of the same picture. And underneath the picture, a description of the candlesticks and a price. It said 229,600GBP.

They looked at each other, eyes wide. "Does that mean," Hannah almost whispered, "that those candlesticks sold for two hundred and twenty nine thousand pounds?"

Lottie was frowning at the screen. "It's a set of six, and it says they're royal. So—"

Hannah was wriggling with excitement. "But even

if ours sold for a third of that – and OK, they're not royal, so take a bit off – that's still, say, I don't know, maybe . . . Lottie, they might be worth fifty thousand pounds!"

"Mmm," said Lottie. "I don't know if it works like that."

"OK, but even if they were worth half of that – even if it was just a few thousand – Lottie, that's amazing!" Hannah was bouncing up and down in her chair now.

Lottie was clicking on links. Suddenly her eyes lit up. "Look, this is brilliant. We can get them valued free! We can fill in a valuation form online and email photos, and then they'll send us an estimate of what they're worth."

"Charlotte!" called her mother from downstairs. "Dinner's ready."

"Coming!" called Lottie.

Hannah was reading the screen greedily. "Send clear colour photographs, front and back. . . photographs of signatures, maker's marks, and any areas of damage... Oh, my goodness, Lottie, we can do this! Can I borrow your camera? I'll take the photos tomorrow morning. In the theatre, before the others come out. They look great on the stage with the painting behind them. Much better than they did in the sitting room in front of the peeling wallpaper."

"It says here they take four to six weeks to reply with a valuation," said Lottie.

"Well, that's OK, I guess. He only just sold the Field Marshall to pay the rent – he must have a while until the next payment's due. How long do you—"

Footsteps sounded, running up the stairs. Lottie closed down the website.

The bedroom door opened. "Come on, you two. Your dinner's ready, Charlotte. How are you, Hannah? How's your poor father today?"

As Hannah put her coat on in the porch she reached into the pocket for her gloves, and her fingers brushed against Jack's matchbox. Her stomach lurched.

"And do you have any idea what caused the fire?" asked Vanessa.

Hannah glanced up. Vanessa was holding her scarf out to her and looking straight into her eyes. Hannah felt her cheeks burning. Could Vanessa read minds?

She took the scarf and busied herself with wrapping it around her neck.

"No. Nobody knows. It's a complete mystery."

Chapter Twenty-Two

Overheard

Tuesday morning, nine thirty. Hannah flicked back through the photographs on the camera. They looked good. Really good.

Her heart fluttered with excitement. Imagine the look on Dad's face when she presented him with the biggest cheque he'd ever seen in his life! How happy he would be when all his problems were solved forever.

She slipped the camera into her coat pocket and looked around the theatre. It was still exactly as they'd left it when the fire broke out. Lottie had brought all the costumes back but she'd clearly been in a state of shock, because she'd just dumped them in a heap on the queen's bed. They stank of smoke.

Hannah began the calming, satisfying work of putting the theatre in order. She smoothed out the creases in the costumes and hung them back on the rail. She replaced the jewellery in the middle drawer of the chest and the props on the props table. She opened up the Book at the Props page to check against her list that everything was present.

The front-of-house door slid open and a shaft of

morning sun fell across the floor. Once again, Hannah felt how wrong it was that the queen's bedroom had a bare concrete floor.

"Hannah?" said Lottie.

Hannah looked up. Lottie sounded nervous.

"Hannah, we've got a problem. A really big problem."

Hannah's blood ran cold. *Another* problem?

Lottie's words tumbled out in a breathless torrent. "The judge just phoned to ask directions to the farm for Saturday and she sounded really nice but she wanted to know where to park and I couldn't tell her to park at the end of the track and walk because if she walked all the way down the track and then saw there was loads of space to park in the yard she'd think we were really rude. And I couldn't tell her it was a secret because what if it's against the rules to have a secret theatre, so I said to park in the farmyard but what if your dad sees her and finds out?"

Hannah stared at Lottie. Her mind was completely blank. What with everything else that was swirling around in there at the moment, the possibility of Dad discovering the theatre hadn't even occurred to her. And she couldn't think of a single thing to say.

She swung round as the stage door was shoved open and the Beans burst in.

"Whoa, that was close," said Jo. "We're going to have to be really careful. Dad and Adam are just down there feeding the pigs."

Adam was an agricultural student. He had done

158

work experience on the farm last year, and he had enjoyed it so much that now he came up nearly every weekend to help Dad.

"Shut the door, quick," said Hannah.

A giant ball of wool squeezed through the doorway.

"Jo, I told you, no animals in the theatre this week. We've got to be professional."

"Jasper's not an animal, he's my friend," said Jo, hugging his fat woolly neck.

Lottie was checking the state of the costumes. "So what are we going to do about the judge?"

"Jasper, get off the stage!" said Hannah. "Jo, get him off."

"What about the judge?" said Jo, throwing both arms round Jasper's vast stomach and dragging him into the auditorium.

Lottie explained the problem. When she had finished, Sam, who was sitting on the floor of the auditorium stroking Jasper, said, "I think we should invite Daddy. He'd like the play."

"Huh," said Hannah.

But Lottie, still standing at the costume rail, put on her concentrating frown and said, "You know, what if Sam's right?"

"*What?*" said Hannah.

"Maybe he *would* like the play. Maybe he'd be proud of you. Maybe, once he saw it, he'd think the theatre was a good thing."

"Oh, yeah," said Hannah. "Great idea. And what if he didn't? What if we invite him and he goes ballistic and orders us to dismantle the theatre and put all his stuff back here? After all the work we've done, and the theatre looking so beautiful, and the judge coming on Saturday—"

"But if we don't invite him," said Lottie, "and he sees the judge arrive and finds out what we've been doing behind his back, he might go even more ballistic and storm into the theatre and shut it all down on the actual day. We can't risk that, can we?"

Jo, who had been crouching down at the auditorium wall fixing a piece of sacking, suddenly put her fingers on her lips and hissed, "Sshh."

They looked at her in surprise. "What?" said Hannah.

"Rustling," she said softly. "Just outside. I think it's a dog."

Everyone listened. There was a definite rustling outside. And now panting too. "It's Tess," whispered Jo. "She can smell us."

The panting turned to whining and the whining to scratching on the auditorium wall. A shout came from the direction of the track. "Tess! Tess! Come back here!"

"Oh, no!" hissed Hannah, rigid with fear. "Dad's going to find us!"

Sam huddled into her side and clutched her arm.

"What can we do?" asked Lottie. Her eyes darted around the theatre, but there was absolutely nowhere to hide and they all knew it.

"Go away, Tess, go away!" hissed Jo.

The whining and scrabbling grew more frantic.

"Oh, no; oh, no," whimpered Lottie. "He's going

160

to kill us!"

"She can't get in unless Dad opens the door," whispered Hannah. "No one say a single word."

"Tess! Tess!" It was Dad's voice from the field. "Come out of there at once! Where is that wretched dog?"

Then they heard Adam's voice. "I guess she's stuck in all those brambles."

"Yeah, I'll go in and see where she's got to."

Frozen like statues, they heard the trampling of nettles and the cracking of brambles. Dad clearly had a stick and he was beating his way to the hen house with it.

Hannah's heart thumped against her chest so hard that it hurt.

There was more slashing of brambles, and then Adam's voice, much closer now. "Found her?"

"There she is. You bad dog!" growled Dad. "What do you think you're playing at?"

He was right outside, less than an arm's length from where the children sat. And here was the tramp, tramp, tramp of Adam's feet too.

Tess scrabbled at the wall again.

Hannah held her breath. Please don't find the door, Dad. Please, please, God, don't let him come in.

"What's up with you?" Dad asked Tess. "Rats?"

"What is this place?" asked Adam. "I never knew there was a shed here."

Dad cleared his throat before he answered. "Used to be a poultry house. Hasn't been used for years. Come away from there, old girl. What a mess you are. Let's take those burrs out of your coat, eh?"

Jasper gave his head a vigorous shake. Jo fixed him with a stern look and put her finger on her lips.

"So you're not going to fight the rent review then?" asked Adam.

"No."

"But it's such a massive increase. I can't believe he's allowed to do it."

"Well, I've spoken to a lawyer and he reckons we wouldn't win if we fought it. It's a big increase, but it's in line with the market. And I've no time for a battle. There's enough to do here. Sit still, Tess, and leave that shed alone! You are a blessed nuisance, girl!"

"You're not really going to sell the cows, though, are you?"

Hannah's stomach churned. Sell the cows!

Jo's face turned white. Sam stared, huge-eyed, at Hannah, and opened his mouth to speak. Hannah put her hand over it and shook her head at him.

"No choice. Got to pay the rent somehow."

"What about next year, though? How are you going to cope without the milk cheques?"

"We'll worry about that when we come to it," said Dad in a tone Hannah knew meant the conversation was over. "Come on, Tess, we've got work to do."

No one moved or spoke as the footsteps and the rustling grew fainter. At last came the distant crunch, clomp, crunch of boots on tarmac. Hannah dropped her shoulders and breathed again.

"Oh, my goodness, that was so close," said Lottie.

"I've never been so scared in my whole life."

"Hannah, Daddy won't really sell the cows, will he?" asked Sam.

"Of course not," said Hannah. But she felt sick inside. Bad enough Dad selling machinery, but selling his animals!

And when there was nothing left to sell, then what?

"He can't sell the cows," said Jo. "It won't be a farm without the cows. I don't believe he really will."

"It just shows," said Hannah, "that we really need to win this competition and give the money to Dad. We just have to make sure our play's the best, that's all."

"Yes, and wipe the smug smile off Miranda Hathaway's face," said Lottie. "It would be worth winning just for that."

At the end of the rehearsal Hannah walked up the track with Lottie. Wisps of white cloud laced the bright blue sky. A kestrel hovered overhead and birdsong poured from the hedgerows. Soon the meadows would be a mass of wild flowers again: birds-foot trefoil, clover, cowslips, buttercups. And her mother's favourite, lady's smock.

Hannah took deep breaths of the fresh clean air. Then an image forced its way into her head: a cavalcade of lorries rumbling up the track, disgorging their loads of concrete over the fields, suffocating the grass and the flowers, burying the insects and starving the birds.

She imagined the cows and pigs and sheep loaded

on to trucks and taken off to market, bleating and squealing and groaning in a terrified, trampled mass. And she imagined the demolition ball swinging over her house: crashing through Mum's bedroom, smashing up the kitchen. She saw it swing through Dad's office, and the piles and piles of paper whirling and swirling through the yard, the bills and the time sheets and the letters and the journals, like a crazy paper blizzard. She saw the bulldozer crunch through her theatre, ripping up the roof and flattening the walls.

And she heard in her head the roaring of the chainsaws, and the sickening crash as the ancient trees were felled.

And then the silence. The silence of nothingness. Nothing but the silent screams of the fields as they lay buried alive under the hardening mass of concrete.

She imagined what her father must be going through right now.

And she felt the matchbox in her coat pocket.

She could just tell him it was Jack's matchbox, couldn't she? She didn't need to mention *why* the boys had been at the farm.

Telling Dad who might have caused the fire wouldn't save the farm. But it might just give him one less thing to worry about.

And she owed him that, at least.

Chapter Twenty-Three

The Antique Shop

Wednesday, two o'clock. The antiquated bus rattled and lurched towards Massingham. Hannah leaned across Lottie and rubbed the steamed-up window with the back of her hand.

Still miles to go. She looked at her watch. "We'll never make it by two thirty. We should have left earlier."

"Don't worry," said Lottie. "Antique dealers can't be that busy. I'm sure it won't matter if we're ten minutes late."

The bus hiccuped to a stop again. An old man shuffled on, water dripping from his umbrella, and, behind him, two Year Ten boys from their school, heads down, saturated hoodies clinging to their backs. Hannah clutched the plastic bag on her lap more tightly.

Lottie was telling her something about Esmeralda's last-act costume, which she had finished that morning, but Hannah had far too much on her mind to be able to pay attention.

It was the right decision, wasn't it? If Dad was planning to sell the cows at the next market – and

Jo said the next market was in two weeks' time – then they couldn't wait for Sotheby's to take four weeks to reply, could they? And that would only be the valuation. It might be weeks after that before the candlesticks were actually sold.

No, they needed the money now. It was cows or candlesticks.

And Dad surely wouldn't be angry with them when he realised they had saved his cows.

Lottie was still talking but Hannah had to lay her worries to rest. "Are you really sure this guy is honest? I mean, what if he gives us five hundred pounds for them and then he sells them for fifty thousand?"

Lottie sighed. "Hannah, my mum's known him for years. She's bought and sold loads of stuff with him. She said his valuations are spot on."

"You didn't tell her anything?"

"Of course I didn't. I just had to pretend to be really interested in antiques all yesterday evening."

"Thanks, Lottie. I am grateful."

"That's OK. It was actually quite interesting. Did you know that..."

Hannah tried to concentrate but Lottie's mention of yesterday evening had sent her mind flashing back. How was she ever going to pluck up the courage to tell Lottie what *she* had done yesterday evening?

If Lottie found out that Jack and Danny had burned the barn down, she would loathe Jack more than ever.

If that was possible.

And what if she started asking awkward questions? Lottie was all too capable of asking awkward questions.

When they got off the bus in Massingham the weather had settled into a damp grey sulk. They walked down the high street under a low, leaden sky.

As they crossed the bridge over the river, Lottie grabbed Hannah's arm.

"There it is!"

She pointed at a black sign with curly gold lettering. It swung on an iron bracket above a pretty bay window. The sign said "Hugh Featherstone Antiques".

Hannah's heart started to thump against her ribcage. Was it possible? Were they really going to walk out of this little shop with tens of thousands of pounds stuffed into their pockets? Oh, my goodness, what if they got mugged on the way home?

Don't be stupid. It would be a cheque, wouldn't it?

But what if the cheque got stolen? Or fell in a puddle?

Lottie tugged at her arm. "Come on. Isn't this exciting!"

The first thing Hannah saw as they walked through the door was an enormous vase of lilies sitting in the middle of a huge polished table. Her nose filled with the smell of them.

A wave of nausea swept over her. She turned and ran out of the door. She stood on the pavement, leaning against the wall of the shop, blinking back tears and breathing in the kind, anonymous smells of bus diesel, river water and hops from the brewery.

Lottie followed her out. "What's up? You've gone white. Are you ill?" She took a sharp breath. "Oh, lord, it's the lilies, isn't it?"

The fact that Lottie remembered tipped Hannah over the edge.

Everyone had sent lilies when her mother died. For weeks, the house had been full of that smell.

Lottie hugged her until the sobs turned into gulps. "Are you OK now?"

Hannah wiped her eyes with her sleeves. "I can't go back in there."

"We've got to. We have to sell the candlesticks, don't we? Imagine, we could walk out of here with a cheque for fifty thousand pounds! Look, I'll go in and ask them to take the lilies away. I'll get them to spray some air freshener around instead."

"How will you get them to do that?"

"I'll think of something."

A few minutes later Lottie returned, grinning. "It reeks of Pledge in there now." She lowered her voice. "I told him we're the people with the valuable candlesticks, but we can't come in because you're massively allergic to lilies. One sniff and you go into catatonic shock."

Hannah smiled.

"Come on," said Lottie. "Let's go."

This time it was the ticking of the clocks that Hannah noticed first. There were clocks everywhere.

Grandfather clocks, wall clocks, mantelpiece clocks. Clocks with wooden cases, silver cases, black and gilt cases. Big clocks, small clocks, clocks with pendulums and clocks with pillars. Clocks with low, sonorous ticks and clocks with frantic staccato ticks, all ticking over each other, each with a different pitch and pace, all clamouring for attention like toddlers in a nursery school. How could anyone work here and not be driven mad?

Hannah had expected the shop to be a kind of glorified jumble sale, but this was more like a miniature stately home. Elegant, ornate cupboards stood against the walls. The centrepiece of the shop was a very grand dining table where the lilies had stood. The surface, so highly polished that it shone like a mirror, reflected a vast crowd of silver: candlesticks, teapots, sugar bowls, cutlery, platters, photograph frames, all jostling for position, all taunting each other: *I'm more important than you. I'm more valuable than you.*

"Told you he was a silver expert," said Lottie.

Hannah clutched the plastic bag more tightly to her chest. Suddenly she didn't want to abandon her great-great-grandmother's candlesticks, which had sat in pride of place on the sitting-room mantelpiece for all these years, to this ambitious, snooty throng of orphaned silver, valued for nothing more than their price tags.

"What's wrong?" whispered Lottie. "Can you still smell the . . . you know?"

Hannah shook her head. Lottie would think she

was mad if she told her what was going on in her mind. She turned away, towards the window. And then she gave a start.

Oh, no.

Not here. Not now. Not with Lottie there.

Maybe they wouldn't see her.

Head down, Hannah moved away from the window towards the back of the shop. She pretended to be studying a chest of drawers, but she couldn't resist a glance back out of the window.

Through the misty panes, Danny Carr's eyes met hers.

Oh, no; oh, no. Why on earth had she turned round? Stupid, stupid, stupid!

"I believe you have some candlesticks you'd like me to value?"

Hannah looked up.

A man had appeared behind the counter. A middle-aged man, slightly stooped, with faded, papery skin, dry, faded hair and a faded yellow jumper. He looked like he needed a good dusting and an airing in the sunshine.

Maybe they had moved on. Hannah glanced out of the window again.

No, they were still there. It was hard to tell through the steamed-up window, but it looked as though they were having some kind of argument.

Please don't let them come into the shop. *Please.*

Lottie nudged Hannah hard. When Hannah looked at her, Lottie raised her eyebrows with a look that clearly said: snap out of it and let's get down to business.

Hannah cleared her throat and held out the plastic bag. It's to save the cows, she made herself think.

The man took the bag and disappeared into a back room.

The shop door clattered open. Hannah's stomach clenched into a ball.

Lottie whipped her head around. From the look on her face Hannah knew it was them.

She turned round.

It was just Danny. And he looked murderous.

Where was Jack? Hannah looked out of the window again. But there was no one there.

"What are you—" Lottie started to say.

But Danny pushed past her and planted himself squarely in front of Hannah.

"You stinking grass," he spat. His face was centimetres from hers. His breath stank of garlic. Hannah kept her head down and took a step backwards, her heart beating fiercely.

"Hey!" said Lottie. "What's going on?"

He ignored her. "You little grass," he hissed at Hannah again. His hands were clenched into fists. "You stinking little grass."

"What on earth—" said Lottie.

He shot his head round and thrust his jaw towards her face. "Back off, loser."

"Get lost, Danny," said Lottie. "Or I'll call the shopkeeper."

"Yeah, course you will. You're both the same,

aren't you?"

Lottie strode over to the counter.

"Watch it," Danny hissed into Hannah's face. "We'll get you back for this."

"Sure you will," said Hannah, her heart thumping. "Like I'm scared of you, Danny Carr."

Danny contorted his mouth and spat at her. Hannah flinched and screwed her eyes shut. A gob of spit landed on her chin and saliva sprayed over her cheeks.

"Ugh, you're disgusting!" shrieked Lottie. "Get out!" She pulled a tissue from her coat pocket and handed it to Hannah. Hannah scrubbed at her face.

Danny turned, wrenched the door open and walked out of the shop. Lottie watched him go. She turned to Hannah, wide-eyed. "What was that about? What have you done?"

Hannah's legs felt wobbly. She plonked herself down on an antique chair. She couldn't tell Lottie. She couldn't face another person going crazy at her.

"Hannah, say something! What on earth is going on?"

Hannah shook her head.

"Tell me! What have you grassed Danny up about?"

Hannah took a deep breath. "If I tell you, you have to *promise* not to say 'I told you so'."

"OK. Just tell me."

"I found a matchbox outside the barn," said Hannah, trying to keep her voice even. "It had Miranda's name and phone number written on it.

And when I was with Jack at the bus stop that day, he was holding the same matchbox."

Lottie gasped. "*Jack* set the barn on fire?"

"I told Dad last night and he rang the police. The policewoman went round to their houses this morning."

Lottie was staring at Hannah, open-mouthed. "I can't believe he burned your dad's barn down. Why didn't you tell me? That is unbelievable. What an evil thing to do. What's going to happen to him?"

Hannah shrugged. "She said she'd tell the school. But I don't know if they'll do anything."

Lottie's face was hard with anger. "That is so evil. He ought to go to prison."

"It was an accident. I know it's awful but it *was* an accident. They said they lit a fire in there, and they thought they'd put it out."

"Why didn't you tell me all this before?"

Hannah squirmed. "Well, I didn't know for sure if it was them until the policewoman phoned. And that was only just before I left today."

Lottie frowned. "How did you know Danny was involved though? If you just found Jack's matchbox?"

Hannah felt herself blushing. She shook her hair over her face and looked at the floor. "Oh, you know . . . those two always hang around together. I just guessed, really."

When Lottie replied, Hannah could tell she was still frowning. "I don't get it. What were they doing at your farm? They've never been up there before, have they?"

173

Hannah made a non-committal noise.

"They are such losers," said Lottie. "I always knew Jack Adamson was a loser."

"You promised you wouldn't say 'I told you so'."

"I didn't. I just said—"

"It was an accident. They didn't set the barn on fire on purpose."

"Idiots," said Lottie. "Lighting a fire in a barn! And then not even putting it out properly! Stupid, pathetic idiots. Oh, come on, Hannah, you can't deny it."

Hannah said nothing. She couldn't argue with Lottie because she would lose, but she couldn't let go of the beautiful pictures inside her head. Jack shredding the blank page of her maths book and scattering it to the winds. Jack kneeling in front of her in the bus shelter and gathering up her possessions. Jack, astoundingly, *not* spreading the dead duck story all around the playground. Jack's cheeky grin, his gorgeous wink, the way he made her laugh. . .

"Ah, young ladies."

They looked up. The man was there again, standing at the counter, holding the candlesticks in his fists. He looked amused, like he was laughing inside at some private joke. It didn't suit him. It made his face twist into weird shapes. He probably hadn't attempted a smile for twenty years.

"Interesting," he said, and Hannah's stomach did a somersault again. "You inherited these, you say?"

"Yes," said Hannah.

"From your great-great-grandmother?"

174

"Yes."

"Hmm." He cleared his throat. "And do you know how your great-great grandmother got hold of them?"

"No," said Hannah, her heart beating fast. Just tell me how much they're worth, she thought. "I think she inherited them too."

He paused, savouring that private joke again. Hannah was beginning to hate him.

"Hmm," he said again. "I think that's unlikely. They may have great sentimental value, but I'm afraid they are not genuine antiques."

Hannah stared at him. "What do you mean?"

"My dear, they're not solid silver. They are mass-produced, silver-plated candlesticks manufactured in the 1950s. The kind of thing you could buy in any high street homeware store."

"But . . . how can they . . . I mean . . . are you sure?"

His voice softened. "I'm sure. I'm sorry." He laid the candlesticks on the counter and began wrapping them up again in the newspaper that Hannah had carefully packed them in. He put them back in the plastic bag and held it out to her.

"I'm sorry to disappoint you." He attempted a smile again. "I hope you weren't planning a trip to the Bahamas with the money."

"No," said Hannah. "Not the Bahamas."

"That's all right then."

The rain was pelting down now – great driving sheets

of it that soaked straight through Hannah's coat and chilled her to the bone. She kept her head down and her shoulders hunched around her ears.

Lottie squeezed her arm. "I'm really sorry, Han. What a shame."

Hannah trudged on. She couldn't speak.

"They really do look like antiques," said Lottie.

Hannah drew in her breath.

Sotheby's!

She had sent off photographs of cheap 1950s candlesticks to be valued by the Sotheby's silver department. And she had thought things couldn't get any worse.

"At least we tried," said Lottie.

The hard knot of misery in Hannah's stomach exploded into anger.

"Why did they lie to her? I can't believe they lied!"

"Who? Who lied to who?"

"Mum's great-grandmother or whoever it was. She lied to my mum."

"Well, your mum got them from her grandmother, didn't she? Maybe her grandmother really did think they were real."

"Well then, her mother lied to *her*. Somebody knew they weren't real. Somebody bought them from a department store and pretended they were valuable. Why would anybody do that?"

Lottie put her arm round Hannah. "I don't know. It's a real shame. But listen. The only thing we can do is to make sure we win the competition. We've got two more days of rehearsals and we'll make it

176

perfect. Then we'll have five hundred pounds to give your dad. And that will help to save the farm. Five hundred pounds has to be a help. Doesn't it?"

Chapter Twenty-Four

One Day to Go

On Friday afternoon, Hannah lay on her bed, absorbed in writing the opening speech for the villain in her new play: an evil landlord determined to destroy the beautiful valley that the poor peasants have tended for ten generations. He plans to enclose the land and force them into slave labour, building him the most magnificent palace the world has ever seen.

"*Silence, paupers, and hear ye my plans!*" she wrote. "*No longer shall ye scrape together your miserable pittances by tending scrawny goats and skinny sheep. This land is mine, all mine, do ye hear? Your pastures will become my pleasure grounds, your meadows my rose gardens. . .*"

Dimly, Hannah became aware of the phone ringing. With a sigh, she slid the play under her bed and ran downstairs to answer it.

"Hannah?" It was Lottie. "You'll never guess what I just found on the skip next door."

"You've been rummaging in a skip? *You?* Lottie Perfect has been rifling through a *skip?*"

"I heard them bringing a load of stuff out so I

178

went to have a look. You've got to come right now and help me carry it to the theatre."

"Now? What is it?"

"It's a surprise. But I promise it's great. And we really, really need it for the play tomorrow. It will make all the difference, I swear. They've gone out now – we need to do it right away."

Hannah considered. She'd been looking forward to having an hour to herself before she had to get the tea. But then again, she would have all evening to write. And if Lottie was getting excited about something she'd found in a skip, then it was probably something worth getting excited about.

"OK then," she said. "See you in twenty minutes."

On her way out of the dining room, Hannah picked up a chair. She might as well take one out now. It would save time in the morning.

Today, for the first time, it felt like spring had really arrived. A high blue sky arched over the farm, from the woods in the north to the pale-blue hills of the South Downs. Daffodils clustered around the mossy tree trunks in the orchard.

Hannah carried the chair along the secret path, where tiny tight pink buds were growing on the blackthorn bushes. She pushed open the front-of-house door and set the chair down in the auditorium. Suddenly, out of nowhere, a wave of pure joy flooded over her. The theatre was beautiful. The weather was beautiful. Yesterday's rehearsal had been perfect. And they were going to win the Linford Arts Festival drama competition.

Hannah could almost believe that the theatre itself was excited about tomorrow's performance. She could sense anticipation in the air. Everything was ready. The auditorium was swept clean, awaiting the rest of the chairs. In the dressing room, the costumes, all neatly labelled, hung in shimmering rainbow glory on their rail. Martha had arranged the make-up neatly on the chest of drawers and the jewellery sparkled on its tray. The Book lay on the props table. Every prop had been checked off the list and set out in scene order.

On stage, the queen's bedroom was immaculate. The worthless candlesticks were back on the dressing table. Hannah pushed all her feelings about the candlesticks to the back of her mind.

"We're going to win, Mum," she whispered. "Wish us luck. We're going to make you proud of us. And we're going to give the money to Dad and help to save the farm. We won't let anyone destroy the farm. I promise you we won't."

"You won't believe this," said Lottie, when she answered the door. "You are not going to believe it."

She grabbed a rucksack from a hook and shrugged it on to her shoulders. "I've altered Jo's Rallentando breeches so they don't keep falling down. I just need to try them on her once we've done this. Now, come and see."

The edges of the skip were built up with jagged pieces of wood. Lottie craned her head over the sides and pulled at something. "Look at that."

It was a rolled-up carpet. The corner that Lottie had pulled back revealed a red background, patterned with a tapestry of blue, white, black and gold. It looked in perfect condition.

"Wow," said Hannah. "What a find."

"I know," said Lottie. "It's like it's meant to be."

Hannah pictured the queen's bedroom, with its wood panelling, draped window, four-poster bed and now a Persian carpet. She drew in her breath with delight and hugged Lottie.

"It's a sign," she said. "We're going to win the competition."

The carpet was unbelievably heavy. They had to keep stopping to shift its weight and shake their aching arms. There were a few people out walking their dogs but nobody asked them why they were carrying a large Persian rug up Elm Lane on a Friday afternoon.

When they reached the farm track, the cows in North Meadow gazed up at them as they staggered past, and went back to chewing the cud. The heavily pregnant sheep in South Meadow took no notice at all.

"Stop, Hannah," gasped Lottie, halfway down the track. "I need to rest."

"Are you crazy? What if Dad sees us? Come on, we're nearly there."

They stumbled through the field and up the secret path, the carpet leaving cracked branches and snapped twigs in its wake. Hannah pulled the front-of-house door back. They lurched into the auditorium and heaved the carpet off their shoulders. It thudded on to the floor and they sank down on to it, panting and rubbing their aching arms.

"Right," said Hannah, springing up. "Let's see how it looks."

Lottie groaned. "Just give me two minutes." She pulled her shoulders back and rolled her neck round. "I can't believe the judge is coming tomorrow, can you?"

"No," said Hannah. "It's amazing, though – it actually does feel like we're ready."

"But there's still one problem, isn't there?" said Lottie, looking at her. "Your dad."

Hannah's stomach lurched. "Come on," she said, standing up. "Let's get everything off stage, then we can lay the carpet down. Bed first."

Lottie got up, brushing dust off her trousers, and they took hold of the tied-together crates at the bottom corners.

"He won't be out tomorrow afternoon, I suppose?" said Lottie, hopefully, as they edged the queen's bed into the auditorium.

"No," said Hannah. "Careful with that post – don't catch the curtain wire. I did try to suggest a couple of things, but he looked at me like I was mad. Right, dressing table next. Let's clear the surface."

They picked up the candlesticks, the queen's hairbrush, perfume bottles and jewellery and took them backstage. Then they got themselves in position to move the dressing table.

"I think we have to tell him," said Lottie, grasping one end.

Hannah let go of the other end. Her whole body shuddered with panic. "We can't! He'll go mad. He'll make us dismantle the theatre and cancel the judge coming and everything."

"But, Hannah, we've been through this. What if he sees the judge arriving and finds out that way and goes crazy? Maybe if we tell him beforehand, we can talk him round."

"But maybe he won't see anyone," said Hannah. "He never noticed anything at the fire, did he? All the guests were there and we were in costume and everything and he never batted an eyelid."

"Maybe because he was a little bit busy rescuing animals from a burning barn?" said Lottie. "We're not going to have that sort of distraction tomorrow. Hopefully."

Hannah desperately tried to think. What if Sam told him? He might not get so mad with Sam.

But that was hardly fair on Sam, was it?

Lottie took hold of the dressing table again. "Come on, let's shift this."

Crab-like, they walked the dressing table into the auditorium.

"How are we going to move the window seat?" asked Hannah. "The window's attached to the seat and the ceiling."

Lottie looked at it. "We need reinforcements. Let's get the Beans. Jo can try on these breeches too, while she's here."

As they emerged into North Meadow, a flash of electric blue in the bushes by the stream caught Hannah's eye. She grabbed Lottie's arm and pointed. "Look. A kingfisher."

The little bird darted to another branch and settled there.

"Wow," whispered Lottie. "I've never seen one before. I thought they'd be much bigger. It's so tiny. Beautiful."

"I must remember to tell Dad. He doesn't think there are any around at the moment. I wonder if your dad's seen it for his bird survey."

Lottie drew in her breath sharply and grabbed Hannah's arm. "I know!"

Hannah stared at her. "What?"

"What if I get my dad to phone your dad and tell him about the kingfisher? He could ask to come up and meet your dad in this field tomorrow, right before the play, to show him. And then he can take him to the theatre – he can say there's a nest in the bushes or something – and all the audience will be here, and the judge—"

Hannah looked at Lottie as if she were mad. "What are you talking about?"

"Don't you see?" said Lottie. "If my dad brings him into the auditorium right before the play starts, your dad can't yell at us and make us stop the play. Not in front of all my family and the judge and everyone. So at least we'll be able to do the performance. Even if he goes ballistic after everyone's gone."

A tiny chink of light pierced the murky grey fog in

Hannah's head. "You know what?" she said. "That might actually work."

"Cool," said Lottie. "I'll call Dad tonight and explain." She stopped in her tracks. "Oh, but we must remember. One of us can do it later."

"Do what?"

"We'll have to take the candlesticks away. And the horse and dog painting."

Thank goodness Lottie had thought of that. If Dad saw Mum's precious candlesticks and her favourite painting hanging in a chicken shed, he would definitely go ballistic. Even if the Queen was sitting in the audience.

Chapter Twenty-Five

Despair

At nine o'clock on Saturday morning Jo put her head round the back door. Hannah and Lottie were standing in the scullery.

"Well?" said Hannah, who had been drumming her fingers on the freezer for the last five minutes.

Jo stepped in. She had a notebook and pencil in her hand. She cleared her throat importantly.

"Secret Security Report Code 07962 from the Great and Mighty Society of Bean. Report delivered at 0900 hours on Saturday 20th March. Mung Bean and String Bean have carried out a full search and the farmyard is officially pronounced a safe zone. Chief Suspect codename A.R. spotted at 0856 hours driving a tractor in the direction of the Waterbrook."

"Good. Stay here and keep watch. We'll be back for more chairs in a minute. Oh, and Martha," Hannah called back into the kitchen, where Martha was still eating breakfast, "remember to be at the theatre by ten o'clock."

"Ten!" said Martha through a mouthful of toast. "Don't be stupid. The judge isn't coming till three."

"No, but we're having a last dress rehearsal at ten.

If you'd stayed to the end of yesterday's rehearsal, you'd have known that."

"Shut your face, scarecrow hair. You're lucky I came at all. If you're not careful I won't even turn up today, so watch it."

Hannah opened her mouth to retort, but Lottie jumped in. "It would be a shame if you didn't turn up when the judge is coming. You're such a good actress, and the judge might be a talent-spotter and recommend you for a film."

"Shut up," said Martha, but the venom had gone from her voice. Lottie winked at Hannah. Hannah smiled back. That should do it.

Hannah picked up two dining chairs and set off across the yard. Lottie staggered behind her, a chair under each arm.

Hannah's stomach was full of butterflies. No, not butterflies – more like elephants trampling around inside her. She couldn't believe this was really happening. A real judge from a real festival coming to their theatre to watch their play!

And a five hundred-pound prize.

Once again she replayed the daydream where she presented her father with the prize cheque. With tears of gratitude in his eyes he would humbly accept the money, which would save the farm and make him look upon Hannah with love and admiration for evermore.

It was a lovely daydream. But when she thought about Dad actually coming to their play, the elephants multiplied, a whole great herd of them stampeding around her stomach.

He has to be impressed, surely? He won't stop us performing the play? He won't explode at us in front of the judge and order us to dismantle the theatre right then and there? He'd never do that, would he?

No, no, he'll love it when he sees it.

I know he will.

He has to.

Taking deep breaths, Hannah set down her chairs at the front-of-house door. Don't worry, she told herself. It will all be fine. And the carpet is just perfect. The stage really does look like a bedroom fit for a queen now.

She pushed the door open and stepped into the auditorium.

Her body turned to stone. She opened her mouth in a gasp. But no sound came out.

"Hannah?" asked Lottie, behind her. "Come on, get inside. My arms are killing me."

Lottie pushed past the chairs into the theatre. And froze.

Hannah stood absolutely rigid. She couldn't move and she couldn't speak. Her eyes huge with horror, she stood and stared at the scene before her.

At the crimson curtains, slashed to ribbons.

At the wooden panelling, scrawled all over with neon spray paint.

At the eyeshadows, blushers, nail varnish and lipsticks, smashed to pieces on the floor.

At the Persian carpet, smeared and splattered with stamped-on make-up.

At the perfume bottles from the queen's dressing table, lying in shattered shards of glass all over the carpet.

Hannah couldn't think. She couldn't take it in. All she could do was stare and stare in disbelief.

With a great gasp, Lottie unfroze. She hurtled through the wings to the dressing room.

"Noooo!" she wailed. "Oh, no, no, no!"

Heart racing, Hannah darted backstage.

A scene of savaged chaos met her eyes. Drawers gaped open, the shoes and bags and scarves hurled across the floor. The jewellery lay trampled to pieces on the concrete and the empty costume rail sprawled on the ground.

This can't be real, Hannah thought.

It must be a nightmare.

Lottie sank to her knees on the concrete floor. In her arms she cradled a bundle of costumes. "Look," she sobbed, holding up a dress. "Look what they've done."

Hannah gasped. A huge slash ran through the queen's gown, slicing it apart from neck to hem.

"And this, look." She held out Esmeralda's blue silk dress. The bodice was peppered with stab wounds.

"Everything," sobbed Lottie. "They're all destroyed. Every single one."

Hannah sank down on the cold concrete floor beside her friend and lifted up the costumes one by one. Dresses, shirts, jackets and skirts; everything was cut and torn and stabbed and ripped.

Fury boiled up inside her. "How could they? How could anybody do this?"

Lottie gasped and grabbed her arm. "Look!"

Hannah raised her head and looked. Scrawled on the mirror in blood-red lipstick were the words: GOT YOU BACK, YOU COW.

They stared open-mouthed at each other.

"Danny!" said Hannah, at the same time as Lottie said, "Danny and Jack!"

Hannah wanted to cry, "No! Not Jack. Jack couldn't have done this."

But she didn't say it.

Because he could, couldn't he?

That's what Danny had meant in the antique shop. "*We'll get you back for this.*"

And they had.

Lottie swept the mutilated costumes back into her arms and buried her face in them. "I can't believe it," she sobbed. "How can anyone be that evil? How can they just ruin everything like that? How could they?"

Still Hannah said nothing. Lottie was right. How could they? How could people be that horrible? She put her arm around her friend while Lottie sobbed into her costumes.

Then suddenly Lottie sat bolt upright and stared at Hannah.

"Wait a minute. How did they know we had a theatre here?"

Hannah's heart stopped. Her head flashed back to that moment on the floor of the bus shelter.

"Do you want to come to our dress rehearsal? It's on my farm."

What had she done? What had she started? How much had she destroyed with that one stupid, stupid invitation? If only she could go back in time. If she could just take back that one little sentence. She would give anything. Anything.

But you can't do that, can you?

You can't delete the past.

Lottie was pacing the theatre with furious energy. "Who could have told them? I haven't told anyone except my family, and you've only told your granny. The Beans would never tell. So who . . . Oh!"

She swung round and stared at Hannah. "Martha!" she shouted. "She hates us and she hangs around with Danny's sister. She told them, just to spite us!"

Lottie's face was bright red. She looked as if she were about to explode with rage.

I have to tell her, Hannah told herself. I can't let Martha take the blame.

But what would Lottie do to her when she found out *she* was responsible? Hannah shrivelled at the thought of it.

"I'm going to kill her!" Lottie said. "Stupid, stupid girl! We should have known she couldn't keep a secret. I hate her. I hate her so much."

The brambles crackled outside the stage door.

Lottie strode to the door and pulled it open.

Outside, in purple leggings and a tight black vest top, stood Martha, her hands on her hips and a scowl on her face. "Jo says why aren't you coming to get the other chairs, you losers?" She stopped. "What are you looking at me like that for, freak?"

Lottie yanked Martha inside the theatre. "Was this you?" She gestured wildly at the chaos. "Did you tell them where our theatre was? Did you know they were going to do this?"

Martha's eyes widened. "Oh, my lord, what's happened?"

"Lottie," said Hannah. "Lottie, don't—"

But Lottie didn't seem to hear her. "Don't pretend you don't know about it!" she screamed at Martha. "You told them, didn't you? You told your stupid little friend about the theatre so Danny could come and wreck it. You told them it was the competition today and he came and destroyed our theatre to get back at Hannah." She grabbed Martha's shoulders and shook them. "How could you? How could you do that?"

Hannah dragged herself to her feet and touched Lottie's arm. "Lottie, I don't think—"

Martha pushed Lottie's hands off her shoulders. "Get off me! What friend? What are you talking about? I didn't do anything!"

Lottie scooped up an armful of mutilated costumes and thrust them in Martha's face. "You know exactly what I mean. Danny Carr's sister. Jade. Did you tell Danny where our theatre was?"

Martha took a step backwards and stared at her accuser, chin up. "You evil pig. How dare you? How dare you accuse me of this? You're disgusting, horrible bullies, both of you. I wish I *had* wrecked your stupid theatre and I'm glad someone else did. And don't think I'm ever going to be in your stupid little play now, because I'm not, so there. I hate you both and I hope you die!"

Chapter Twenty-Six

Confessions

They stood motionless as the sound of Martha's running feet faded away.

There was a terrible silence. Then Lottie slowly turned to Hannah. "You know what? I've got a horrible feeling she didn't do it."

Hannah's insides felt like swirling soup. "What do you mean?"

"I'm just thinking . . . her face when she saw all this. She looked . . . shocked."

Tell her, Hannah said to herself. You have to tell her.

But no words came.

"But if *she* didn't tell them," Lottie said, "then who did? They can't have found it by accident. Unless they followed us." She stared, wide-eyed, at Hannah. "That must be it! They followed us one day and found out where it was! Don't you think? Hannah?"

The stage door rattled with three loud knocks. Hannah's stomach flipped over. Nobody ever knocked at the door.

Was it Dad? Had Martha gone and told him

everything? Already?

"Cooeee! Charlotte, Hannah!"

Lottie's mum! Relief surged through Hannah. Lottie pulled a face and pushed the door open a fraction.

"What do you want?"

"Lovely to see you too, light of my life. I thought you might be in need of sustenance, with your busy day ahead." She held out a box of biscuits. "Where's Hannah?" She pulled the door open further and stepped in. Her eyes widened and her mouth fell open. "Good grief! What on earth has happened here?"

They said nothing. But Vanessa's eyes fell on the message on the mirror.

"'Got you back'?" she said, and there was fear in her voice. "What does that mean? Who's got you back for what? What's going on here?"

They stood there, silent. Vanessa waited for a minute. Then she fetched three chairs from the auditorium and placed them in a circle.

"Right," she said. "Sit down and tell me everything."

The girls stayed standing. Hannah could feel Lottie looking at her but she couldn't meet her gaze.

Lottie was obviously fed up with Hannah's silence, because she sat down and said, with a distinct edge to her voice, "It was Jack Adamson and Danny Carr, from our class. They did it to get back at Hannah because Hannah found out they started the fire in the barn and she told the police."

195

Vanessa actually seemed lost for words for a moment. "Jack and Danny burned the barn down?" she said eventually.

"Not on purpose," Hannah blurted out. Lottie let out a snort and Hannah wished she had kept her mouth shut. "They lit a fire in there," she explained to Vanessa in a tiny voice. "And they didn't put it out properly."

"What idiots!" said Vanessa. "What absolute irresponsible idiots." She shook her head. "Your poor father. How dreadful for him. I hope they get properly punished. And then to do all this!" She gestured at the wreckage. Then she frowned. "But how did they find your theatre?"

Lottie went through all her theories of how the boys could have found out. Then she looked at Hannah. "What do *you* think? Why aren't you saying anything? What is wrong with you?"

Vanessa was looking at Hannah too. Hannah's heart was thumping so hard against her ribs that she felt dizzy.

She had to speak. It was now or never.

In a strangled voice, she said, "It wasn't Martha. It was me. I told Jack where the theatre was."

Lottie stared at her, her eyes getting bigger and bigger.

"*What?*"

Gripping the back of the chair, with her eyes fixed to the floor, Hannah told them everything. How she'd invited Jack to the dress rehearsal. The conversation between Jack and Danny that she'd heard outside the theatre. And the part they already knew – how she'd found the matchbox and eventually told her father.

She didn't look at either of them as she spoke, but when she finished, she glanced up at Lottie.

She wished she hadn't. Lottie was glaring at her, eyes blazing with fury.

"You traitor! How *could* you? You stupid, stupid cow! All the time I thought it was someone else, someone who hated us, and it was *you*! What was the point of all the secrecy, all the work we did, if all the time you were just going to ruin it? What was it all for?"

She was standing up now, gesturing wildly and shouting into Hannah's face. Hannah slid on to the chair and curled up in a ball. She wished she could just dissolve. "I'm sorry," she said. "I'm so, so sorry. I was so stupid and if I could do anything to take it back I would."

"But you can't," snarled Lottie. "So what's the point of saying it? Of course you're sorry now, when everything's ruined. But that didn't stop you inviting your precious Jack to our dress rehearsal behind everybody's backs, did it?"

Vanessa stood up. Now she's going to start shouting at me too, thought Hannah. And I deserve it, I know I do.

But Vanessa put her hands on Lottie's shoulders and pressed her back into her chair. "That's enough, Charlotte," she said. "Calm yourself down." Lottie pushed her mother's hands off, but she sat down, with her jaw jutted out and her arms folded.

Vanessa turned to face Hannah. Hannah stiffened up all over. But instead of shouting at her, Vanessa knelt down, put her arms around her and gave her a hug. Then she moved back, but she stayed kneeling and kept her hands on Hannah's arms as she said, "Now, Hannah, you have got to stop blaming yourself. You didn't do anything wrong."

"Oh, sure she didn't," said Lottie.

Vanessa whipped her head round. "Be quiet, young lady." She turned back to Hannah and her voice softened. "Think about it. All you did was invite somebody to your play. A friend – or so you thought. *You* didn't burn the barn down. You didn't vandalise the theatre. And you couldn't possibly have known he would do those things either."

"Yes, she could," said Lottie. "Everyone knows Jack Adamson's a pathetic loser."

"Well, he's always seemed perfectly charming to me," said Vanessa. "And he's a lovely-looking boy."

Lottie snorted. Vanessa stood up and fixed her with a gaze. "And another thing, young lady. Who did you invite to your dress rehearsal and your performance today?" Without giving Lottie a chance to reply, she started counting on her fingers. "Your mother, your father, your auntie, your uncle, your cousins. And who did Hannah and her sisters and brother have to come and watch them? One person. Their grandmother, who, lovely as she is, is eighty years old and very frail. So just try to put yourself in your friend's shoes for once, Charlotte, and maybe you'll show a little more understanding of why she invited somebody else to her play. All right?"

Lottie scowled. But the tightness in Hannah's throat slackened a little.

Vanessa stood up and clapped her hands together. "Right," she said. "Now that we've sorted that out, the question is, how are we going to get all this mess fixed before the judge arrives?"

They stared at her.

"Don't be ridiculous," said Lottie. "There's nothing we can do. There's no way we can get it cleaned up in time. You saw the costumes. They're slashed to pieces. We'll just have to phone the judge and tell her not to come. And Miranda Hathaway will win the competition, like she wins everything."

"So don't let her!" said Vanessa. "Come on, you two. Everyone will help. Rachel's old sewing machine must still be in the house somewhere. I'll take it home. With Charlotte on hers too, we can mend the costumes and the rest of you can clear up in here."

"But the judge is coming at three," said Hannah. "And the theatre's completely wrecked. Even if we tried to mend stuff it would never look as good. There's no way we could win now."

"Hannah Roberts," said Vanessa, "that's not like you. You're not someone who gives up."

But the full force of what had been done to them suddenly hit Hannah like a demolition ball. She curled herself up on the concrete and wrapped her arms around her head. "I can't do it. It's ruined. The theatre won't ever be the same now."

Vanessa crouched down and put her hands on Hannah's shoulders. "Hannah, those boys have done a terrible thing, but you can't let them win. The way you're responding now, that's exactly what they want. They wanted to demoralise you and make you give up. You must rise higher than them. Show them they can't defeat you."

Hannah didn't move. "They have defeated me. They win."

From her curled-up ball, Hannah heard Vanessa give an exasperated sigh. "Well, I'm going to take these costumes out to the car and then I'm going inside to find that sewing machine. Come home and help me when you're ready, Charlotte. And, Hannah," she called from the door, "if I have to squeeze into the queen's costume myself and perform in front of the judge, then I will. But I couldn't do it half as well as you could, and it wouldn't be a pretty sight. Is that really what you want?"

Chapter Twenty-Seven

Hope

After what seemed like a very long time, Hannah felt Lottie's arm on her shoulder.

"I'm sorry I yelled at you."

Hannah's tensed muscles melted in surprise and relief. "Don't say sorry. You've got nothing to be sorry about." Her voice came out muffled through her knees. "I deserved it. I'm so, so sorry. But I know it's no good saying that."

"Well, you were unbelievably stupid," said Lottie. "But I know you're sorry."

Hannah uncurled herself a tiny bit. "Thank you."

"I'm still mad at you."

"Yes."

Lottie stood up and started to pace around the dressing room. When she spoke again, her voice was back to normal. "You know what? I think she's right. We should fight back. We can't let them defeat us."

"I can't do it. I haven't got the energy."

"Hannah, imagine how we'll feel in the future if we don't do this. If we just let them win. And, quite frankly, since you got us into this mess, you, more than anyone, should be helping to get us out of it."

She slipped through the wings on to the stage. "Look, we *will* be able to clear it up, you know. It looks worse than it is. I mean, there's loads to do, but if we get the Beans in, there'll be four of us to do it." She looked at her watch. "And we've got nearly five hours before the judge arrives."

A chink of light sneaked into Hannah's head. She lifted her face from her knees. Then she saw the shattered make-up and the crushed jewellery. "But what about all this? You can't mend make-up."

"No, but we can borrow some. Mum's got loads of make-up. I'll put it back before tonight. She'll never know."

Lottie was so brave. Hannah could imagine Vanessa's reaction if she caught them using her Chanel eyeliner to draw moustaches on to ten-year-olds.

"And we don't really need jewellery," said Lottie. "I mean, I know it's great to have it, but we can manage without."

"But she's a queen," said Hannah. "She has to wear jewellery."

"Oh, come on, Hannah. It'll be a challenge. You like challenges." She started to gather up the rest of the costumes from the floor. "I'm going to go home and help Mum mend these. You find the Beans and start clearing up in here."

Maybe. Maybe it would be possible. Maybe they could actually put on their play.

But then, like a sledgehammer, it struck her.

"Lottie, we can't. Martha won't be in it. We can't

do it without her."

Lottie stopped in the act of picking up Prince John's jacket. "Maybe that was just a threat? She's threatened it before and she always turns up in the end."

"Not after what you said to her just now. I'm telling you, she definitely won't come back this time."

Lottie put the costumes on the chest of drawers, picked up the broom and started to sweep the shattered jewellery into a pile. "Well then, we'll have to ask my cousin Alice to be Esmeralda. She's coming to the play anyway."

"What, the one who never took her eyes off her book last time?"

"Yes. She's got a really good memory. I bet if we gave her a script now she'd know the words by three o'clock."

Hannah narrowed her eyes. "Isn't she the one whose school play you went to see and you said she was the worst actress you'd ever seen in your entire life?"

Lottie shifted her eyes away. She picked up a heap of broken jewellery and tipped it into a bin bag. "I never said that."

"You said she was so atrocious you were ashamed to be related to her. You said if they'd put a plank of wood on stage it would have been more realistic."

"I must have been exaggerating. She's not that bad. At least she won't mess around like Martha."

"At least Martha can act."

"But there's no way Martha's going to come back. So what's the point of even saying that?"

"Unless. . ." Hannah glanced at Lottie. "Unless you apologise to her."

Lottie's eyebrows shot up. "Me?!"

"You were the one who accused her."

"Yes, because *you* hadn't told me the truth."

Hannah paused and took a deep breath.

"Yes. You're right." She stood up, and she felt some of her strength come back. "OK. If we're going to do this competition, we've got to do it properly. I'm going to apologise to Martha."

"Really?"

"Yes. If we're going to do this play, it needs to be the best that it can be."

Now Lottie took a deep breath. "Right. I suppose I'd better come with you. I guess I'm going to have to apologise too. Even though the whole thing's your fault."

Chapter Twenty-Eight

Apologies

Martha's bedroom door was shut.

"Martha?" called Hannah.

No reply. Hannah tried the door. Locked.

"Martha?"

"Get lost, pigface!"

Hannah took a deep breath. It felt like preparing for an Olympic pole vault.

"Martha, I'm so sorry we accused you of telling about the theatre. We know it wasn't you now. We should never have said it was. We were just upset that all our things were ruined."

She waited for an answer. None came.

"Sorry, Martha," said Lottie. "We're sorry we said it was you and I'm sorry I yelled at you."

Still no sound.

"Go on," whispered Lottie. "Apologise more."

There was nothing else for it. She was going to have to grovel.

"Martha, we're really, really sorry we accused you. We were just being mean and we shouldn't have said it. We were really upset and we took it out on you, and we shouldn't have. Please forgive us. Please be in the play. It won't be any good without you. You're a really good actress and we need you in it. It would be such a waste if you missed it now, after all the rehearsals and everything. *Please*."

Still nothing. Hannah looked at Lottie.

"Your turn. Grovel to her."

Lottie scowled at her. "If you'd told me it was *you* who told Jack where the theatre was," she hissed, "then I'd never have yelled at her."

"I tried to, but you were too busy yelling."

Lottie pulled a face at her and turned to the locked door. "Martha, I'm really sorry I yelled at you and accused you of telling the boys. I know you wouldn't have done anything so horrible. I was just really upset about the costumes being destroyed. But we can get it all mended. My mum's going to help and everything. So please be in the play. We really need to win it, you know we do, and we can't win without you. You're the main part."

There was absolute silence from Martha's bedroom. Hannah and Lottie looked at each other in despair.

"Right," Lottie whispered. "Tell her it was your fault. Tell her you invited Jack and Danny to the play."

"What!" hissed Hannah. "No way."

Lottie gave her another hard stare. "If you don't tell her, I shall."

Hannah had thought that nothing could be worse than confessing her stupidity to Lottie.

But she was wrong.

This was worse.

Hannah faced her sister's locked bedroom door and, knowing that at least she would never in her whole life have to do anything more humiliating than this, she told her everything.

When she finished, she stepped back from the door and waited for the shouting.

It didn't come.

Bedsprings creaked. Hannah didn't dare breathe. She glanced at Lottie.

The key turned. Slowly the door opened. Martha stood there, hatred in her eyes and tear stains on her cheeks.

Her voice was slow and quiet. "You evil, evil cows. You," she said to Hannah, "are a liar and a coward, and you, Lottie Perfect, are a mean nasty bully. I hate you both."

"Martha, I'm so sorry," said Hannah. "I should never have let Lottie blame you, I know that. That was cowardly, you're right. And I did a really stupid thing inviting Jack to the play. But we're going to clear it all up before the judge comes—"

"And the judge will be so impressed with your acting," Lottie said. "You never know, she might recommend you for a film part or something."

"GO AWAY!" screamed Martha.

Hannah and Lottie leapt back as if they'd been jabbed with a cattle prod.

"I hate you all and I hate your stupid theatre! I'm never ever talking to you ever again!"

"But, Martha, the play's to raise money for the

farm," pleaded Hannah. "If you won't be in it, we won't win the prize and the farm won't get any money."

"You won't win a prize anyway, you freaks!" screeched Martha. "Your poxy little play in your poxy little shed is never going to win a prize. I don't know why you're even bothering. I hate you both, you ugly, evil pigs!"

"I hate you too!" screamed Hannah. "You're mean and selfish and none of us will ever speak to you again!"

She turned and ran down the front stairs and out of the front door into the garden. Her head felt as if it was about to explode.

"Well, you were right," said Lottie when she caught up. "She'll never come back. But we can't let her ruin it. I'll call Alice and get her to come up now so you can rehearse her. What's the time?"

Hannah looked at her watch and her heart started racing. "Half ten already!"

"Right," said Lottie. "I'm going home to mend the costumes. I'll send Alice straight over. See you as soon as I'm done."

With a huge mental effort, Hannah pushed the image of Martha's tearstained face out of her mind and turned her attention to the job in hand. There were the walls to scrub, the carpet to clean, the props to mend, a new princess to rehearse and . . . "Curtains!"

Lottie's eyes widened. "What are we going to do?"

"I'll take the other pair down."

"Hannah, you can't!"

A thought struck Hannah. "No, you're right. We can't let Dad see them. We should have taken the others down yesterday."

"What are we going to do, then?" asked Lottie.

"I'll get my bedroom ones. They're tatty but they'll have to do. Go on, you go and mend the costumes and I'll get the Beans and clean up the theatre. And be back by two," she called to Lottie's retreating back. "We need to have a proper rehearsal with your cousin."

Chapter Twenty-Nine

Arrivals

By two o'clock Hannah and the Beans had swept the floors, cleaned up the dressing room, hung the new curtains, scrubbed the carpet and painted over the graffiti on the panelling. The paint was still wet but as long as they didn't touch the back wall it would be all right. Thank goodness they hadn't left the candlesticks and the painting in the theatre. Hannah had completely forgotten to take them away last night, but Lottie must have remembered. Hannah shuddered to think of what Danny might have done if he had got his hands on them.

Hannah took a deep breath and silently repeated the mantra that she had been chanting in her head all afternoon. We're going to win. We have to save the farm.

She looked at the tense, earnest girl standing in front of her. Trying to get Alice to act was like rehearsing Martha at her most annoying.

Except Alice wasn't doing it on purpose.

Hannah summoned up all her reserves of cheerfulness and energy. "OK, let's try again. This is a really important scene, remember? It's the first time Esmeralda has stood up to the queen. So she's being very brave and determined."

Looking at the floor, shoulders hunched over, Alice muttered in a flat monotone, "*I have made up my mind, Mother. I totally refuse to marry that odious Prince Rallentando. If I cannot marry Prince John, then I will marry neither.*"

She looked at Hannah hopefully. Hannah forced a smile. "Great! Well done. OK, let's go on."

"Hannah! Open the door!"

Hannah ran to the door and pushed it open. There was Lottie, almost hidden behind a huge bundle of costumes.

"Take some of these. My arms are killing me."

Hannah gathered up an armload. "Have you done them all? Are they OK?" She laid them down on the queen's bed. "Wow, they look like new."

Lottie dumped her bundle on the bed. "On most of them we could just sew up the rips, but on some, like this –" she held up Esmeralda's dress "– I sewed a new bodice on top of the holey one. The skirts are quite full so hopefully the mended bits won't show too much."

"They're amazing," said Hannah. "Nobody will ever notice they've been mended. I can't believe you've done them all."

"Well, my mum did a lot," said Lottie. She looked around the theatre. "It's looking great in here, too."

Jo looked up from where she and Sam were scrubbing the auditorium floor. "This nail varnish won't come off at all."

"Don't worry about it," said Hannah. "We'll just put a chair there. It's much more important to have a last dress rehearsal now Lottie's here."

"And I've got make-up," said Lottie, tipping up a carrier bag on to the bed. Expensive-looking lipsticks, eyeliners, mascara and blusher rolled all over the costumes.

"You are so dead when your mum finds out."

"She won't find out. Not until later anyway. She's coming up at half two, by the way, and she's going to wait in the yard to meet the judge and bring her over here. And my dad's arranged to come up and see your dad at two forty-five, to walk round the meadows and discuss bird habitats. But he's actually going to bring him into the theatre. And by then the judge will be here, and your granny and all my family, and he won't be able to do a thing."

Lottie sounded so confident. And Hannah had been swept along by her confidence when they had first made the plan. But now. . .

Now she was quite sure that if Dad didn't like what he saw when he walked into the theatre, then fifty festival judges wouldn't have the power to stop him closing it down right there and then.

The rehearsal was terrible.

Appalling.

Quite frankly, thought Hannah, Lottie's cousin Alice might as well be a cardboard cut-out. There's absolutely no hope of us getting a prize now. The most we can hope for is to perform the play without completely embarrassing ourselves.

And even that's a lot to ask.

"Oh, well," said Lottie, as Hannah checked that all the props were back on the table. "They say a bad dress rehearsal means a good performance."

"Huh. I shouldn't think whoever said that had ever seen a dress rehearsal that bad."

"Ssshh," said Jo. "Who's that?"

Hannah listened.

It was Vanessa's voice.

Hannah's stomach flipped over. Lottie's mum was bringing the judge into the theatre.

The front-of-house door opened. The others moved downstage, trying to peek through the curtains to get a look at the judge. But Hannah couldn't move. She stood completely still, full of dread. Her stomach churned.

And then she really thought she was going to be sick. For, somewhere in the thicket outside the theatre, she heard the unmistakable sound of her father clearing his throat.

So the plan had worked.

And here he was.

"It's Dad," whispered Jo. "Oh, I hope he likes it."

Sam's face lit up and he gave a little jump of excitement. "Daddy's come to see our play!"

Lottie, despite her apparent confidence, had turned white. She stood rooted to the spot, gnawing her thumbnail.

Alice didn't look up from her script.

Hannah couldn't breathe. What would he do

when he came in? What would he say? Oh, why had they taken this ridiculous risk? There was no need to have brought him here. He was so unobservant, they could have carried on doing plays for years and he would never have noticed. She felt sure of that now, now that he was heading up the path, now that there was absolutely no turning back.

And suddenly, like a flash of lightning in her head, she realised.

She had agreed to this plan because, deep down, she actually *wanted* him to see the play.

She wanted him to notice her.

And then the stage door squealed back on its runners. Hannah swung round and her heart stopped. There in the doorway, wearing an ancient tweed jacket lightly dusted all over with pig meal, stood her father.

Chapter Thirty

Reactions

His mouth fell open. He said nothing at all. For the first time in her life, Hannah saw her father completely, utterly lost for words.

The children stood frozen to the spot, their eyes fixed on him, waiting in petrified silence for his reaction.

And then the strangest thing happened. At the sight of Dad's dumbstruck face, Hannah found herself desperately wanting to laugh.

Giggles welled up inside her. She bit her cheeks until they hurt. She mustn't laugh now, she just mustn't.

Finally he found his voice. "What's all this then?"

Hannah couldn't control herself any longer. Into the midst of the silence, she let out a gigantic snort.

Once she had started, she couldn't stop. All the tensions and emotions of the last few hours came bursting out of her. She laughed until tears poured down her face. She slid down the side of the chest of drawers and doubled up on the floor, howling helplessly.

She felt Lottie grab her by the shoulders and shake

215

her. "Stop it, Hannah!" she hissed. "Stop it! What are you doing?"

Hannah forced herself to stop. She looked up and saw her father, still in the same position, staring down at her as if she were a strange wild animal.

There was a horrible silence. She knew she had to say something. She scrabbled to her feet.

"Sorry, Dad," she said. It sounded so lame. "It wasn't you. I just – I don't know—"

He cut her off. "What's all this? What's going on here?"

"It's our theatre," said Hannah, her heart thumping. "We've turned the shed into our theatre."

His eyes narrowed and his jaw set harder.

"Come and see the stage, Dad," said Jo, tugging at his sleeve. "It's amazing. Look, there's a carpet and real wood panelling and everything. You have to be quiet on stage, though, cos the judge is out there."

Hannah's stomach did a somersault.

"Judge?" he said. "What judge?"

Everyone was frozen still, but their eyes looked to Hannah.

"Well," she began eventually, her heart pounding so hard she thought everybody must be able to hear it, "you see, we've entered our play into a competition – in the Linford Arts Festival – and the judge is here to watch it. And Granny and all Lottie's relations, too. So we thought you might want to watch as well. If you've got time, I mean. If you don't mind. . ." Her voice faded out.

"If I don't mind! If I don't *mind*! How many times

have I told you not to go messing about with the farm buildings? And then you come here, behind my back. . ." He looked around the theatre. "Where have you put everything that belongs here?"

Hannah gulped. "In . . . in other sheds."

"In other sheds! Haven't I told you never to move anything?"

"But you weren't using any of it," said Hannah. "It hadn't been used since. . ." She braved his fierce stare. "Since . . . you know. . ."

"It's none of your business whether it's been used or not. It's a poultry shed, not a *theatre*."

Sam, who had been clutching Hannah's hand all this time, said in a tiny voice, "So aren't you going to watch our play then?"

Dad made a noise like a growl as he turned around sharply. "No, I am not. Fooling around with plays! Some of us have work to do."

Twigs snapped as he stamped his way down the path. Nobody moved.

"Well," said Lottie eventually, "it could have been worse, I suppose. I mean, he didn't actually ban us from doing the play, did he?"

Hannah was about to make a sarcastic retort when there came a loud "Cooeee!"

Hannah jumped like she'd touched an electric fence. Lottie's mum was peering round the panelling, a bright smile on her face. Oh, no. Did the audience just hear all that?

"Mum!" hissed Lottie. "What are you doing on stage?"

"I just wanted to wish you the best of luck,

darlings. I've been talking to the judge and she seems terribly nice. Although I've had to separate her from *your father*, Charlotte." She stage-whispered this to Lottie, rolling her eyes. "Honestly, he was boring the poor woman to death about bird-watching. I don't know why he can't appreciate that *nobody* is interested."

Lottie scowled at her.

"Anyway, sweethearts, everybody's here now. Except Arthur. I thought he might be with you. I sent him backstage so he could wish you luck. He must have been so impressed with what you've done. Is he on his way back round now?"

Nobody said anything. Perhaps Vanessa guessed the truth, because her voice rose to a new level of brightness.

"All right, darlings, we're all rooting for you out there. I'm sure it's going to be absolutely marvellous. Break a leg, all of you!"

She disappeared again. Still nobody moved, but Hannah sensed everyone looking to her expectantly.

She glanced at her watch and the hairs on the back of her neck rose up.

It was three o'clock.

Hannah summoned all her strength. "OK, everybody, time to go! Alice, don't worry, you'll be brilliant, and we'll all help you if you get stuck. Remember, everyone, don't look at the audience. Forget all about the judge and everything. Just *act* and enjoy it. Let's make this the best we've ever done it and let's win that prize."

218

Chapter Thirty-One

The Performance

Jo and Lottie took hold of the curtain strings. Alice and Sam stood in the wings stage left to wait for their cues.

Hannah laid her head on the pillow, closed her eyes and gave a thumbs-up sign. Lottie and Jo pulled the curtains open.

Appreciative murmurs came from the audience. Hannah gave them a few seconds to take in the splendour of the scene. Then she opened her eyes and stretched elegantly upright. She raised her chin and called, "*Maid! MAID! Come here at once! I command you!*"

And as soon as Hannah started to speak in the queen's voice, she *was* the queen.

"*Coming, Your Majesty,*" called Lottie. She appeared instantly, with Sam in his footman's costume behind her.

"*I have been waiting ages for you, maid! Calling until my face was blue and my throat hoarse!*"

The audience laughed. Hannah breathed in the laughter like oxygen.

"*For my breakfast,*" she said, fixing Lottie with

219

a haughty gaze, "*I need tea, avocado, bacon, eggs, kidneys, grapes and cheese. That will be all.*"

"*Yes, ma'am.*" Lottie curtsied and flicked her hand at Sam. He left to fetch the breakfast tray.

"*Now, maid,*" said Hannah. "*As of course you know, my daughter, Princess Esmeralda, will be sixteen on her next birthday. She will be married then.*"

In the back of her mind, Hannah thought she heard the stage door creak open.

"*Why on her sixteenth birthday, your majesty?*" asked Lottie.

Alice, in the wings, jerked her head up from her script like a startled rabbit and gawped backstage. What was going on?

"*It has long been the custom of my family—*" began Hannah.

A whirlwind of fury shot into the wings.

Martha! Oh, my goodness, it's Martha!! What is she doing? She's come to ruin the play! Oh, no; please no.

"*It is not your place to question this,*" Hannah said.

In the wings, Martha grabbed Alice's arm, yanked her off the barrel and ripped open the Velcro at the back of her dress. Alice's face contorted with indignation. Her arms flailed around her back and she slapped blindly at Martha's fingers.

"*Is that clear, maid?*" finished Hannah. Luckily they had rehearsed this scene so many times that every word and gesture came automatically, while inside her head she was praying over and over: don't scream, you two. Don't say anything aloud.

"*Yes, Your Majesty,*" said Lottie. Lucky Lottie. With her back to the wings, she had no idea of the pantomime being played out behind her.

"*Unfortunately there are no suitable princes in this area.*"

"*There is Prince Alfred—*"

Martha leapt on to Alice's back and wrestled her to the ground.

What if they roll on to the stage? Get backstage! Now! Where's Jo? Why isn't she doing anything?

"*Have you taken leave of your senses, maid?*"

Alice waved her hands in the air in a desperate gesture of surrender. Martha climbed off her back and dragged her towards the dressing room. What was she going to do now?

"*I want you to send two men to search the country for suitable princes. They must be back within a year.*"

"*But, Your Majesty—*"

"*Silence, maid! Do you want to be imprisoned for treason? Now, go and start the search today.*"

"*Yes, Your Majesty.*"

Sam, in his footman's livery, entered with a laden breakfast tray. "*Your breakfast, ma'am.*"

"*Take it away. I don't want it. Whatever made you think I did?*"

Drawing strength from the audience's laughter, Hannah swanned over to her dressing table. Out of the corner of her eye she saw Martha, in the

221

wings, climbing into Esmeralda's costume. Oh, my goodness. What was she doing now?

"*Now, I must choose my dress,*" said Hannah. "*Let me see. Bring me my purple silk. No, no, not that one. My green damask, I think. And call my daughter.*"

"*Yes, Your Majesty.*"

As Lottie exited into the wings, Martha paused in the act of fastening her dress to give her a nasty twisting pinch on the arm. Lottie's face contracted in shock and pain. She shot a murderous glance at Martha, but Martha had already glided onstage, her face serenely innocent.

"*Come in, Esmeralda, my dear,*" gushed Hannah.

Martha bobbed a pretty curtsy and said sweetly, her eyes demurely lowered, "*You wanted to see me, Mama?*"

The play went beautifully after that. Hannah was so caught up in the action that she didn't look at the audience at all, just drank in their laughter and approval.

Apart from one strange moment.

In Scene Two, the queen is briefly lost in thought, trying to devise a test for the princes. As Hannah directed her faraway gaze at the auditorium ceiling, she thought she saw her father standing at the back by the door. But she had to whip her head round immediately to snap at the maid, and when she next got a chance to sneak a look, there was nobody there.

Had she dreamed it? Was it some sort of mirage?

Did she so want him to see her play that her mind and eyes had played a trick on her, like a parched traveller in the desert convinces themselves there is an oasis in the distance?

"Wow!" said Lottie as the curtains swished across the stage and the audience's applause turned into chatter. "Can you believe how well that went? *So* much better than the dress rehearsal. Hannah, you were amazing. And so was Martha." She turned to Martha. "Well done."

Martha stuck her tongue out.

"Sorry again for yelling at you, Martha," said Lottie. "You were fantastic in the play. Thank you so much for being in it."

"Yes," Hannah said. "You saved the day. Thank goodness you came."

"Shut up, losers," said Martha.

Lottie's mum poked her head through the curtains. "Darlings, that was *wonderful*. Absolutely marvellous. Such fun. And Mrs Butler just asked me to say could you all come through to the auditorium once you've changed, so she can talk to you about your play."

Hannah's stomach turned over. What would she say? What if she said it was the worst thing she had ever seen and how dare they waste her time by having the nerve to enter this prestigious competition with their ridiculous little play in a shed? She sat down in the auditorium with a lead weight in her stomach.

The judge smiled around at the circle of nervous

faces. Only Martha managed to look completely unconcerned.

"Well, congratulations, all of you," said Mrs Butler. "Now, I need to clarify at the beginning that I can't give you any indication yet as to whether or not you've won a prize. The prizes will be announced at the festival's closing ceremony next Thursday, which I hope you can all attend. But we do like to give you some feedback about the play now, as there isn't time for that at the prize-giving. So I would like to start by saying how impressed I was with your production."

Hannah's heart leapt. Relief flooded over her.

"It's particularly impressive," continued Mrs Butler, "because I can see from your programme that you've done the whole thing yourselves. I gather you've had no adult input at all, is that right?"

They nodded.

"And one of your parents told me that your theatre was badly vandalised last night and you've had to spend the morning repairing it."

More nodding.

"Well, I think that shows quite extraordinary commitment and resilience. A lot of people would have given up if that happened to them. You're obviously a very strong team. And I have to say, I can't see any evidence of the damage so you clearly did an excellent repair job."

Yes, yes, Hannah wanted to say, but what did you think of the play? Is it good enough to win a prize? Tell us!

"So I guess what you really want to know," said Mrs Butler, "is, what did I think of your play?"

Sparrows chirped loudly in the bushes. Inside the theatre, the silence was terrifying.

Mrs Butler beamed at them. "Don't look so frightened. I loved it."

She loved it!

Their play, that she had written, and the judge loved it! A little spring of joy bubbled up inside Hannah.

"I thought the script was excellent," Mrs Butler said. "It was very funny, a nice fresh take on the fairytale genre, with some lovely characters. It was well cast and well acted and the pace was just right, which shows very good direction. Your scenery was excellent – so atmospheric with the panelling – and the costumes are quite stunning. Did you really make those all yourself, Lottie?"

"Well, Hannah helped," said Lottie. "And my mum helped mend them."

Hannah couldn't let Lottie give away the credit.

"She pretty much did it all herself. And she designed everything."

"I think that's absolutely amazing," said Mrs Butler. "You're extremely talented, Lottie. Very few adults could do that."

Lottie went scarlet. Hannah beamed at her.

"And finally, I want to say how well organised your whole production was. Your programmes are beautiful, you've created a lovely atmosphere in your theatre and you all knew exactly what you were doing. So very well done, all of you."

Mrs Butler smiled round at them and bent down to pick up her bag. "Well, I do have to go now. I've got to be at another performance at five. Though not in a hen house this time. I think yours is unique in that respect. Hannah, would you show me to my car? And Martha too, if you wouldn't mind. I don't want to get lost in the undergrowth."

"What a beautiful place this is," Mrs Butler said as they crossed the field. "It's like a valley lost in time. I didn't think farms like this existed any more – with all the old hedgerows and barns, and chickens pecking about the yard, and the cows and sheep and pigs in the fields. And the birdsong! I've never heard so many birds. It's just magical."

Hannah wanted to say: "Then give us the prize so it won't get covered in concrete." But she just said, "Thank you."

Mrs Butler got into her car. Then she looked at Hannah and Martha and said, "I didn't want to single out anybody's acting in there, but I did want to tell you two that you are both very talented actors."

For the second time that afternoon, Hannah just laughed. It was a laugh of sheer surprise and shock. A professional judge had told her she was a talented actor!

"I mean it," said Mrs Butler. "If it's what you really want to do, you stick with it. And the writing too, Hannah. That was a very sophisticated script, directed with an extremely sure touch. Quite exceptional. I shall be looking out for your name in the theatre reviews ten years from now. I can see you with your own company – an actor/writer/director in the Brechtian mode."

Hannah stood there, wide-eyed. It was impossible to take in.

Was the judge making fun of her? She didn't seem to be.

Her own theatre company! Imagine that!

Writing plays and acting in them and putting them on – for a job!

Was that really possible? Could she, Hannah Roberts, really do that?

Mrs Butler seemed to think she could.

What did "in the Brechtian mode" mean? She must look that up.

"And now I must go or I'll be late for the next show," said Mrs Butler. "It was a pleasure to meet you all, and we'll see you next Thursday at the prize-giving. Goodbye!"

As they said goodbye, Hannah glanced at Martha. Her face was flushed with pride. Hannah felt a rush of affection for her sister. She caught her eye and smiled at her.

Martha scowled and curled her lip, and as soon as Mrs Butler started her engine, she stalked off into the house without a word.

Hannah stood in the yard, staring at the car as it bumped up the track. Her whole world was expanding. She could be an actor! She could be a writer! She could write plays and star in them on the West End stage! She could be rich and famous and she could buy the farm and save it forever from anybody who wanted to take it away from them. And her wonderful new life would begin next Thursday, when she would accept a cheque for five hundred pounds at the Linford Arts Festival prize-giving and present it to her father.

Chapter Thirty-Two

The Prize-Giving

The Linford Conference Centre was a big disappointment.

It was the biggest building Hannah had ever been inside. But there was no red velvet, no gilded wood, no sparkling chandeliers. Just rows and rows of drab grey seats facing a wide stage with bottle-green curtains.

Hannah had told Dad that Lottie's mum was taking them all out for the day. Which was true – she just hadn't said where they were going. And Vanessa had said she'd get them fish and chips afterwards, which was enough to bribe Martha into silence. Not that Dad asked any questions anyway.

Had he been at their play? Or *was* it a mirage?

Nobody else had seen him there. He hadn't said a thing about it since. And none of the children had mentioned the play to him either. His reaction when he'd come backstage hadn't exactly made them want to bring up the topic. And the last thing Hannah wanted to do was remind him that he hadn't actually banned her theatre.

So nothing was said.

Like on so many other subjects.

When they had arrived at the conference centre, the cavernous auditorium was nearly empty, but now the rows were filling up. Dozens of groups of children and teenagers kept pouring into the vast space, and the noise level rose and rose with the laughter and the chatter. But all Hannah could think about was the phone call she had overheard that morning.

Dad was talking on the dining-room phone when she came downstairs. "Sixty cows and ten heifers," he was saying. "Yes, plenty of room in the yard. Good, good. Yes, we'll give you a hand loading up. We'll see you Monday evening then."

Hannah's heart raced as he put the phone down.

"Who was that?" She had aimed to sound casual but her voice came out about half an octave higher than usual.

Dad didn't look at her. "Oh, just some bloke from Lincolnshire."

Hannah wasn't going to let him get away with vagueness. "Why's he coming on Monday? What's he loading up?"

He cleared his throat. "We're selling some livestock."

Hannah's throat felt so tight she could hardly get the words out.

"Cows?"

"Yes."

She forced herself to ask another question.

"All of them?"

He gazed out of the window. "Yes."

Hannah had to ask one more question. It came out all croaky.

"And the calves?"

Her father seemed to look right through her.

"No point keeping the calves, is there?" He cleared his throat again and left the room.

Hannah had to grip the back of a chair to stay upright. Her knuckles were white.

So it's really going to happen.

He must be absolutely desperate for money if he's selling his cows to pay the rent.

But what will he do next time the rent is due?

Will there be anything left to sell?

And if not . . . what will happen to us?

Hannah was brought back sharply to the present. A voice she knew only too well sliced its way through all the thousands of other voices in the conference centre.

"Budge up, Ems, there's dozens of us to fit in."

Oh, that's just perfect.

Miranda and Emily and a big group of people who must be members of their drama group were squeezing their way into the seats right across the aisle. Hannah bent down and shook her hair into her face, but Miranda's eagle eye zoomed straight in.

"Oh, hi, guys!" she cooed. Hannah registered the sweeping up-and-down appraisal of her clothes, followed by a barely disguised smirk. "Isn't this just sooo exciting? I can't wait for the results, can you?"

Without waiting for a reply, she turned to the boy

on her right and started up a conversation, tossing her glossy auburn hair and trilling her fake laugh.

"I can't believe," muttered Lottie, "that in all this massive building they chose the seats right next to us."

Hannah allowed herself a private fantasy of the outrage on Miranda's face when the judge announced that the winner was the Secret Hen House Theatre. Then she cringed. How ridiculous it sounded. Why hadn't they given their theatre a more sophisticated name? Honestly, look at all these people they were competing against. How had she ever let herself think her theatre might win?

At two o'clock precisely the house lights went down and the curtains opened. The Mayor of Linford, wearing a big gold chain, stood centre stage. Behind her was a long table at which sat what must be the judges. Scanning the row, Hannah saw Mrs Butler, and at the thought of her kindness, she felt a bit better.

But she knew, from the programme in her hand, that they were going to have to wait for ages. The drama prizes were right at the end of the youth section.

The music awards were announced first, then the dance ones. And for each category there was a long speech by the judge, then the actual prize-giving, and finally a performance of the winning piece.

Hannah shrivelled further and further into her seat as she watched perfect performance after perfect performance. How had she ever had the presumption to enter this competition? All these people looked and sounded like professionals.

Would they be rehoused in one of those tower blocks they had passed on the way into Linford?

What would Dad do in a block of flats?

Hannah pictured him endlessly pacing the rooms, day after day, as angry and depressed as a caged swallow, gazing out of the windows at the fields far, far in the distance.

And what about Sam? It had taken him ages to settle into school. What would happen to him if he was taken away from the farm and had to start all over again in a city?

And Jo. How would Jo cope without her animals?

And what would happen to Jasper and Lucy?

If Mum were still here, Hannah thought, then maybe we would have a chance. She could comfort Sam in the way Hannah remembered she used to comfort her – sit on the floor and gather him in her arms and rock him backwards and forwards and tell him, don't worry, everything will be all right. She would run her hands through Jo's curly hair and say, never mind, we'll get you a pet. She might even understand Martha's moods and tantrums and manage to calm her down.

And she would smooth out Dad's frown and give him a hug and make him laugh again, just like she used to.

But Mum wasn't here. And how could they survive this without her?

The final dance performance was called *The*

Devastation of the Immortal Soul among the Incarnadine Forces of Modernity. A group of solemn-faced teenagers dressed in blood-soaked bandages writhed, wormlike, on to the stage, to the sound of a single drumbeat.

Hannah felt giggles rising in her throat. She bit her cheeks and fixed her eyes on the carpet. She mustn't laugh, especially with Lottie's mum sitting right behind her. She bit her cheeks harder.

But then she made the mistake of looking at Lottie. Lottie was leaning slightly forward, watching the stage in a ridiculously exaggerated impression of someone who found every movement deeply meaningful. Her fingertips were pressed together and she was nodding earnestly, a frown of concentration on her face. When she realised Hannah was looking at her, she met Hannah's gaze and raised her eyebrows.

Hannah was biting her cheeks so hard they hurt. Her insides were nearly seizing up with the effort of not laughing.

And then she looked at the stage.

A boy in a gold Lurex catsuit with a garland of sunflowers round his neck was crawling among the dancers, unwinding the bandages with his teeth. Lottie made a strange noise in her throat. Hannah's shoulders started to shake. Her face went bright red and tears of laughter poured down her cheeks.

Finally the drumbeat stopped and, after a second, people clapped dutifully. Under cover of the applause, Hannah bent double in her seat and howled with laughter.

Vanessa leaned forward and tapped her hard on the shoulder. Hannah took deep breaths and wiped her eyes. The applause died down and Lottie nudged her. She looked at the stage for more entertainment, but instead the Festival Chairman and the Mayor of Linford stood centre stage.

Hannah's stomach did a giant back flip.

This was it. The drama prizes.

"Ladies and gentlemen," said the chairman, "I have great pleasure in inviting Fran Butler, the Chair of our Theatre panel, to announce the winners in the festival's youth drama category."

Every fibre in Hannah's body tensed to breaking point.

But Mrs Butler began yet another speech about the festival and the prizes and how it was all judged and organised and on and on and on. After what seemed like hours, she said, "And now the bit you've all been waiting for – the winners!"

And then she pulled an envelope out of her pocket, and Hannah could neither move nor breathe.

"Our first category is the under-fourteens section," she said.

Lottie gripped Hannah's hand.

Hannah's hands were sweating. If they won, they could give the cheque straight to Dad and he wouldn't have to load his cows on to a lorry on Monday morning. Not all of them anyway. Five hundred pounds must be enough to save some of the cows.

Fran Butler had really liked their play. And they

had done it all themselves. That had to count for something. They would win. They just had to.

"We had some very strong entries in this category," said Mrs Butler, "but in the end we had to decide between two excellent and very different productions. We can only have one eventual winner, but we wanted to single out both of these productions for a special mention. One of these was the Linford Youth Theatre, with their performance of *Plague*."

Hannah and Lottie exchanged glances. Miranda's group. Of course.

Miranda's row rippled with excitement.

"This play," said Mrs Butler, "was a subtle and thought-provoking meditation on a particularly tragic episode in our country's history, performed with astonishing maturity and professionalism, using music and physical theatre with imagination and accomplishment."

Hannah heard this with a heavy heart. How could they ever have thought they could compete against the Linford Youth Theatre? She didn't even know what physical theatre was.

"The other play in our final two," said Mrs Butler, "was *By Her Majesty's Appointment*, written and performed by the Secret Hen House Theatre."

What?

Had she heard right?

Hannah looked at Lottie. Lottie's eyes sparkled and she was grinning an enormous grin.

She *had* heard right! She couldn't believe it. They were in the top two!

"This play," Mrs Butler was saying, "was a delightful comic fairytale, performed with verve and sparkle. What really deserves special mention is the fact that every aspect of the production – costumes, scenery, writing, direction and even the conversion of the building from a chicken shed into a theatre – was done entirely by the five members of the company, whose ages range from six to eleven. This was terrific ensemble work by a talented and passionate theatre group."

Hannah felt as if she was about to take off with happiness. Here they were, in this enormous place with all these people, and their play in a shed was being singled out for special praise!

Vanessa leaned forward and put her arms round Lottie and Hannah. "Well done!" she whispered. But Mrs Butler was speaking again.

"After a lot of deliberation," she said, "we did decide on our winner. The Wilmot-Fawcett Shield and a prize of five hundred pounds for the best production in the under-fourteen age range is awarded to. . ."

Hannah's heart stopped. She sat rigid as stone, gripping Lottie's hand.

". . .the Linford Youth Theatre!"

The group across the aisle erupted into celebrations. They punched the air, cheered, whooped and hugged each other.

Hannah pulled her hand out of Lottie's and clapped fiercely. She looked along the row to the Beans and Martha. "Clap!" she ordered.

So that was it.

The cows would be sold to pay the rent, and when the next rent day came round, there would be nothing left to pay it with.

And their farm and their home would be demolished.

Chapter Thirty-Three

The Lunch Queue

On Monday night Hannah buried herself in the bedclothes and stuffed cotton wool in her ears. She tried to fill her mind with poems she knew by heart, so there would be no space left in it to hear the heartbreaking moos from the prison truck. But every poem she knew was about land and animals and they just made her feel worse.

The cattle lorry was three tiers high. The men drove the cows up the steep ramps, cramming them into a prison of slats and steel. Once they were all loaded and the doors were slammed shut, they would be hurtled hundreds of miles away to a massive dairy farm in Lincolnshire. Hannah couldn't bear to think of it. Their huge bewildered eyes, their cries of pain when they lost their balance and fell against each other as the lorry swayed and bumped up the motorway.

And when they stumbled off the lorry in Lincolnshire, frightened and confused, who would be caring for them? There weren't many farmers like Dad any more. His cows went on to that lorry as animals with names. But they would come off it as units of production.

When Hannah dragged herself out of bed on Tuesday morning she felt as if she'd run an overnight marathon.

And it was the first day of the summer term.

"Why isn't Daddy having breakfast with us?" asked Sam, looking up from his cereal bowl.

"I don't know," said Hannah. "I'll go and call him."

The farmyard was eerily quiet. The pig-shed door was closed and the chickens were still shut up.

Hannah crossed the yard to the milking parlour.

The sliding door was open. Her father stood in the silent parlour with his back to her, facing the blackboard where the cows' names were chalked up. He held a cloth in his hand.

As she watched, he started to rub out the names of his cows.

He did it very slowly, as if his arm was stiff and heavy. Daisy, Buttercup, Clover, Chocolate, Primrose, Lily; one by one the names disappeared.

When he had finished he didn't turn round. He just stood there, facing the blank empty board, the cloth dangling from his hand.

"Dad?" said Hannah. Her throat was so dry that her voice came out croaky.

He didn't move.

She tried again. "Dad?"

This time he turned round. When Hannah saw his face it felt like somebody had punched her in the stomach.

His eyes were swimming with tears.

Hannah hadn't seen him cry since the day her mother died.

For a minute, he stared at her blankly. Then he cleared his throat. "What do you want?" he said. He sounded irritated.

"Nothing," she mumbled. "Breakfast's ready." And with feet like lead she trudged back to the house.

The school dining hall stank of spaghetti bolognese. Hannah and Lottie leaned against the gloss-blue walls, edging along silently as the queue inched forward. All Hannah could think of were the cries of distress from the cows in the lorry and her father turning to her with his eyes full of tears.

Jack was showing off to a group of hangers-on a few places ahead of her. Behind the Year Eights, Miranda and Emily were gazing up at Jack like devoted puppies. Strangely, Danny wasn't with him. And they hadn't sat together in assembly either. Hannah remembered them arguing outside the antique shop. Had they fallen out?

Normally Jack's presence so close to her would have sent Hannah into a flurry of self-consciousness. But today she didn't care if her hair was frizzy. She didn't care whether he was looking at her or not. She wouldn't even have cared if there was a spot the size of Mount Vesuvius glowing on her chin.

"Hey, Roberts!"

Hannah didn't look up.

"Hey, Roberts! What's up? Forget to wash the

mud out of your ears?"

"Leave her alone, Jack," warned Lottie.

Jack ignored her. "Sorry your theatre didn't win the prize. Did the sheep forget their lines?"

Miranda giggled. Hannah stared from Jack to Miranda and back again, her face blazing. Of course. Miranda would have told Jack all about the prize-giving. They would have been sniggering about it all morning.

"Well, they did come second," said Priya. "That's pretty good actually. There were loads of entries."

Hannah shot her a look of surprised gratitude. But Jack was still talking. "Or was it the cows who let you down? Did Ermintrude refuse to put her frock on?"

Miranda giggled again.

"It's true," said Jack. "Old Farmer Roberts really does give his cows names. They're all chalked up in his milking shed. He probably tucks them up in bed at night too."

And then, just like that, it happened.

Hannah looked at Jack and it was like she was seeing him for the first time.

Not a witty romantic hero. Not a rebel with a heart of gold.

Just a pathetic thirteen-year-old coward who set people's barns on fire and ran away.

"Isn't that right, Roberts?" said Jack. "Does he sing them lullabies too?" He started warbling in a high falsetto. "Goodnight, my darling Buttercup, cow of my dreams. Sleep tight, my dearest Ermintrude—"

A volcano erupted inside Hannah.

Without knowing what she was doing, she swung back her arm and punched Jack square on the chin, sending him crashing into the wall. His startled face flashed before her eyes, and then the next punch landed on his left cheek and he roared in indignation and pain.

With a strength she never knew she had, Hannah pinned him to the wall by his shoulders. "You evil piece of scum! How *dare* you? How dare you insult my dad like that after you destroyed his barn? How dare you burn our barn down and run away, you horrible stinking coward! How dare you destroy our theatre, you and your pathetic friend! You're vile and evil and sick and you've ruined our lives. I hate you!"

Jack stared at her, open-mouthed. As Hannah paused for breath and loosened her grip, he lurched forward as if to make a dash for it.

"Don't you dare!" shouted Hannah. She jammed her knee into his crotch.

He let out a howl and doubled up. Hannah shoved him back against the wall, cheeks and eyes blazing.

"Trying to run away? Of course you are. That's what you do, isn't it? You destroy things and then you run away because you can't face up to what you've done. Do you know what you've done? Do you?" She was screaming into his face now. "You've destroyed my family and you've destroyed our farm. Is that what you wanted? Is it? Are you happy now? Was it fun? Was it a laugh?"

Still pinning Jack to the wall, she wheeled round to face Miranda, frozen in shock.

"Why aren't you laughing, Miranda? Don't you think it's really funny? Isn't it great that my dad's going to lose his farm? Isn't that really, really hilarious?"

Firm hands grasped her shoulders and an adult voice said, "Hannah, Hannah, stop. Stop it right now. Let go of Jack."

The words hit Hannah like a nail punctures a tyre. She started to crumple. She allowed the teacher to prise her hands from Jack's shoulders. She was surprised at how tight her grip had been – her fingers actually ached.

As she was led out of the room and her surroundings began to swim back into focus, she suddenly realised that the entire dining hall was silent.

Every single pair of eyes was staring at her.

Chapter Thirty-Four

The Head's Office

Mr Collins leaned forward in his chair and frowned across the desk at Hannah. She looked down at her lap. She wondered if the Head even knew who she was.

She had never been in his office before. It was cold and sparse, painted a greyish-blue colour. There were bookcases filled with folders and dull-looking documents, and three grey metal filing cabinets. A cork board on the wall was covered with laminated notices pinned to it at precisely spaced intervals. Mr Collins's desk was completely bare.

"I gather from Miss Haywood," he said eventually, "that you were involved in a serious incident in the dining hall this lunchtime." He spoke in exactly the same way as he did in assembly, as if he were weighing up each word carefully before he uttered it.

Hannah didn't know whether she was supposed to reply. She nodded. It felt like it wasn't really her in that chair at all. Everything that was her had been sucked out and all that was left was a great big blob of nothing. It was as if she were watching a film of all this happening to somebody else. Nothing Mr

Collins could say or do could hurt her now. After all, she wouldn't even be at this school soon.

But then the Head's secretary poked her head around the door and said, "Mr Roberts is here."

Dad? He's called Dad into school? Hannah's stomach turned over.

So she did have some feelings left then.

She gripped the sides of her chair and fixed her eyes on the floor as her father walked in. She couldn't even bear to imagine the next few minutes.

"Thank you for coming in so quickly, Mr Roberts," said the Head. "Please, take a seat."

He gestured to the one other free chair. It was uncomfortably close to Hannah's. Hannah caught a whiff of pig manure as Dad sat down, scattering wisps of straw on to the grey carpet.

"I am sorry to inform you," began the Head, "that your daughter was involved in a serious incident this lunchtime in which she physically assaulted another student."

Hannah could feel her father's impatience as he shuffled in his hard little chair. "What do you mean by 'physically assaulted'?"

The Head paused for an irritatingly long moment. It was as if he found it a real effort to come out with the unadorned truth.

"I am afraid," he said eventually, "that your daughter hit another student."

"Who?" demanded Dad.

Mr Collins cleared his throat. "I don't think that is relevant to the issue."

"Of course it's relevant," Dad scoffed. He turned to Hannah. "Who did you hit?"

Hannah glanced from the Head to Dad and back again before replying, "Jack Adamson."

"You hit Jack Adamson?"

"Yes."

"Huh."

Hannah could have sworn she saw a flicker of amusement cross her father's face.

"Apparently, Hannah, you accused this boy of vandalising a theatre on your farm," said Mr Collins.

Oh, no, no, no! Why oh why had she gone and told the *entire school* that she had a theatre on her farm? How stupid could she be?

"He did *what*?" said Dad.

"Let's not jump to conclusions, Mr Roberts," said the Head. "I was not intending to use any names until the facts had been established. I have since been informed by another student that in fact the boy Hannah attacked was not involved in the vandalism at all; that in fact the vandalism was committed by a completely separate person."

"*What?*" said Hannah. "Who? Who told you that?"

Mr Collins frowned at her. "Hannah, as I just said, I am not going to jump to conclusions or reveal any names until I have thoroughly investigated this matter. I shall be interviewing all the relevant people in the course of the afternoon. I just need to confirm with you whether your theatre was indeed vandalised."

The sound of Mr Collins even mentioning her theatre was hideous. Her beloved secret theatre, dragged out in public and trampled to ruins.

"Hannah, I need to know the truth."

Hannah took a breath. "Yes. It was vandalised."

"And what exactly was done to it?"

Hannah squirmed. This was torture. "The costumes were slashed, the make-up was ruined, the jewellery was broken, the scenery was graffitied, the props were ripped."

Dad's face blazed with fury. "They did all that to your theatre? Why on earth didn't you call the police?"

Hannah stared at him. Why *hadn't* they called the police? The idea had never occurred to her. "I don't know," she said. "I suppose we just wanted to get it all ready in time for the competition."

He looked at her as though she was mad. "What was so important about the competition, for goodness' sake?"

Hannah met his eyes. Why not tell him? It would make no difference to anything now.

"There was five hundred pounds prize money. If we won, we were going to give it to the farm. To pay the rent. But we didn't win, and now the cows have gone."

He just stared at her. Was he angry? Shocked? Confused? She couldn't tell.

Mr Collins cleared his throat. "Well, I don't think we need all the details now. As I said, I shall be interviewing the relevant people to get to the bottom of this matter. I need to know, though, if you know who was really responsible for the vandalism."

"No," said Hannah.

"You have no idea?"

"No." It was bad enough that she had publicly accused Jack – and probably falsely, it seemed now. She wasn't about to start making any other accusations. She had said quite enough for one day.

"I see. Well, what we need to focus on now then is the appropriate punishment for your behaviour at lunchtime. And then I shall ask your father to take you home for the rest of the day."

Dad kept his eyes fixed on the road as he drove her home. His profile, when she dared to glance at it, revealed nothing.

"Well, now you know everything," said Hannah. "But don't worry, we won't be doing any more plays."

Her father shot her a single sharp glance before turning his eyes back to the road. "Don't be stupid, girl," he said. "You're not going to let those idiots defeat you, are you?"

Hannah stared at him, open-mouthed.

Was he saying they could keep their theatre?

She was petrified to ask in case that wasn't what he'd meant. But she had to know.

With every muscle tensed, she said, "Do you mean we can keep the theatre?"

He kept his eyes on the road ahead and took his time before replying. "I just said, don't let a couple of halfwits dictate what you do."

Hannah stared at him for a long moment, letting this extraordinary change of attitude sink in. A surge of joy, like you get on the first warm day after a long winter, bubbled up inside her.

They could keep their theatre! They could do another play!

And then she remembered.

In a few months' time the theatre, along with the rest of the farm, would no longer exist.

Chapter Thirty-Five

Granny

Teachers are ridiculous. They go on and on about how great it is to read for pleasure. Then, when they want to give you a really bad punishment, where do they send you?

To the library.

One day's library detention. It could have been worse. She had to go to her teacher at the start of each lesson and collect her work, then return it at the end. She had to eat lunch alone, like a leper. And she wasn't allowed to talk to anybody at all, all day.

Just before afternoon registration, Lottie sauntered innocently into the library and dropped a folded piece of paper on to Hannah's desk. It said, in Lottie's super-neat handwriting: *Meet me at tennis courts entrance after school. Important news!*

"What news? Tell me!" Hannah mouthed back.

Of course, Mrs Trimble took that moment to look up. "Hannah Roberts, I hope you are not communicating with anybody. And you, young lady," she said to Lottie, "I hope you are not attempting to communicate with Hannah while she is in detention. Go to registration now, please."

Lottie winked at Hannah and left. Hannah dug her fingers into her forehead. How could she wait until after school?

Battered by bags and jostled by elbows, Hannah pushed her way through the crowd to where Lottie was leaning against the tennis-court fence.

"Well?" she said. "What's happening?"

"Nice to see you too," said Lottie.

"Just tell me!"

Lottie started walking towards the gates. "Guess what? Danny's been suspended."

Hannah stopped in her tracks. "Suspended? For what? For the vandalism?"

Lottie tugged at her elbow. "Keep walking. Well, everyone's talking about it, but no one actually knows anything. But in geography, Priya looked out of the window and saw Danny walking out of school with his dad. And then at break this rumour started going round that he'd been suspended."

Hannah's head was whirling with so many questions that she didn't know where to start.

"But why? Who started the rumour? What about Jack? Who went to the Head?"

"What?"

"Mr Collins said another student had been to see him and said it wasn't Jack who did the vandalism, it was someone else."

"That's weird," said Lottie. "Who else would know about the vandalism? Unless it was actually Jack who went to the Head. I bet he grassed Danny up so he wouldn't get the blame."

Hannah grabbed her arm. "Oh, no!"

"What? What's wrong?"

"My granny. Look, it's Granny. Oh no. . ."

"Why, what. . .?"

But all Hannah could hear was the terror thumping in her head.

Because there was Granny at the school gate. She was leaning on her stick, looking tinier and more frail than ever in the throng of teenagers.

Granny had never, ever come to school to meet her before.

What had happened? Was it Dad? Sam, Martha, Jo? The farm? They hadn't been thrown off the farm already, had they? They couldn't have been. Dad had just sold the cows. He must be able to pay the rent.

What if it was Dad? He wouldn't have done anything stupid, would he?

Please, please, don't let it be Dad, she prayed. Anything else you like, but let my dad be OK.

"Goodness, Hannah, you look as white as a sheet," said Granny as Hannah reached her, out of breath. "Are you all right?"

"What's happened? Who's hurt?"

Granny squeezed her shoulder. "Oh, sweetheart, don't worry. Nobody's hurt. I just need to have a chat with you. Sorry, Lottie, is that all right?"

"Sure," said Lottie. "I'll call you later, Han."

Granny turned in the direction of her bungalow. "Let's go and have a cup of tea."

"Tell me now," said Hannah. "Whatever it is, tell

253

me now."

Granny shook her head. "Too many people. You know what the gossip's like in this village."

Hannah felt herself boiling over. "No one's listening to us! You have to tell me. *Please.*"

Granny looked at Hannah. "All right. But we'll walk the back way."

They turned left down Mill Walk, a tree-lined lane with grassy verges. The noise from the school gates faded into the background. A blackbird trilled from a tree. Hannah's heart thumped painfully against her ribs.

"Your dad came round this morning," Granny said.

There was nothing unusual about that. Dad went round to see Granny every Tuesday morning. He always said it was so he could check up on the mother-in-law and she always said it was so she could check up on the son-in-law.

"And?" said Hannah.

"He didn't want me to know," said Granny, "but I dragged it out of him."

"Dragged what out?"

"Well, you know he sold the cows yesterday."

"Yes."

"The problem is, he got much less for them than he'd expected."

Hannah's throat was so tight that every word felt like pushing a boulder uphill. "Was . . . was it enough to pay the rent?"

"Just about. This time. But the problem is—"

"Next time. Now the cows have gone, there's no money from the milk and there's nothing left to sell, so how will he pay the rent next time? Especially since the landlord's doubled it."

"How do you know all that?"

Hannah shrugged. "I heard a few things." She didn't add: I think about nothing else these days.

"The problem is," said Granny, "that it's not just the rent. There are other things that have to be paid for too."

"Like what?"

They had reached Granny's bungalow. She unlocked the door. "Come on, sweetheart, let's get you a cup of tea."

"So what else has to be paid for?" said Hannah, as Granny filled the kettle.

"Well, he lost his barn and all its contents in the fire, didn't he?"

The fire that was my fault, thought Hannah.

Granny opened a packet of biscuits and shook them out on to a plate.

"The problem is, the contents of the barn weren't insured."

She set the mugs out and poured the water into the teapot. She looked at Hannah. "Oh, darling, you're completely white. Come and sit down."

She took the tea tray into the little sitting room. Hannah sat down heavily on the sofa.

"I don't know if I should be telling you this," said Granny. "You're too young to take on all these worries."

"No! Tell me! I want to know. I hate that nobody ever tells me anything. Dad never talks about anything. Nobody told me anything when Mum was ill. It was all secrets, secrets. It's horrible. And it doesn't make anything better. All the horrible things still happen." She picked at a loose thread on the embroidered sofa cushion. "If we'd won that stupid competition, everything would be all right."

Granny put her arm around Hannah. "I'm afraid it would take more than that."

"How much more?"

"Do you really want to know?"

Just like she had in the Head's office, Hannah felt a strange sense of calm. Everything was over now, so how could knowledge hurt her?

"Tell me everything," she said.

Granny pushed the plate of biscuits in Hannah's direction. Hannah shook her head.

"Well, to start with, the rent is twenty-eight thousand pounds a year."

"Twenty-eight thousand pounds!"

"Yes. Seven thousand pounds, four times a year."

Hannah tried to take this in. "But how can anyone pay that much?"

"Well, it's very difficult. Before the rent was doubled, your dad always managed, by selling crops and milk and stock, and doing contracting work for other farmers. But now. . ." She sighed again. Hannah kept her eyes fixed on the cushion.

"He's worked so hard," said Granny. "And he kept going, he made it work, up until now. All that time, when everybody else ripped out their hedges and poisoned their fields with chemicals and turned away from mixed farming to specialised intensive units, he stuck to his principles and respected the land, and it was hard, hard grind for very little money, but he just about managed to keep it going."

There was a crack in Granny's voice and Hannah took her eyes off the cushion for a second to glance at her face. Her stomach tumbled over as she saw that Granny was blinking back tears. She fixed her eyes back on the cushion, picking fiercely at the embroidery with her fingernails.

"But . . . well . . . once you have to sell your assets to pay your rent. . ."

She didn't finish the sentence. But Hannah finished it in her head.

Then it's all over.

Hannah buried her face in the cushion.

She felt Granny's hand stroking her hair. "I'm so sorry, darling. I'm so sorry. I hate telling you like this. I just thought – well, I'm afraid it looks like you really will have to leave the farm, and I knew your dad would find it too hard to tell you, and I really didn't want you hearing it from some village gossip."

Hannah shivered. "What about the others? Are you going to tell them too?"

Granny got up stiffly and bent down to turn the electric heater on. The bars began to glow red. Outside, a car door slammed and somebody coughed.

"Not yet, I think." She straightened up slowly. "I

wanted you to know first. Partly because, when the others do get told, you might have to be the strong one."

"But I can't be the strong one!" cried Hannah. "Why do I always have to be the strong one?" She buried her face in the cushion again. She wished she could sleep for a hundred years.

She heard Granny rummaging around in a cupboard. After a while, the cupboard door shut and Granny said, "Hannah, look at this."

Hannah raised her head from the cushion and rubbed her eyes. Granny was holding a scrapbook. It had a faded blue cover, scuffed up around the edges.

Hannah sat up. Granny put the scrapbook on her lap.

"When I saw you in your play," said Granny, "you reminded me so much of your mother. I know she would have wanted you to have this."

Hannah's heart beat faster. She opened the scrapbook.

On the first page was glued the programme of a play and a piece cut out from a newspaper. *Linford Evening News, 18th November 1981,* was written above the cutting in Granny's handwriting. The headline said: "Comic Feast from Local Drama Group".

Hannah looked up at Granny. "Rachel's reviews," said Granny. "From when she was in the village dramatic society."

Hannah turned back to the short article. Her heart skipped a beat when her eyes lit upon her mother's name.

"The production was greatly enhanced by a wonderful performance from sixteen-year-old Rachel Southwood. We hope to see more from this gifted young actress."

Hannah turned the page. She searched the next cutting for Mum's name. "The vivacious quality of Rachel Southwood's acting is a joy to behold," it said.

Hannah read on. There were so many programmes and reviews. Mum seemed to have been in two or three plays a year.

The last review was dated 5 May 1991. "Rachel Southwood's acting goes from strength to strength."

The rest of the pages were blank.

"For your reviews," said Granny.

"Huh," said Hannah. "Not much chance of that now."

Granny gave her a fierce look. "Don't give up. Never give up the thing you love."

"Mum gave up. She gave up when she got married."

"That's because she'd found the thing she really loved," said Granny.

Hannah stared at her. "But drama. . ."

Granny smiled. "Being a farmer's wife and a mother. That's what really fulfilled her. It was what she'd always wanted. You're more passionate about theatre than Rachel ever was. And more talented too, I think. You've been lucky enough to find the thing that makes *you* happy, that lights you up inside.

Some people never do. Don't let it go."

"But what if—"

Granny put a hand on Hannah's shoulder. "You'll find a way. Whatever happens, I know you'll find a way."

Chapter Thirty-Six

A Revelation

Thursday morning was bright and sunny. Lottie and Hannah shot out of the science lab at morning break to grab their favourite bench in the corner of the playground.

"I've nearly finished the next play," said Hannah.

"Really? But what about. . .?"

"Do you want to come up after school and read it through? And we could start designing the set. The others are going to Granny's for tea."

Hannah had been invited too, of course. She had said she had too much homework. Actually, she couldn't face being with the others at Granny's house, having to pretend everything was fine. She needed to take her mind off all that.

"Let's get a costume book from the library at lunchtime," she said.

Lottie elbowed her hard in the ribs.

"Ow! What was that for?"

"Look!" hissed Lottie. "No, keep your head down. Over there."

Hannah looked to where Lottie was pointing. It was easy to spot him, the only person in the playground not wearing navy blue and grey. His eyes darted around as if searching for somebody.

"Danny! What's he doing here? Isn't he suspended?"

Danny's eyes caught Hannah's.

"Uh-oh," said Lottie. "Looking for you, I think."

He was heading straight for their bench, head down, fists clenched.

His stocky frame loomed over Hannah. His face was contorted with rage.

"There you are, you sneaking little grass. Thought you'd go crying to the Head, did you? Thought you'd go snivelling to Collins about how I trashed your wendy house? You stinking little sneak."

Hannah sat rooted to the bench. Was he going to hit her? He looked angry enough.

"So it *was* you who vandalised our theatre, then," she said.

"Said I'd get you back, didn't I? Did you like your surprise?"

Drawing strength from Lottie's presence, Hannah stood up to face him. "You're a sad little coward, Danny Carr. And for your information, I never mentioned your name to Mr Collins."

A small gaggle of people was gathering around the bench. Danny leaned in towards Hannah, his face bright red, eyes flashing. "You're lying, you cow!"

Hannah looked straight into his scowling face. "I'm not lying," she said. "I didn't turn you in."

"Yeah?!" he screamed. "Then who did?"

"Actually," said a voice behind him, "it was me."

Danny jerked his head up. Hannah and Lottie swivelled round.

Behind the bench stood Emily Sanders.

Emily? Emily had turned Danny in? *What?* When? Why?

Danny gaped at her. Then he gave a kind of spluttering laugh. "You? Don't be stupid."

Emily looked at him, her hands gripping the bench. "I thought what you did was disgusting. And you're such a coward, you were just going to let Jack take the blame for it. So I told the Head it was you."

"You stinking grass!" Danny looked like he was about to explode.

"Don't get mad at me," said Emily. "I didn't burn a barn down or trash anybody's theatre. You're only getting what you deserve."

Danny swung his arm back. But as it came flying towards Emily's face, Jack Adamson sprang forward from the group of onlookers and grabbed it.

Across the playground boomed the voice of Mr Matthews, the head of PE. "Danny Carr! Come here this instant!"

Danny shook off Jack's hands, turned on his heels and legged it towards the main gates. Mr Matthews stepped into his path. "Not so fast," he said. "What do you think you're doing on school premises, young man?"

The onlookers shifted their attention to this new drama. As Danny was marched towards the Head's office, Hannah, her head full of questions, turned around and caught Emily's eye.

"Not here," Emily whispered. "Cloakroom."

"So?" said Lottie, huddled on the wooden bench. "Tell us everything."

"Well, after Hannah went nuts with Jack in the dining room, we asked him—"

"We?" asked Hannah.

"Me and Miranda. We asked Jack if he really had vandalised your theatre. And he wouldn't say. But we knew it wasn't him."

"You knew?" said Lottie. "How?"

"Me and Miranda met up with him and Danny one day in the holidays, just after the fire in your barn. And Danny said to Jack, let's trash their theatre to get back at Hannah for telling the police. But Jack said, no way. He feels really bad about the fire anyway—"

Lottie snorted. "Sure he does. Shame he hasn't actually apologised or anything then, isn't it?"

"I think he's too embarrassed," said Emily.

"Coward," muttered Hannah.

"So Danny said he'd do it on his own. And we never thought he really would. But then in the dining room on Monday, after Hannah got taken out, Danny started boasting about how he'd vandalised it. And I was looking at him and I just suddenly thought, you are a horrible, horrible person. I couldn't believe I'd actually thought he was fun and cute."

Just like me with Jack, thought Hannah. Except Jack didn't actually do the vandalism.

"Jack was looking at him like he was a piece of

dirt, and he said, I can't believe you did that. And he and Danny had this big row, and Danny said, Well, go and run off to Collins then, and tell him it was me. And Jack said, I wouldn't do that. I'm not a grass. So Danny went off in a mood, and Miranda and I told Jack he had to go to Mr Collins and say it wasn't him, otherwise when you went in there, he'd get all the blame and Danny would just get off scot free. But he wouldn't tell on Danny."

"So you did," said Lottie.

"Yes."

They sat in silence. Emily looked more and more uncomfortable. Finally she said, "Erm, OK. I'd better go . . . the bell will ring any minute."

She hitched her bag on to her shoulder.

Hannah looked up. "Thank you, Emily. That was really nice of you."

"That's OK," said Emily. "He deserved it. And I'm really sorry about your farm. I know how you feel. Well, a little bit." Her eyes welled up. "My parents are selling my horse. You know Manor Stables is closing, and there's nowhere else around here to keep him. Everywhere we could afford is full and everywhere else is too expensive or too far away. So, anyway . . . I mean, I know it's not the same, but. . ."

She shrugged and wiped her eyes.

"I know," said Hannah. "It's horrible to lose the thing you love."

The bell jangled right above their heads. Emily stood up. "I've got to go. Miranda will be wondering where I am."

Chapter Thirty-Seven

Hunting

It was a glorious afternoon as Hannah and Lottie walked down the farm track. Puffy cotton-wool clouds perched in the great blue sky that arched over the valley. The hedges were a mass of white blossom.

Hannah clutched Lottie's arm. "Listen. Up in the wood. The first cuckoo. Tell your dad."

"Let's get some pens and paper," said Lottie. "Then we can take the costume books to the theatre and start designing."

As they passed through the dining room, Hannah checked the phone. There was one new message. She dialled to pick it up.

It was a very posh male voice. "Good afternoon, Mrs Roberts. This is Sebastian Milsom from Sotheby's speaking."

Sotheby's? Hannah cringed. Oh, no. They were phoning to say how dare she waste their valuable time by sending in photographs of worthless candlesticks.

How embarrassing. How utterly humiliating.

Unless...

Could they be . . . might they be . . . could it be possible?

Despite the disastrous trip to the antique shop, Hannah had still nursed a tiny flicker of hope. What if that valuer had been wrong? After all, he only ran a poky little shop in Massingham, didn't he? He wasn't a London auctioneer. Maybe Sotheby's would know differently.

"I've just received your auction estimate request form," said the voice. "I'm so sorry to disappoint you, but I am afraid I have to tell you that the candlesticks you wished to have valued are mid-twentieth-century reproductions, and therefore not something we would be able to sell for you."

So.

There it was then. Her last tiny flicker of hope was gone.

Nothing could save them now.

Hannah felt as if there was a great big stone lodged in her stomach. Every single door was shut and locked against her. She had tried every way she could think of to save the farm and nothing had worked.

She couldn't possibly think about another play now. All she wanted to do was flop down on her bed and cry.

But the message carried on.

"I am, however, extremely intrigued by the oil painting behind the candlesticks in your photographs. It looks like a rather fine picture. The artist's signature is visible in one of the photographs, and, if it is genuine, I think you might have a rather good Ben Gunn there. I would very much like to come and have a look at it, if I may. I wonder if you'd be so kind as to give me a ring so that we can arrange a convenient time. My number is. . ."

Hannah stood stock still, clutching the receiver. She couldn't take this in.

"What's wrong?" said Lottie. "Hannah, what is it?"

Hannah couldn't speak for a minute. When she did, her voice came out all quavery.

"It was Sotheby's. He thinks the painting might be good."

"Painting? What painting?"

"The horse and dog. He says the candlesticks aren't worth anything but he likes the painting in the background. He wants to come and look at it."

Lottie's eyes widened. "The painting? That's amazing! He wants to come and see it? Wow, that was quick. We only sent it off last week. Wow, Hannah, he must really like it. When's he coming? Oh, wow, how exciting!"

But Hannah still felt dull and heavy inside. She couldn't seem to feel the same excitement as Lottie. She couldn't allow herself to. She had got so excited before – first about the candlesticks, and then about the competition. She couldn't take the disappointment a third time.

"It might not be worth anything. He said 'if it is genuine'. It's probably a fake – just a copy or something. Anyway, he never said he thought it was valuable."

Lottie's eyes were shining. "He wouldn't come all the way here if he didn't think it was valuable."

"He's coming to check if it's a fake."

"This is so exciting, Hannah! It might save the farm! How amazing, that it was just in the background like that, and it might be valuable! Who does he think it's by? When's he coming?"

"I have to phone him back. Where did you put the painting?"

"What do you mean?"

"You know, when you took it out of the theatre. The night before the play. Did you put it back in the sitting room?"

Lottie gave her a blank look. "What are you talking about?"

Panic flooded through Hannah.

No, no, this couldn't be happening.

"You know!" she shouted. "You said you were going to take the painting and the candlesticks out of the theatre. So Dad wouldn't see them when he came to the play. So where did you put them?"

"Stop yelling at me," said Lottie. "I didn't put them anywhere. I thought you'd taken them out of the theatre. You said—"

"I didn't take them!" shouted Hannah. "I didn't touch them!"

They stared at each other. Hannah felt dizzy. She leaned on the arm of the chair.

"So. . ." she said, "you didn't move them, and I didn't move them, but after the theatre was vandalised, they were gone."

The colour drained from Lottie's face and her eyes became enormous.

"No," she whispered. "You don't think . . . you don't think Danny did something to them?"

Hannah's heart was pumping. "He can't have done. They weren't smashed up in the theatre like everything else, were they?"

"So do you think he took them? Maybe he thought they were valuable too."

"He might have nicked the candlesticks, but he can't have walked home with a massive great painting under one arm."

"So where would he have put it?"

Hannah took a deep breath. Calm down, she told herself. I need to think.

"I reckon he's hidden it on the farm somewhere, just to taunt us."

"Right," said Lottie. "Let's search."

They searched the granary, the bull pen, the loose boxes, the deserted milking parlour and the old cow stalls where Dad shut up the poultry at night. Then Hannah searched the pig shed while Lottie ran down to the empty sty where Dad kept the bedding straw.

Within seconds, she called, "Hey, Han, come here."

Hannah dashed out of the pig shed, banging her head on the door frame.

"Ow," she moaned, racing down the path clutching the sore patch.

She ducked inside the end sty. "Where is it?"

"Look at these. They're hilarious."

Lottie pointed. Sheets of paper covered in pencil

drawings were sellotaped all over the walls.

"Not the painting?"

"Oh, sorry," said Lottie. "Did you think. . .?"

"Of course I did."

"Oh. Sorry. No. But you've got to see these."

When Hannah moved closer to the wall, she saw that the drawings were strip cartoons. The first one she looked at showed long, thin, green things wearing tracksuits, with beads of sweat dripping from their skinny faces. The caption read "Runner Beans".

The next one showed big, fat, bean-shaped creatures carrying big, fat, bean-shaped babies. Underneath the cartoon was a caption in Sam's handwriting: "Broad Beans".

She had to call Lottie over to see the next one. The tall slim beans were wearing berets. Strings of onions hung around their necks. "'French Beans'," read Lottie. "That is actually quite funny."

Hannah was looking at a picture in Sam's six-year-old hand. This time the beans were coloured brown and were lying on the beach under a bright-yellow sun.

"Look, Lottie."

Lottie came over. "*Baked Beans.*" She laughed. "Well, I think we've discovered the top secret headquarters of the Great and Mighty Society of Bean."

"Not the painting, though."

"No."

They walked back across the yard to the old stable block. This was Hannah's last hope. Please let it be there, she prayed.

As they approached, a swallow, quick as an arrow, darted through the stable door. Hannah drew in her breath.

"They're back!"

She tiptoed to the door and pointed at a spot high on the far wall. Through the gloom, you could just make out a mud nest. "They come back every spring," she whispered. "All the way from Africa. We had fourteen pairs last year."

Suddenly she thought: what if they come next year – fly halfway round the world to get here – and their nests have been destroyed?

"Come on," said Lottie. "It's got to be in here."

Hannah leaned over the open top half of the stable door and drew the bolt on the bottom half. They stepped on to layers of dusty straw, littered with battered buckets and empty sacks. The shaft of afternoon sunlight that shone through the door lit up thousands of dust motes suspended in the air.

Hannah couldn't possibly pick up a sack without first giving whatever might be lurking underneath it the chance to get away. On the other hand, she couldn't bear to frighten the nesting swallows by making a noise. She hovered, paralysed, over the first sack.

Lottie solved her problem by grabbing a dented old meal scoop, bashing it on a metal bucket and shouting, "Come out, come out, wherever you are!"

The swallow darted straight out of the door again, squeaking in alarm. There was no other movement.

They worked their way through the stables, uncovering a lot of dried-up chicken dung but not much more. It must be here, Hannah kept repeating to herself. It must be here.

Jasper pushed through the half-open door to join them. "You're missing Jo, aren't you?" said Hannah, ruffling his wool. "She'll be back soon."

There was an old door propped up in the last bay. This is it, she thought. It's behind here.

They pulled the door away. A hen squawked and flapped away from them. Three smooth eggs lay in the straw.

Nothing else.

Waves of panic flooded over Hannah. She grabbed on to Lottie.

Lottie squeezed her shoulder. "It will be all right. We'll find it. It's got to be somewhere."

"But we've searched the whole farm. It isn't here."

Lottie looked at her watch. "I should go. My mum's coming home early. Look, wherever it is, one day won't make any difference. We'll get the Beans to help look tomorrow. And if we don't find it, we'll go to Danny's house and ask him. And we'll tell him we'll go to the police if he doesn't give it back."

The panic waves subsided slightly. At least that was a plan.

"What's Jasper eating?" said Lottie.

Jasper had his front hooves propped up on a chicken crate. He was nibbling something hanging from a hook on the wall.

"Get that out of your mouth, Jasper," said Hannah.

She yanked it away. "Honestly," she said, holding it up for Lottie to see. "A leather stirrup strap. That sheep will eat anything."

Lottie was looking at the hook. "There's a whole bridle. How many years has that been hanging there?"

"Probably from when they used to have shire horses. Before Grandfather bought the Field Marshall."

"Emily would love it here, wouldn't she?" said Lottie.

"Mmm," said Hannah. Then she drew in her breath and stared at Lottie. She looked around the stable block. At the four bays, each with its manger and saddle hooks still fixed to the walls.

It wouldn't take much. A coat of whitewash, bit of a scrub, move the junk out.

Lottie was looking at her, eyes narrowed.

"Hannah? What are you thinking now?"

Midnight. Hannah turned over again in bed and bashed her pillow into shape.

What if Danny had destroyed the painting?

If it was destroyed, it would all be her fault.

And if he hadn't destroyed it, and they went to his house and confronted him – what if he then did destroy it anyway, out of spite, or fright?

These thoughts went round and round in her head all night, and when she met Lottie on their bench in the playground before school, she hadn't slept at all.

Lottie was brimming over with excitement. "I looked at loads of livery yards on the Internet. And I rang the numbers and spoke to some of the owners. I pretended I had a horse I wanted to stable and I asked what they charged."

"And?" said Hannah.

"It depends. Some of them are really posh, with sand schools and jumps and stuff, but some just have a stable and a field. I reckon, if we cleaned out those stables, you could get maybe twenty-five pounds a week for each horse."

"Twenty-five pounds a week per horse?" said

Hannah. "So with four horses, that's a hundred pounds a week."

"Yep. Five thousand two hundred a year. Not bad, eh?"

Lottie frowned at Hannah. "What's wrong? I thought you'd be excited."

"It's great," said Hannah. "Thank you so much for doing all that. It's just – oh, you know. It still won't be enough to save the farm. But if we had some money from the painting . . . I'm just so worried about it. I mean, what if Danny has – you know. . ."

The bell rang for registration.

"Don't worry," said Lottie, picking up her bag. "We'll get that painting back if I have to rip Danny Carr open from head to toe to find it. And I'd enjoy that."

Hannah's stomach lurched. Jack, with his guitar case slung over his shoulder, had just come through the gates.

He hadn't even looked at her since she'd attacked him in the lunch queue. She had been waiting all week for a chance to speak to him alone.

She almost chickened out. But she knew she would never have peace of mind until she'd done it.

"You go on in, Lottie. I just need to speak to Jack."

"Jack! Why on earth would you want to talk to him?"

"I just have to. I'll see you in the classroom, OK?"

Lottie shrugged. "Whatever you say." She hoisted her bag on to her shoulder and walked away.

Her heart pounding, Hannah forced herself to

walk up the path towards the gate. Jack looked up as she approached. When he saw who it was, he looked back down at his feet and dug his hands deeper into his pockets.

A surge of power, like electricity, swept through Hannah. She felt as if she had grown twenty centimetres taller. Imagine, Jack Adamson feeling awkward in her presence!

She stood right in front of him. "I just wanted to say I'm sorry for accusing you of vandalising our theatre. I shouldn't have said it. I was upset and I took it out on you, but I shouldn't have. And I know now that you didn't do it. So I'm sorry."

He was scraping at the tarmac with his foot. She waited for a minute but he said nothing. She started to walk off.

"Wait a second," he said.

She turned round. "What?" Her eyes met his briefly and her stomach gave a little lurch.

No, she told herself sternly. Do not succumb.

"You shouldn't be apologising," he said. He was looking at the ground again. He shuffled a stone from foot to foot. "I should have apologised to you. For the fire. We were idiots, lighting a fire in there."

"Yes. You were."

"We thought it was out. When we left. But. . ."

He tailed off.

Hannah continued to look at him expectantly.

Finally he met her eye and said, "What?"

"You haven't actually said sorry."

"Oh."

She waited while he scuffed his feet around on the tarmac.

"Sorry," he said.

"Thank you. I accept your apology. Goodbye."

And, with her head held high, Hannah turned on her heel and walked into school.

He caught up with her in the foyer. "Hey, Roberts."

Hannah turned around and felt that flutter again as her eyes met his. Why did someone so gorgeous have to be such an idiot?

"What?" she said. There was no way he was going to know she still felt anything for him.

"Was there anything missing from your theatre after Carr did it over?"

Hannah's heart thumped. "What do you mean?"

"He was boasting about how he had some stuff of yours in his bedroom. Said he was going to flog it on eBay." He shrugged. "Just his usual crap, I guess."

Hannah gave a casual laugh and turned away. "Must have been. What would we be doing with anything valuable in our theatre?"

And with her pulse racing, she walked down the corridor. She didn't break into a run until she was around the corner and out of his sight.

Chapter Thirty-Nine

The Rescue Mission

"Get lost," said Martha. "No way."

She was sitting on her bed painting her toenails purple. Hannah and Lottie had coaxed her to open the door a few centimetres, but they were not allowed on pain of death to set foot over the threshold.

"Martha," said Hannah, "you've got to do this. Do you want the farm to be demolished? Do you want to move to a tower block in Linford?"

Martha looked up from her left foot. "Yes. I do, actually. That's exactly what I want. A nice warm flat in a big town with things going on, instead of this boring grotty old dump. *And* my shoes wouldn't get covered in chicken dung every time I stepped out the door."

Hannah pulled a face at Lottie. "OK, you hate the farm. But what about Dad? How do you think he would feel? And Jo, and Sam? What about poor little Sam?"

Martha shrugged. "Not my problem." She started on the other foot.

Hannah sighed with frustration.

Lottie took a step forward. Martha shot her a

look. Lottie held her palms out in front of her and stepped outside the door again. "Fine," she said. "If that's your attitude, that's fine. If you're happy to share a bedroom with Hannah and Jo, don't help us."

Martha scowled as she dipped the brush in the bottle. "What are you talking about, loser?"

Lottie shrugged. "I'm just saying, that's all. It's only fair to warn you. Flats aren't very big. You'd probably have to share a room with at least one of your sisters. Most likely both."

Martha jammed the brush back into the pot and screwed the lid on as if she were wringing Lottie's neck. She swung her legs off the bed and sprang upright.

"Fine," she spat. "But you owe me. Big time. And if that poxy painting is worth nothing, like I bet it is, and we move to Linford, my stinking so-called sisters can sleep in the corridor for all I care. There's no way on earth I'm ever going to share a room with either of them."

Hannah and Lottie crouched behind an evergreen shrub at the side of Danny's garden. Dusk was turning to dark and new stars were appearing in the sky every minute.

"They're taking ages," whispered Lottie.

"Well, it might be a long job," said Hannah. "They've got to get Danny out of his room and then they've got to take his—"

Lottie grabbed her arm. "Look!"

Hannah jerked her head up. At Jade's bedroom window a torch was flashing on and off very fast.

The all-clear.

They scrambled to their feet and crept along the path to the back door. Hannah pushed down on the handle. Her heart stopped as she waited for the creaks and rattles that would bring Danny's parents running. But this door wasn't like the farmhouse doors. The handle slid down smoothly and the door opened without a sound.

Feeling like a criminal, Hannah stepped inside Danny Carr's house. Lottie was so close behind that Hannah could feel her breath on her neck.

They were in a little room that housed a freezer, a washing machine, a jumble of shoes and boots, and a row of hooks heaped up with coats and scarves. Hannah consulted the map they had drawn using Martha's descriptions of the house.

They had to go through the door straight ahead of them into a kitchen.

And then along the hall and up the stairs, right in the centre of the house. Then on to the landing and into the second room on the right. Danny's bedroom. Which, if Martha and Jade had done their job properly, would be empty.

Empty of Danny, anyway. But hopefully containing two silver-plated candlesticks and one great big oil painting.

The door from the kitchen into the hallway was open. The *EastEnders* theme blared out from what, according to Hannah's map, must be the living room.

Was the programme starting or ending? She glanced at her watch.

Seven thirty. Just starting. So they should have a clear half-hour. That would be enough time, wouldn't it?

They crept through the hallway.

Oh, no.

The living-room door was wide open. They were going to have to walk right past that gaping open door to get to the stairs.

Which way did the TV face?

Why hadn't she checked that with Martha?

Please let it face the door, she prayed. Please, please let them have their backs to us.

Hannah crossed her fingers and took a step forward.

What on earth would she do if Danny's mum or dad came out now?

Feeling sick, she leaned her head very slightly round the living-room door.

Danny's mum was sitting on a sofa, facing the TV, with her back to the door.

Thank you, thank you, said Hannah to herself.

She crossed the open doorway in one light stride. Lottie followed.

Now for the stairs. They were carpeted and they didn't make a sound under the girls' feet. In a nanosecond they were on the upstairs landing.

There were four doors leading off the landing. They were all painted shiny white and they were all shut. Music and raised voices came from the first room on their right – Jade's, it said on the map.

Let's hope they've hidden his laptop really well in there, thought Hannah.

The next room was Danny's. With a glance at Lottie, Hannah opened the door. They nipped inside and Lottie closed the door behind them.

Danny's room was laid out exactly as Martha had described it. The only thing that surprised Hannah was how tidy it was. For some reason, she had expected it to be a tip.

From their questioning of Martha, they had worked out that the painting could only be in one of two places.

Unless he had already got rid of it.

Or destroyed it.

No. She couldn't let herself think like that.

The wardrobe was in the far corner. Lottie pulled open the doors.

Hannah recoiled at the sight of the clothes piled up on the shelves. She had no desire to get this close to Danny Carr.

On the landing a door opened and slammed back against the wall.

"Touch my stuff again and you die, you little weirdos!"

It was Danny's voice.

Hannah stopped breathing. There was no time to think. They dived into the wardrobe. The screws from the handles stuck through a bit at the back. They grabbed on to them and pulled the doors shut, plunging themselves into darkness.

Danny's bedroom door crashed open and springs creaked as someone flung themselves on to the bed. There was the sound of a laptop being switched on.

Oh, no.

Martha and Jade had clearly hidden Danny's laptop somewhere pathetically easy to find. And now he would spend the entire evening in his room playing computer games, and they would slowly suffocate in his wardrobe.

What a way to die.

Hannah's leg was all twisted up underneath her. Lottie's foot was digging into her hip. She couldn't stay in this position much longer.

CRACK!

Hannah jumped so hard that one elbow bashed into the side of the wardrobe and the other hit Lottie in the jaw. The wardrobe doors swung open.

GUNFIRE?

In the *house*?

What? Who?

Danny was already out of the room and storming into Jade's, swear words pouring out of his mouth. His mum was running up the stairs, screaming, "Danny! I've told you not to fire that rifle in the evenings!"

"It wasn't me!" yelled Danny. "It was Jade's nutter friend!"

So *that* was who.

Hannah grinned. Great work, Martha.

"Quick," hissed Lottie. With admirable presence of mind, she had already sprung across the room and shut the door.

Hannah refocused. She dropped on to her stomach beside the bed. There wasn't much space underneath it. She stretched her arm out and swept it around.

Her fingers brushed against something hard and bumpy. Whatever it was ran for over half the length of the bed and then turned at a right angle.

The picture frame!

"It's here! Get the other end."

Lottie lay down and stretched out her arm. "Got it. OK, pull."

They eased the frame out. Hannah closed her eyes. What might he have done to it?

She felt Lottie's hand on her arm. "Look, Hannah. It's all fine."

Hannah opened her eyes and saw the beautiful bay hunter and the springer spaniel. She wanted to kiss them. She had never been so glad to see anything in her entire life.

Lottie swept her arm under the bed. "Aha." She pulled out a candlestick and went back in for the other. She pulled a carrier bag out of her coat pocket and put them in it. Then she took hold of one side of the picture frame.

"Come on."

Hannah took the other side. "What do you reckon, just race down the stairs?"

"Go for it."

They scrabbled to their feet and on to the landing. There was an almighty row going on in Jade's room. "She's nuts!" Danny was shouting. "She should be locked up."

"Well, what do you expect," screamed his mother, "if you leave a loaded air rifle lying around the house? I have just about had it up to here with you, Daniel Carr. You're grounded for a month."

She stormed out of the room and started down the stairs. Lottie, nearly at the bottom, sped up, but Hannah, three steps above her, caught Mrs Carr's eye and froze. Lottie tugged at the picture. "Come on," she hissed.

Mrs Carr gaped. One pink-slippered foot dangled above the top step. She stood there, gawping at Hannah, Lottie and the large gilt-framed oil painting.

Danny, an air rifle tucked under his arm, appeared at the top of the stairs. He saw the girls and the painting, and the colour drained from his face.

Hannah felt the same surge of power that she'd had when she had squared up to Jack on the school path.

"Oh, here's Danny," she said. "He'll explain everything. Bye, Mrs Carr."

As she and Lottie carried the painting out into the night, they heard Danny's mum say, "Will someone just tell me what the heck is going on in my house tonight?"

Chapter Forty

A Visitor

Monday afternoon. Rain pelted down from leaden skies. Raindrops bounced off the farm track and soaked Hannah's trousers. She had walked home from school as fast as she could, and not just to get out of the rain. She must phone the man from Sotheby's straightaway to arrange a time for him to come and look at the painting.

As she crossed the yard, Dad stepped out of the pig shed with a bucket in each hand. "Oh, Joanne, er, Martha, er, Hannah. Good. There's a lamb in the Aga needs feeding. Triplet. She couldn't feed all three. I gave it a bottle a couple of hours ago but it can't take much at a time. There's some colostrum in the scullery."

Hannah skipped off to the house. The rain was pouring off the roof, splashing on to the ground from the leaking gutters. Never mind. The first bottle-fed lamb of the year, and it was going to be hers.

The bottom door of the Aga was ajar. Inside it was a cardboard box. Hannah eased it out of the oven and scooped up the tiny lamb that lay in it on a handful of straw. She could feel his ribs and his quick shallow heartbeat under his nubbly wool.

The lamb looked at Hannah and gave a little bleat. She stroked the top of his head and his big soft ears.

The back door rattled and the others tumbled into the scullery. Their school bags thudded on to the freezer.

Hannah kissed the top of the lamb's head. "You're mine," she murmured, as the others clattered up the back stairs without looking into the kitchen.

Hannah measured two scoops of colostrum formula into a baby's bottle, screwed the teat on and settled down on a stool with the lamb on her lap. His body was warm and comforting, like a hot-water bottle. But he was too weak to suck very hard, and when the doorbell rang ten minutes later she was still trying to coax him to take a little more milk.

Hannah stood the bottle on the table, cradled the lamb in the crook of her left arm and pulled the scullery door open.

On the doorstep, in the pouring rain, under a large black umbrella, stood the smartest man she had ever seen. He had short brown hair, which might have been wavy if it wasn't so neatly cut. He wore a navy-blue pinstriped suit with a perfectly knotted red tie. A lovely expensive smell wafted from him. He carried a black leather briefcase and his highly polished brogues bore no signs of mud. Had he blown in on the east wind, like Mary Poppins?

He smiled at her. "Good afternoon." He transferred his briefcase to the same hand as his umbrella and held out his other hand. Hannah held out hers.

Nobody had ever offered to shake her hand before.

"I'm Sebastian Milsom, from Sotheby's auctioneers." He transferred the briefcase back to his right hand. "I have an appointment with Mrs Roberts. I'm afraid I'm a little late. I couldn't find the entrance to the farm."

"Hannah," called Jo from the landing. "Have you got the scissors?"

Hannah stared at the man in complete confusion. He must have read her expression, because he said, "I'm sorry. Perhaps it was your sister I spoke to on the telephone?"

Jo galloped down the staircase. "Ah, what a cute lamb," she said, and then stopped short as she registered the immaculate stranger.

"Jo, this is Mr Milsom," said Hannah. "From Sotheby's."

Jo clapped a hand to her mouth. "Whoops. I did mean to tell you."

Hannah gave her a look. Jo grabbed the scissors from a pot on the shelves and ran back up the stairs.

Hannah turned back to the man and gasped in horror. Jasper, who must have rammed his way through the half-open gate, was standing behind Mr Milsom, nibbling the edges of his briefcase.

"Jasper! Shoo! Shoo!" she said, pushing with all her strength on his woolly shoulders.

But Mr Milsom just laughed. "What an enormous sheep. Are they all as tame as that?"

"No," said Hannah, desperately trying to shove Jasper's great bulk away. "He was an orphan lamb.

My sister reared him. Get off, Jasper."

Mr Milsom looked from Jasper to the skinny little lamb in Hannah's arms, and back again. "Golly. What on earth did she feed him?"

Hannah gave up trying to move Jasper. It would be easier to move Mr Milsom. She smiled brightly. "Come in. Mrs Roberts isn't here at the moment, but I can show you the painting."

"That would be wonderful. Thank you so much."

Hannah led him through the kitchen, acutely aware of the mountain of paper on the window sill, the greasy tools dumped next to the overflowing laundry basket, the black dust coating her mother's wedding china on the dresser. But as they passed through the big tiled hall Mr Milsom said, "What a lovely old house you have," and Hannah wanted to hug him.

Sam's and Jo's faces appeared at the top of the stairs. They each held a pencil and a notebook that had "Bean Spy Club" written on the cover. When they saw Hannah and Mr Milsom they nudged each other and giggled. Hannah glared at them. "Go away," she mouthed.

They didn't go away. They sat down on the top step and started to scribble in their notebooks. Hannah led Mr Milsom into the sitting room and shut the door.

"Here it is," she said, her heart thumping.

His eyes opened wide. Was that a good sign?

He moved very close to the painting, making appreciative little murmurs. Hannah wasn't sure whether she should stay.

"Would you like a cup of tea?" she asked.

He gave her a warm smile. "That would be lovely, thank you."

When she returned with the tea, having put the lamb back in his box, Jo, Sam and Martha were huddled outside the sitting-room door, trying to look through the keyhole.

"Go away!" hissed Hannah, flapping her arms at them. "Shoo!"

"Don't shoo me," said Martha. "I'm not a hen."

"I'm hungry," said Sam. "What's for tea?"

"I'll get it in a minute. Now, *please* go away."

She walked into the sitting room. Mr Milsom was writing in a smart black notebook. She put the tea down on a side table. He looked up and smiled at her.

Her heart thumped, but she had to ask. "So . . . is it real? Is it really by Ben Gunn?"

He looked at her kindly, but he said, "I really need to speak to your mother or father."

Hannah hadn't planned for this. She had to distract him. "When is your next auction?"

He put down his notebook and picked up the mug. "Our next sporting sale – that's where we would sell a Gunn – is in four weeks. But it's too late to get your painting into that sale, unfortunately. The catalogue's about to go to print."

"So when's the one after that?"

"November."

"But that's too late!" cried Hannah.

He frowned. "Too late for what?"

"For . . ." What could she say? If she answered that question, she would have to tell him everything.

"What is it?" he asked.

And he sounded so concerned.

So she told him everything.

The whole story.

Well, nearly.

And he sat on the torn Victorian sofa and sipped his tea and listened.

"The next rent is due on Midsummer's Day," she finished. "And if Dad can't pay it on time they're going to throw us off the farm. So November's too late."

The back door rattled open. Hannah went rigid.

"Hannah!" called Dad.

Mr Milsom stood up. "Ah, good, is this your father?"

"No!" hissed Hannah. "He doesn't know."

Mr Milsom's eyes widened into circles.

"You can't let him know," whispered Hannah. "He won't let me sell it."

Mr Milsom took a deep breath and put his hand on the desk to steady himself. He looked hard at Hannah.

"Miss Roberts, you cannot sell this painting without your father's permission. That, I am afraid, is against the law. If we are going to sell it, then I shall have to speak to him."

"But he'll kill me!"

Mr Milsom put a gentle hand on her shoulder.

"Miss Roberts, if your father is one-tenth as impressed as I am by the story you've just told me, I would imagine that killing you will be the last thing on his mind."

Chapter Forty-One

The Sale

Who would have believed it?

It had helped that Dad took to Sebastian Milsom right from the start. Dad was a man of instant likes and dislikes. If he disliked you, everything you said was nonsense and everything you did was laughable. But if he took to you . . . well, you could do pretty much anything. You could probably strip naked and start worshipping the goddess Diana in the pig field and he would think you were thoroughly sensible.

So when Mr Milsom told Dad that he had a rather good Ben Gunn painting hanging in his sitting room, and that selling it might be a rather good idea, and that maybe, just maybe, as an incredibly special favour to Hannah, he could rush through the paperwork and squeeze their painting into the Sporting Art Sale in four weeks' time . . . well, Dad took notice.

And so on Thursday 6 May Hannah found herself, as in a dream, walking through the front door of Sotheby's on New Bond Street.

The first thing that struck her was how extraordinarily quiet it was. It was nothing like she had expected. Sotheby's was more like a church than an auction house. Even though there were a lot of people milling around, everybody spoke in hushed voices and seemed to float across the carpeted floors.

And it was so clean! All the walls were painted white and cream, and there wasn't so much as a smudge on any of them. Cream-coloured roses in glass vases stood on the gleaming surfaces. In a pristine café off the reception area, people in immaculate suits drank frothy coffee from white china cups and murmured into mobile phones. The men all looked like Sebastian Milsom. The women had perfect hair and elegant hands.

Thank goodness Dad had made an effort. He was wearing his wedding suit and a clean white shirt, and he'd combed his hair and shaved.

They walked upstairs on thick cream carpet to the auction room. It was smaller and less fancy than Hannah had imagined. There were plenty of empty seats but Dad, as he did everywhere, plonked himself down in the back row.

"Can't we sit nearer the front?" said Hannah.

"No, these will do."

A smart-suited man and a woman with long, shiny auburn hair walked down the aisle to the front row. The man sat down and crossed his legs. The woman tossed her auburn hair and. . .

Wait a minute.

No. Don't be silly.

"Do you want a look at this?" Dad pulled out a glossy catalogue from the battered leather document case he had brought with him and handed it to Hannah.

Well, at least she might find out something this way. Dad had been as vague as usual when she had asked him how much the painting might sell for.

Hannah flicked through the thick shiny pages. There were hunting scenes, shooting scenes, racing scenes . . .

And here it was. Almost at the end of the catalogue. It was labelled "Lot 37". Hannah looked at the writing on the facing page. She skimmed the dates and the section called "Provenance".

She looked at the figures at the bottom of the text. £30,000–£40,000.

She stared at the numbers.

"Dad?"

"What?"

"Does that mean," Hannah whispered, "that our painting is worth thirty to forty thousand pounds?"

Dad cleared his throat. "Well, that's what Mr Milsom thinks. We'll see. It all depends on somebody wanting it."

"Thirty to forty thousand pounds!"

"All thanks to you," he said.

Hannah stared at him, amazed. Was he *praising* her?

He avoided her gaze, but he carried on. "You didn't run away from the problem. You faced up to it and you tried to solve it." He paused and then, in a quieter tone, he said, "Your mother would have done the same."

Hannah couldn't bear him being nice to her. She shook her head. "No. I nearly destroyed everything. The theatre *and* the farm. If the painting doesn't sell, it *will* all be destroyed. And it will be my fault."

"What are you talking about?"

Hannah twisted her fingers together. "I invited Jack to our dress rehearsal. It was supposed to be a secret but I invited him. And that's why he and Danny burned the barn down – because they got bored and went off and lit a fire instead. And that's how Danny knew where the theatre was to come and vandalise it."

She held her breath.

"So?" said Dad.

Hannah looked at him. "What do you mean?"

"So you invited people to your play. You didn't invite them to burn down the barn or vandalise your theatre, did you?"

"No."

"Well then, it's not your fault, is it? Gracious, girl, the nonsense you do talk."

He shook his head, took the catalogue from Hannah and started to read it.

It was just what Vanessa had said, only in slightly different words.

When Vanessa had said it, she hadn't quite believed her.

But she believed Dad.

Hannah's shoulders dropped about ten centimetres. It felt like an enormous weight had been lifted from them. A weight that had been there for such a long

297

time that, until it was taken away, she hadn't even realised how heavy it was.

The auburn-haired woman in the front row turned her head to scan the room.

But it wasn't a woman.

It was Miranda Hathaway.

Unbelievable.

Miranda Hathaway, at the same auction!

Miranda saw Hannah and her jaw dropped. She blinked a few times, as if she was trying to clear an obstruction from her eye.

Hannah stopped herself from laughing just in time and smiled instead.

"It was that rent rise that caused all the problems, anyway," said Dad.

Hannah looked at him, wide-eyed. He didn't seem to be talking to anybody. He was looking straight ahead.

Was he confiding in her?

"If we'd sold the thresher, it would only have covered the rent for a few more months, and then the cows would have had to go the next time," he said.

Out of the corner of her eye, Hannah could see Miranda. She had stopped blinking. Now she craned her head forward and mouthed, "What are you doing here?"

Hannah was tempted to say, "Waiting for the disco to start," but that would just confuse Miranda. "Selling a painting," she mouthed back.

Miranda treated Hannah to one of her sweeping

up-and-down looks, as if to say, Don't be ridiculous; somebody as badly dressed as you can't possibly have a painting to sell. She frowned, turned away and took her father's catalogue off his lap.

Hannah turned back to Dad. "So what are you going to do? I mean, even if we sell the painting, it won't pay the rent forever, will it?"

"No," he said. "With any luck, it'll buy us some time. But we're going to have to make a lot of changes to the place."

Something in his voice made Hannah look curiously at her father. He had mentioned making changes as though he actually relished the idea. She couldn't remember when she had last heard him sound enthusiastic about anything.

Miranda turned round again. "Which lot?" she mouthed.

Hannah had never been so pleased to answer a question. "Lot thirty-seven."

Miranda started leafing through her catalogue. Hannah sat back to await the reaction.

A tall, slim man in glasses entered the room and stepped on to a platform at the front. He must be the auctioneer.

And then in walked Sebastian Milsom. He stood next to the auctioneer and opened up a laptop on a little table. He glanced round the room and when he saw Hannah he beamed at her. Hannah beamed back. She started to enjoy it all. She looked around at the other people in their smart suits and jewellery. She wanted to say, "Look at lot thirty-seven! That's ours! We're selling that!"

Miranda turned round again. She had a disbelieving sort of frown on her face. She held up the catalogue with the page open at Lot 37. "Really?" she mouthed.

Hannah nodded, straight-faced. Inside her head, she was jumping up and down with glee.

Miranda stared at the page, and back at Hannah. "How come?"

And Hannah just shrugged nonchalantly, as if they had dozens of paintings worth thousands of pounds hanging on the farmhouse walls.

Miranda tossed her head and turned back to face the auctioneer.

The first picture was lifted on to an easel at the front by two immaculate assistants in white gloves. And the auction started.

The bidding was very discreet. You had to hold up a sign called a paddle with your number on it if you wanted to bid, but half the time Hannah couldn't see anybody raising their paddles at all. What secret signs were these people using? She kept her hands in her lap and didn't dare catch the auctioneer's eye in case she accidentally bought a work of art.

Much of the bidding seemed to be done over the phone. There was a row of telephones on a counter along the right-hand walls, and Sotheby's assistants perched on stools talking to the distant bidders.

Lots came and went very quickly. In no time at all, the hammer went down for Lot 36. The two assistants brought Dad and Mum's Ben Gunn painting into the room and placed it on the easel.

Goose pimples prickled up all over Hannah's body.

"We have here," said the auctioneer, "a fine Ben Gunn."

Sebastian Milsom glanced up from his laptop for a second and smiled at Hannah. Hannah smiled back at him.

Miranda caught the exchange of glances. She looked curiously from Mr Milsom to Hannah and back again, as if trying to work out the connection.

Dad sat very straight, clasped his hands in his lap and kept his eyes fixed on the auctioneer.

"May I start the bidding at twenty-eight thousand pounds?" said the auctioneer. "Thank you, madam."

The bidder was a woman in a pale-pink dress.

"Do I see thirty thousand pounds?"

A small man in a navy suit, a striped shirt and a spotty tie raised his paddle a few centimetres and nodded.

"Thirty-two?"

This time it was a telephone bidder.

"Thirty-four?"

The man with the spotty tie again.

"Thirty-six?"

The auctioneer paused while an assistant murmured down the phone. She looked up and shook her head. He looked out into the room again.

"Thirty-eight?"

The woman in the pink dress raised her paddle.

"Forty?"

The man in the spotty tie.

"Forty-two thousand?"

It was just the two of them bidding now.

"Forty-four thousand?"

Time slowed down.

"Forty-six thousand?"

There was a pause, before the woman in the pink dress slowly raised her paddle.

"Forty-eight thousand?"

The man in the spotty tie raised his paddle.

Hannah felt dizzy.

"Fifty thousand?"

The woman shook her head and put her paddle in her lap.

"Do I see fifty thousand pounds anywhere?"

The room was as silent and still as a gallery of statues.

The auctioneer tapped his hammer on the lectern. "Sold, for forty-eight thousand pounds. Lot thirty-eight. . ."

Time went on, presumably. Their painting was taken off the easel by the white-gloved assistants, another painting was put in its place and the bidding continued. But for Hannah, time had stopped. Dazed and dizzy, she turned to her father.

"We can pay the rent now," she whispered.

Slowly he turned to her and focused his blue eyes on her green ones. A grin spread across his face.

"Yes," he said. "Nearly two years' rent."

"And then?"

"And then there are going to have to be changes."

Hannah took a deep breath. "Actually," she

whispered, "I've had an idea about that too."

When the auction finished, Miranda and her father walked out down the aisle as Hannah and Dad were still gathering up their things. Miranda stared at Hannah. She looked completely confused. I had you nicely tucked away out of sight in a box labelled "Farm Girl", she seemed to be thinking. Now you've messed everything up and I don't know how to treat you any more.

Hannah smiled at Miranda. Good luck figuring that one out, she thought, because there is so much of the world that you don't understand, Miranda Hathaway.

Chapter Forty-Two

New Beginnings

"Get that animal's filthy stinking paws off my new shoes!" screeched Martha.

Jo clutched the silky cocker spaniel puppy to her chest. "Don't be so mean. She smells a lot better than you do. Budge up, Sam."

"Right, you lot, let's get a move on," said Dad, yanking open the driver's door.

Hannah disengaged Sam's hands from his new John Deere baler long enough to fasten his seatbelt, and ran around to the passenger door.

She heaved out a bag of pig nuts and dumped it at the side of the yard.

"Hi, Hannah," called Emily. She was wheeling a barrow full of horse manure from the stables to the dung heap. Her cheeks were bright red and her hair looked like a bird's nest, but Hannah had never seen her look so happy. "Hey, my friend Rosie from the other stables is thinking about renting one of your stables. Can she come up and have a look around tomorrow afternoon?"

"Sure, great," said Hannah. "I'll be here. See you!"

She brushed some of the straw off the passenger

seat and jumped in.

"Where are we going anyway?" asked Martha.

"Got a couple of things to do," said Dad, starting up the engine.

They bumped slowly up the track, the windows open to inhale the scent of new-mown grass. Adam had mown North Meadow yesterday for the first cut of hay. Swallows darted, weaved and dived through the grazing sheep in South Meadow. They passed the ancient oak tree that stood alone in the middle of the pasture. New life had sprung out of its hollow shell, and a choir of birds sung from the shelter of its branches. And over the farm arched the huge sky, pale at the edges of the valley, shading to a deep bright blue in the centre.

Dad pulled up at the postbox opposite Lottie's house. He handed Hannah a small brown envelope. "Shove that in the post, will you?"

Hannah looked at the address. "The rent cheque?"

"Yep." He grinned. "It's not even due for another week. That should give old what's-his-name a bit of a shock when it lands on his desk."

"Did you pay the whole year's rent?" asked Hannah.

Dad grunted. "Not on your life. They can wait until it's due. Besides," he said, glancing at Hannah, "there's a couple of other things we need to buy. Some new curtains for the sitting room, for example."

Hannah turned rigid.

He'd noticed? But why hadn't he said anything?

He chuckled. "Don't worry. Your mother would

305

have been delighted to see her curtains in a theatre."

Well.

What else had he noticed that he'd never said a word about?

Hannah hopped out and posted the rent cheque.

"Hey, Han!"

Lottie was leaning out of her bedroom window. "How long will you be out for? Can I come up later? We could start building the set."

"Dad said we'll be an hour," said Hannah. "So better make it two. Meet you in the theatre. I'll bring the script. It's all finished."

"Great, see you soon," said Lottie. "Have fun!"

Dad drove out of the village and took a route Hannah didn't know, along narrow winding lanes shaded with beech and chestnut trees. The verges, covered with cow parsley, were a froth of white lace.

Dad turned into a gateway and stopped the car in a neat and tidy farmyard.

"What are we going to do here, Daddy?" asked Sam.

Dad got out and opened the back door. He ruffled Sam's hair. "We're going to start farming again, boy."

Hannah watched her father as he leaned over the railings, stroking the beautiful chocolate-brown calves. His eyes were bright. He looked younger than he had for years.

"So you're not going back into dairy then?" asked Mrs Thompson, the farmer.

"No point. Milk prices are so bad, small herds just aren't viable any more. I thought we'd run some Sussex beef calves instead."

Mrs Thompson nodded. "Good idea. People like rare-breed meat these days."

"I've been talking to the local butcher, and he'll take all we can produce. Wants the lamb and pork too."

Mrs Thompson laughed. "Is that student of yours putting new ideas into your head? I hear you're taking him on full time. I bet you could do with some help."

Dad smiled. "He's a good lad, Adam. Wants us to apply for the Countryside Stewardship Scheme too. Put the arable back to grassland and concentrate on stock-rearing." He leaned over and let a calf lick his hand. "You're a pretty little thing, aren't you, eh?" He straightened up. "He's got some funny ideas, mind. Planning to set us up with a computer, for goodness' sake."

"Good Lord," said Mrs Thompson. "It sounds like you're going to be dragged into the twenty-first century at last."

"Well, it's about time," said Dad. "Things have stood still for too long at Clayhill."

When they got home, the others disappeared up to their rooms. Hannah rummaged in the cupboard to find something for tea. She emerged with two cans of baked beans, to see Dad standing in the doorway holding a long thin cardboard package.

He held it out to her. "This came today."

"For me?"

He nodded.

Hannah put the beans down on top of the cupboard. She pulled the tape off the parcel and opened it up. There was a layer of bubble wrap under the cardboard. She pulled that off too. Then she drew in her breath. "Oh! Oh, it's beautiful!"

It was a black metal sign. Around the edge was a border of brambles, with a silhouette of a hen in the bottom left-hand corner. And inside the border, in elegant curving iron letters, was written *The Secret Hen House Theatre*.

Hannah ran her hands over the smooth cold metal. She pictured the sign nailed to the door of her theatre. "It's gorgeous. It's so beautiful."

Then she looked at her father. "But how did you know? How did you know the theatre's name? And how did you know our logo – the brambles and the hen?"

Dad pulled a grubby piece of paper from his pocket and unfolded it.

It was the programme of *By Her Majesty's Appointment*.

So he *had* come to their play. It hadn't been a mirage. And he had kept the programme all this time. Not only kept it, but had a sign made from the design. He had done all that for her.

"Thank you, Dad. Thank you so much."

"There's something else," he said. "Up in your room. Something I thought you should have."

Hannah ran upstairs, the sign under her arm. She opened her bedroom door.

A tingle spread all over her body. Under the window stood her mother's bookcase, filled with her mother's books.

Hannah let out a cry of delight. She ran across the room and knelt in front of it. She hugged the bookcase and stroked the spines of the books – the row of tatty scripts from the plays Mum had acted in, with her handwritten notes in the margins; the theatre handbooks; the biographies of actors and actresses; and the big green hardback that Mum had won as a school drama prize: *The Complete Works of William Shakespeare*.

Hannah propped her new sign up on the window sill above the bookcase. She looked at the bookcase and the sign and the farmyard outside, with the lichen-covered tiles glowing in the afternoon sun, and she was so happy that she felt as though she was glowing too.

Then she took out her mother's scrapbook from under her bed. She turned the pages until she reached Mum's final review. At the top of the facing page, she wrote: "The Secret Hen House Theatre. Our First Production". She glued in the programme for *By Her Majesty's Appointment*. And below it she pasted the Linford Arts Festival report from the local paper. "Farm Theatre Wins Judge's Praise", it said.

Hannah closed the scrapbook, kissed it and stood it next to Mum's theatre books on the bottom shelf of the bookcase. Then she picked up her beautiful sign and the exercise book containing her new script. With a sigh of pure happiness, she closed her bedroom door, ran down the back stairs and skipped across the farmyard to meet Lottie.

Acknowledgements

This book was inspired by my childhood adventures in the Lucky Horseshoe Theatre. Thanks to all the members of the theatre, and especially to Elizabeth Pratt, who co-wrote *By Her Majesty's Appointment* with me when we were thirteen, and kindly allowed me to use extracts from it in this book.

I was lucky enough to grow up with three fantastic siblings. Enormous thanks to Hazel, Mary and Mark, loyal and hilarious companions through life. Thanks to Mark also for his advice on farming matters.

To my wonderful parents, Robert and Ruth Peters, who gave me a love of reading and a childhood on a farm, thank you so much for your unfailing support.

I am very grateful to Gabrielle Blond, Jo Courage, Brian Courage and Fiona Courage, who kindly read the story in its earliest form and gave me encouraging and helpful feedback.

This book would not have found a publisher without the advice and inspiration I received from SCBWI events. Heartfelt thanks to all the amazing volunteers, and especially to Sue Hyams, retreat co-ordinator extraordinaire and all-round lovely person.

To the writers who offered such helpful comments on my work throughout the revision process – Joe Friedman, Candy Gourlay, Miriam Halahmy, Paolo Romeo and Christina Vinall – many, many thanks. Thanks in particular to Nino Cirone, who generously read draft after draft of the manuscript and always gave exactly the right advice at exactly the right time.

Huge thanks to Kate, Kirsty, Adrian and everyone at the fabulous Nosy Crow, for making my dreams come true.

Big thanks and hugs to my children, Freddie and Dorothea, whose enthusiasm and enjoyment have made the journey even more exciting.

Lastly, and mostly, and always, an enormous thank you to my husband, Oliver, who suggested that I write this book and whose unwavering support, encouragement and belief made it all possible. Thank you for everything.